Jack the Ripper: The Murder of Madam Athalia

ISBN 978-0-6480789-5-1

Aenghus Chisholme

Connect with Aenghus Chisholme: www.aenghuschisholme.com

Cover by Susan Krupp

Also, by Aenghus Chisholme

Merlin the Sorcerer AD491

Guinevere the Queen AD494

Sir Gawain and the Green Knight AD499

Arthur the King AD517

Murder on the Mary Celeste

The Best Things in Life Begin with the Letter B

This book is dedicated to all people fascinated by the story of Jack the Ripper.

Contents

Chapter 1: Friday the 31st of August 1888, 1:00am

Mary Ann Nichols tried as hard as was possible to hide her forty-three years beneath thick layers of makeup. She was only partially successful. The rest of the illusion of youth would have to be provided by the dim gas lights interspersed in the narrow streets of Whitechapel. She tried to guess the age of the man that she had successfully solicited for her favours. She regarded him quickly so as not to seem as if she was too curious. She did not want to scare him off. There was good money to be earned from a quick liaison with this stranger. And money is what she needed. In the distance Big Ben could be heard striking one o'clock in the morning.

The man was dressed well; he was perhaps in his mid-thirties. He had a beard and a cap that looked as if it were that of a sailing ship's captain. It was not uncommon, but also not particularly common either. It was just different enough to gather the attention of a passer-by; but not enough to garner any real interest. He certainly spoke as if he were a highly-educated individual. And there was an accent too; American for sure. But she did not mind. He was more pleasant than some of her more recent 'conquests'.

Mary Ann was not bothered by the fact that he was saying very little. It would suit her if he did not say another word for the entire encounter. Her mind was on that of her children that she so desperately needed the money for. There was her eldest, Henry Alfred. However, her first-born was to another man. It was lucky that when he deserted her that her next husband so readily accepted

Henry as his own. Only his surname would ever betray that he was not the father's son. She often told people that her first husband had died at sea. It was a lie but may also have very well been the truth for all that she knew. He did after all run off and leave the country by taking a job on a ship. Mary Ann ran through the images of her other children, Edward, Percy, Alice and Eliza. They all meant so much to her, as did her husband William.

William worked as hard as he could, but his wage was not enough to support such a large family in the heart of London. Not nowadays. Mary and William were determined that their children fare better than they had done. So with much angst it was agreed that she would sell herself to men to help bring in more income to assist with the upkeep of the family. They both knew that she was now well-past child-bearing age. There was no danger of her falling pregnant to any of these men. That had removed a huge objection from William. He would not entertain the thought of her brining more mouths to feed into their already strained family situation.

Her role as a servant in a large well-to-do family home in Islington did not bring in enough money to support them. William's job at the markets gutting fish and preparing them for market barely offered any more. So it was decided that casual prostitution was as the only way to supplement their incomes. Also, it was best to do it now before she became so old that no amount of makeup of poor lighting would assist her in obtaining any men willing to pay for the use of her body.

"What did you say that your name was ducky?" she asked suddenly realising that she had no idea.

"I am sure that I did not say, my dear" was his reply. It was almost terse, she thought, but was not entirely sure.

His attitude did not matter to her though, only the colour of his money.

"This way" he pulled on Mary's arm directing her down an alleyway. She regarded the scene ahead. It was rather bleak. There were not enough lamps to see very much at all. The cobbled streets glistened with freshly fallen rain. It was lucky that it was not raining now she thought. But something about the complete absence of people made her nervous.

"Where did you say that your...." She thought for a moment to recall exactly what he had called it.

"Your city residence was?" Mary finished asking her question unaware that a note of unease had crept into her tone.

"Bucks row" he replied in a semi-gruff manner. Mary looked around. She knew the area. This was Thomas Street that they had just turned into. She was sure that Buck's row ran off the end of it. Somehow the fact that they were heading in exactly the direction that he said that they would, reassured Mary. She relaxed, even pulling her bearded-man a little closer to her. They had been walking arm in arm just like a civilised couple would. There was no need to advertise that she had just met this man. Keeping up appearances was all a part of her act. She wondered what the residence would look like. Would it be furnished with fine pieces? Would there be paintings on the walls by artists of some note? She was pondering these things when she looked up and saw the street sign. It was almost impossible to read in this light but was visible enough to confirm that they had reached their destination.

Turning into Buck's row Mary could see that it was a very long street with the high walls of a school on one side and a station on the other. There would be no trains at this time of night. The street was completely empty of life. More unusually there were precious few windows looking down onto this section of the street. In fact there were none at all. It was impossible to see where this man's residence could be. This could hardly be considered to be a residential area at all.

She turned to him to demand more information as to the exact whereabouts of their ultimate destination? Mary was keen to get this over and done as the night was wearing-on. There was no possibility of making more money before retiring for the night because she was due at work tomorrow bright and early.

She barely had time to perceive the shiny knife lunging toward her before it severed her throat on her left side. She made to scream but something had covered up her mouth making it impossible to make anything other than stifled noises. She tried to scream without success. The knife lunged again this time making an equally deep gash in the right-hand side of her throat. The pain was unbearable. Now there was something covering her nose as well so she could not even draw-breath to attempt another scream.

The man regarded Mary. He was pleased with the absolute symmetry of the gashes on her throat, both of which poured out blood with wild abandon. He thought that she needed something more definite in order to terminate her life with as much horror as he could. Releasing her nose and mouth so that she could at least take a breath ready to scream, he waited for the second that she had stopped inhaling and then jabbed her in the stomach five times in rapid succession.

Mary fell to her knees. She clasped her stomach then her throat and then looking in terror at her assailant realised that there was absolutely no escape for her. Frantically she tried to push him away. It was a futile attempt. He was strong, much stronger than her. She could feel her life's-blood oozing out of her veins and covering her dress.

With a monumental effort on her part she managed to lift herself from her knees and made as if to run away but she instead fell into a heap on the cobbled street.

"There is no escape for you, silly woman. Do you think that you can out run me? Do you imagine that you are strong enough to ward me off? Noooooooo" his tone was mocking.

Mary managed to scramble to her feet once more only to be thwarted yet again by his intercession. He grabbed her roughly by the waist and flipped her over as if she was a rag-doll. She landed with a thud on her back on the street. Dazed and feeling cold she yet again made to scream. She saw the knife once more lunging toward her. He plunged it into Mary just as she tried to scream. It interrupted her and instead she made a sickening belching sound. Her eyes widened in terror as he cut a jagged line across the side-ways length of her stomach. Mary's eye sight began to dim. The pain that she was in was unbelievable. The last thing that she saw was his hand extending to reach deep inside of the newly cut opening in her mid-section. She had just enough life left in her to see him draw out an internal organ of some description. Mary did not know what it was but in that instant prayed for death rather than endure more of the torture that had been so cruelly inflicted upon her.

Mercifully her prayer was answered. Mary Ann Nicholls died as the man inspected her lower abdomen intestines. He looked at them closely. There was something in his expression that would be identified as distain if anyone had been looking. But he was alone on the street with his dead victim. As if deciding that Mary's innards were not what he was looking for he brutally shoved them back into her and stood up.

He surveyed the scene. Not a person in sight. Excellent; he had chosen the street with some precision. There were no witnesses to concern him. Shaking his hands as if that would somehow remove the blood that covered them, he reached inside his jacket for a handkerchief. Wiping them as best as he could he then returned the blooded piece of cloth to his inside pocket; it would have to do. He pushed his hands into his pockets and retraced his steps moving back toward Thomas Street. His work was done

Chapter 2: Madam Alice Athalia

Alice Annie Athalia was an old woman. She had reached the age of eighty years and was very proud of each one of them. Right now she was sleeping in her capacious bed in her even more capacious bedroom, in an imposing four-story residence in Kensington. She was dreaming. A knife lunged at her and cut her in the neck. Alice groaned in her sleep as the imagery danced before her in her mind. Again it lunged and cut her neck again. Again she groaned. Madam Athalia was in danger of being awoken by the vividness of this nightmare. But then it was as if her viewpoint changed and she was standing outside of her body. It was no longer her that was being attacked it was somebody else. She stood, unable to move, unaware if she even had limbs at all.

A bearded man in a Captain's sailing hat and large overcoat was stabbing a woman to death. Athalia was horrified. She could not scream. She could not raise her hands to her mouth. Somehow only her disembodied eyes were present here. And without realising how she knew, she knew that those eyes did not have eyelids for her to close. She would be forced to watch this horrendous attack.

Unable to turn away she saw the poor woman fall whilst trying to escape. The man violently spun her over on to her back before plunging the knife into her abdomen again and again. Athalia would have done anything at that moment for the gift of speech; she needed more than anything right now to scream for help to offer some assistance no matter how little to the woman being murdered before her eyes. But no such mercy was offered to her and none at all shown to the bleeding woman lying on the ground.

The sight of the attacker driving the knife into his victim's stomach and sawing it open like a sack of grain was more than Athalia could bear. Still, that was not the end of the horror. The murderer reached in and pulled out her innards and drew them up to his face to view them more closely.

Anything that could have deflected her attention from this unbelievably gruesome sight would have been welcomed. This time however, it was as if her silent plea had been answered, Athalia heard a distant scream. There was something familiar about it. There was a brief pause and then again it came. It was her voice; she was the one screaming.

Alice Athalia woke up in a fright. She sat upright in bed gasping for breath ready to scream once more. Looking around her, she could see the comforting surrounds of her bedroom. The window was slightly open, there was cool breeze blowing the curtains. Enough light was trickling through to readily identify the rest of the room. Everything seemed perfectly normal.

Now, there was another sound that Alice recognized. She had heard it many times before. It was the sound of footsteps coming down the main hallway towards her bedroom door. For just a moment her heart seemed to skip a beat as she imagined that it could be the murderer from her nightmare. A rapid knocking came at the door.

"Madam Athalia, are you alright?" it was the voice of her live-in butler Burton. Alice tried to compose herself as best she could before answering. Nevertheless her voice betrayed her true demeanour when she responded to him.

"I am well thank you Burton." She responded. Clearly identifying in her tone that she was anything but well Burton insisted.

"Are you sure Madam Athalia? You sound quite distressed!"

Dear Burton, Alice thought to herself. She was too old to stand upon ceremony and they had been together too long for pretence.

"You may enter Burton" she directed. Burton did just that opening the door and striding through before turning to face Alice in her bed. He held an oil lamp before him and extended it to shed more light into the cavernous room. He could see that all indeed was well.

"What is the matter Ma'am, I heard you scream twice?" his concern was obvious.

"I do apologise for waking you Burton. It was nothing but a bad dream. Thank goodness too! A very vivid and quite gruesome nightmare; the likes of which I do not believe I have ever had before. But it is over now and I am awake." She paused briefly before asking. "What time is it, do you know?" Burton did indeed know as he had passed a grandfather clock in the hallway on his way to the main bedroom suite.

"It is fifteen minutes past the hour of one o'clock in the morning Ma'am." He answered with assuredness.

"I see; far too early to rise then?" responded Madam Athalia in an almost absent-minded vocalisation of her inner thoughts.

"Shall I prepare you some hot milk; to help you back to sleep Madam Athalia?" Burton's offer did not tempt Alice at all. Now that she was awake she could feel that the nightmare had upset her stomach. The memory of which was doing even more to cause nausea.

"You are very kind Burton, but I do not need anything thank you. I shall endeavour to return to sleep and put the whole incident behind me. You are a good soul to worry so much about me." Alice praised his thoughtfulness and kind-heartedness.

"Well then if there is nothing then, I shall leave you in peace." He said. He was reassured that Madam Athalia was indeed well and now wished to exit her chamber so as to afford her the privacy that she should expect in her bedroom.

"Good night Ma'am" he said as he left the room.

"Good night Burton" she responded in kind. Looking around her Alice wondered how on earth she was going to sleep after such a tumultuous dream. She did not want to ponder the contents of it, but was simply unable to not do so. Trying her best to make herself comfortable once more she reviewed the memory of the dream as if it were a book that she needed to read once more in order to extract more details from it.

"What a bizarre dream to have" she said aloud to herself. It simply did not make sense. All of her life she had communed with the dead. She had seen many things in her dreams, but nothing so horrifying as this. It was different, but she could not put her finger on exactly how it was different. Perhaps it was the fact that she was the one trying to pull a vision from the ethereal plane. It was always up to her to seek out the dead and call forward a spirit to commune with. But this nightmare came out of nowhere. For all intents and purposes, she was retired now and the need to call upon her psychic abilities was no longer sought.

Up until this night, she had been enjoying her retirement. It was only on a rare occasion that one of her equally as old long-term clients would seek her professional abilities. But the longer that she lived, the fewer they became. At no time in all of her life, had a vision sought-out her. Is that what it was; a vision that had made itself known to her for some reason? Athalia contemplated the possibility. She was still doing so when she drifted gently off to sleep.

***

The next morning at breakfast Athalia was still pondering the macabre dream that had disturbed her night so abruptly. Burton was making his usual fuss of setting down her toast and lightly boiled egg along with the butter and other condiments that were part of her morning ritual. Alice looked through the glass of the conservatory at the very private rear of her property. The gardens were looking pristine. Autumn would soon make its presence felt and the leaves would fall. It would be a shame to see the end of such a wonderful summer; but this was the last official day of the season.

"No ill-effects from your nightmare I trust Ma'am?" Burton unintentionally broke into Alice's thoughts.

"Hmm?.. No, no Burton; none at all. Thank you for your concern." Alice reached for the morning edition of 'The Times' newspaper. It had been properly folded and placed on the table for her. Picking it up she began to read the headline without really paying attention to any of the headlines. At least in the beginning, then something caught her eye. She read the story through her magnifying glass.

"The police still have no clues in the murder of Martha Tabram whose body was found at George Yard on the seventh of August." Athalia finished the summation of the story.

"I recall that story Ma'am. The body was stabbed thirty-nine times was it not?" inquired Burton.

"Yes" replied Athalia "Stabbed many times; absolutely shocking" Athalia pondered her dream once more and the multiple times that her dreamt assailant plunged his knife into the hapless woman victim. Burton did not notice that she had become deep in thought and interrupted her line of thinking.

"It was such a grisly murder of a woman-of-the-night; who could have done such a dreadful thing, regardless of her occupation?" His question snapped Alice back to the present.

"Yes indeed. The police seem to need help solving this one." Her own response to Burton's statement lit the ember of a thought inside Athalia.

"Please forgive me Madam Athalia. This is hardly breakfast conversation. What will you be doing today Ma'am" he asked trying to change the subject.

"I believe that I shall write a letter when I have finished breakfast Burton." Alice said giving Burton something to latch on to.

"I shall see that your writing materials are laid out in the library Ma'am". He offered his immediate attention to her soon to be task.

"Excellent Burton; thank you" she responded. She would write a letter to the Metropolitan Police Department, the same one that was stumped about the death of the prostitute earlier in the month. Scrutinising the article for more information she noted that it was the Criminal Investigation Department in Whitechapel that was asking the public for any and all information that may relate to the case. This dream was after all in some small way related. The way in which multiple stab wounds were involved gave her dream some new substance. A letter explaining her credentials and the upsetting dream may not be the hard-evidence that they were seeking, but it would make her feel better to write and tell them about it anyway. With a definite plan in mind she could now enjoy her breakfast properly.

Chapter 3: Junior Detective Inspector Samuel Gates

Junior Detective Inspector Samuel Gates was an ambitious young man. He had pushed himself through the ranks of the police working all hours to get noticed by his various superiors during his career. All had found him to be an alert and exceptional worker in all of the roles that he had fulfilled. He had managed to gain a small reputation within the police force as the one that had his sights set on the top job and would probably get to in fullness of time. Such a favourable view from so many had helped him get to the rank that he now held, much sooner than any before him. Although he was the youngest of all of the Junior Detective Inspectors; his compatriots knew that Samuel Gates was the one to go to if you were absolutely facing an almost unsolvable crime. He would be the one that was more than likely going to come up with some idea that could help the situation or at least point you in the right direction for the next stop on the journey of solving a criminal case.

His blonde hair and blue eyes gave him a very innocent look that belied his blossoming intelligence. This was a man that had truly found his calling and was exactly where he wanted to be.

Samuel thought that he was coming to just another work day at the Criminal Investigation Department of the Metropolitan Police Force. However, the moment that he entered the building up the stone stairs and in through the arched doors he knew that something was amiss. The office was positively buzzing with activity. There was urgency in the way that the various clerks, constables and other staff were moving. They all shared a similarly grim expression too.

He was about to ask the nearest person to him when Police Sargent Plymothwood approached him. The Sargent was easily identifiable by his oversized moustache that was by far the largest and most elegantly groomed bundle of facial hair in all of the Whitechapel constabulary.

"The boss is looking for you Mister Gates." He stated in a similarly grim tone to the expression that he wore. It would have been more comedic under different circumstances having a moustache deliver the news. It always looked to Samuel that Sargent Plymothwood never seemed to open his mouth at all because it was all but invisible beneath the tufts of dark hair. However the thought that Senior Detective Inspector Edmund Reid wanted to see him erased any thoughts of humour from Samuel's mind.

"What has happened?" he asked curious as to why the scene around him was so frenetic.

"Murder last night, a bad one at that. I'll let Mister Reid tell you all about it. He is in the briefing office."

That was all of the encouragement that Samuel needed to move hurriedly toward the briefing room. He would not normally be summoned to the room prior to the regular morning meeting between the Senior Detective Inspector and his staff. This must be an exceptional circumstance concluded Samuel. He moved through the building dodging people as best he could and knocked on the door of the briefing room. Not waiting for a response he entered.

Inside were two people, a uniformed Police constable that Samuel did not recognise; he was still trying to learn the names of all of the staff since his promotion and assignment to the large Whitechapel force. And of course the man that had sent Sargent Plymothwood to fetch him.

"You wanted to see me Sir?" asked Samuel as he approached.

"Ah, good yes Gates, exactly the man that I wanted." He had clearly finished with the constable and motioned for him to leave them. He left giving an acknowledging nod to Samuel as he did so.

"A murder last night in Buck's row near the station and school; body was discovered at approximately three-thirty this morning. Woman, we are still trying to ascertain her identity stabbed multiple times in the neck and stomach and then sliced open like a prized-pig ready for the spit". Edmund Reid's choice of phrase was nothing if not inappropriate given that a woman had been murdered, but Samuel was not prepared to object. He instead leant forward seeking more information. Reid continued

"Valuables, such as they were, left on the body, so robbery was clearly not the motive. In her belongings was this." He held up a piece of paper. Samuel looked at it.

"It is a bill of payment for something" he said squinting at the poorly written receipt.

"Exactly, made out to one Mary Ann Nichols, and there is an address. I want you to find out if the body that we have in the mortuary is that of Mary Ann Nichols by going to her address." Samuel looked up at the wall clock. It had just turned eight o'clock in the morning. He took the paper from Reid and studied it. The address was not that far from their Whitechapel police station.

"Find out before the morning briefing at nine o'clock and report back to me" ordered Reid. Suddenly the urgency was more palpable. He took the paper from Reid and gave a quick assurance that he would do exactly as was required.

"Yes sir; straight-away sir!" Samuel tried his best to remain at a dignified pace leaving the briefing room, not wanting to appear flummoxed. This was the sort of thing that Junior Detective Inspectors were called upon to do and he couldn't wait to get to the job that he had trained and worked hard to achieve.

***

It was easy to find the address that was written on the bill of receipt. The block of units was very working-class. Samuel walked up to the front door. Coincidentally somebody was exiting just as he arrived. The woman looked at him in the manner that one would when seeing somebody that you do not know attempting to enter your home. He nodded a friendly 'Good Morning' and waved his police badge at the woman with the suspicious look upon her face. She immediately changed her attitude and inquired of him:

"Is there something that I can help you with luv?" she asked in a very cockney accent.

"Flat number two?" he asked in return.

"That way luv at the end of the hall on the left; 'ere, is there trouble?"

"Not really for me to say Ma'am, just routine business" his reply garnered disappointment from the woman who was clearly looking for something more scandalous than just pedestrian police work. However interesting a visit from the police may be, it clearly wasn't enough to keep her from her day so she nodded dismissively and carried on out the door.

Samuel found the door that he was after and knocked decisively. The door was opened by a man dressed in a shirt, suspenders and dark pants. He seemed a little dishevelled.

"Who are you?" he demanded in a gruff tone. Samuel produced his identification and shoed the man. He squinted at the credentials and changed his tone immediately.

"Can I help you officer?" he asked, and Samuel thought that he detected a note of trepidation.

"I am looking for the husband of Mary Ann Nichols." Samuel watched very closely for the man's reaction. He was not disappointed. The man visibly cringed. Closing and opening his eyes he proceeded with a much more conciliatory tone.

"You've found him you 'ave. William Nichols at your service. What's she done officer? Nothing that deserves the old clink I 'ope?" he looked as innocent as he possibly could and failed at doing so. There were children playing noisily in the flat behind him. He turned around to scald them with a 'Quite!' before turning back to Samuel.

"Mary Ann did not return home last night?" Samuel's question was a leading one. He hoped to gather more information from William than he was perhaps willing to part with. And hopefully without being aware that he was doing so. Mr Nicholls could not help the look of guilt appearing on his face. He clearly did not want to admit that his wife was out the night before.

"She works late at that big house you know? Sometimes she doesn't get back until after midnight. I have been worried sick about 'er I 'ave. Maybe she finished so late that they let 'her stay in the servant's quarters. She could be walking through that door any minute now." He was clearly covering up something and Samuel could easily guess what.

"Does your wife work on the streets Mr Nicholls?" Samuel felt that the direct approach in this instance may be called for. William's face fell. Samuel had the answer that he needed. Mary Ann was a prostitute, maybe a casual one at that. Mr Nicholls had told him that she had a day job as a servant in a 'big house' but with the number of children that Samuel could see in the background maybe that did not pay enough to make ends meet? Casual prostitution was rife in this part of London. It was beginning to add up. Mary Ann was soliciting for business when someone attacked her and knifed her to death. What he needed now was a positive identification so that he could take that back to the morning briefing. Time was short.

"I'm going to need you to come with me and claim Mary Ann Nichols please Sir." Samuel subliminally gave away that something was amiss by being so gentle with the delivery of his message. Even if he was not explicitly aware of it, William saw that Samuel seemed to have softened his questioning approach.

Curious and trepidatious at the same time he turned to the children.

"Henry; watch the children. I have to go with this police officer." Clearly the children did not understand and then gathered around behind William asking in a cacophony: 'but why' and 'where are you going' and 'when will you be back' amongst others.

"Not long, I'll be back as soon as I can". He was crotchety with them. He did not have time to field the plethora of what was sure to be never-ending questions from the children at a time like this.

"Hand me my coat and hat Alfred" he ordered what appeared to be the eldest of the children. Alfred obeyed and fetched William's hat and coat. Putting them on as quickly as he could, he left behind him more objections from the children before pulling the door shut. William checked his pockets for the door keys and satisfied that they were present indicated that Samuel should lead the way down the narrow corridor.

As they were leaving the building Samuel took the time to draw the pocket watch from his waistcoat and look at the time. He had wasted too much time getting to the address. He hailed a handsome-cab. Time was of the essence and he needed to get to the mortuary and have William positively identify the body of his deceased wife so that he could still make the morning briefing.

William looked a little perplexed at being treated to a ride in a handsome cab. Samuel opened the door and indicated that William should get in first. Whilst he did so Samuel tapped the leg of the driver and motioned for him to lean down from his driver's seat perched above the cab.

"The mortuary, and hurry, police business" said Samuel only loud enough for the driver to hear.

"Right you are!" replied the cabbie. He climbed into the cab and shut the door. The cabbie cracked his whip above the large brown horse bringing it to a rapid trot. Inside the cab William gave Samuel a curious look. This was a better place for Samuel to break the news that he had to impart. The thought of doing so back at the flat with the deceased children within earshot was not something Samuel was willing to do.

"Mister Nichols, I am afraid that I have very bad news for you. Please prepare yourself for a shock. We are not going to the Metropolitan Police Station to post bail on your wife for solicitation. We are headed to the mortuary so that you can positively identify the body of a woman who was found murdered this morning. The only clue to her identity was this receipt found amongst her possessions." He handed the piece of paper to William.

"What!? Murdered!? Mary!? No! No! You aren't serious. She can't be dead!" He took the paper from Samuel, his hands trembling. Holding it as if it were diseased he studied the contents. A look of realisation dawned upon his face.

"This is the receipt for her new hat, the one that she wore out last night to..." he cut himself off realising that he almost admitted that his wife was out last night soliciting for sex. He choked back tears. Closing his eyes he wished that he was anywhere else other than right here and right now facing this horrible situation. The sound of the horse shoes and carriage wheels rattling over the cobbled streets filled the cabin.

"Murdered?" said William after a time "How?"

"Stabbed" replied Samuel. He wanted to say something different but could not find the words to soften the blow of how Mary Ann met her end. This brought a new set of gasps from William. He took some time to compose himself.

"She were only forty-three she was; before 'er time. She went before 'her time. What are we going to do?" William closed his eyes again and fought back a new barrage of tears that he could feel welling up inside him. The remainder of the cab ride was done in silence. Samuel did not have the heart to ask any more questions at this time. There would be plenty of time for further investigative work. But first things were first. Proper police protocol needed to be observed. Right now it was imperative that the body be positively identified. That was his primary task. It was the one step that he needed to take to hopefully solve this heinous crime.

***

The Mortuary was an imposing gothic revival building somehow aptly suited to its purpose by the old-world design. William and Samuel exited the cab. Samuel paid the drive who tilted his hat and rode away. William could not even remember walking up the steps and thorough the doors. He could only barely remember Samuel talking with someone and finding out the exact whereabouts of the body. They were led by an attendant and walked through hallways and corridors until they came to a door which was opened and the tow of them ushered in. Inside was a table. A white sheet covered the body that was visible beneath it. Blood stained the sheet toward the mid-section.

At a signal from Samuel the attendant pulled back the sheet exposing Mary's head. William held his hat tightly in his hand and leant forward. The dead face of his wife lay there on the table. He began to cry openly.

"Mary, oh my dear Mary what have they done to you?" he managed to say between tears, wails and sobs. Satisfied that they had the positive identification that was required, Samuel indicated that the attendant should replace the sheet.

There were many questions swimming through Samuel's head that he desperately wanted to ask Mr Nichols, but now did not seem either appropriate or expedient. He did not expect William to be in a state to answer questions for a while yet. He spoke to both William and the attendant, only expecting the attendant to fully digest what he was saying.

"We will need you to come to the Whitechapel station and answer some more questions please Mister Nicholls."

Surprisingly William answered.

"No, not yet please. Let me have some more time with 'er?"

Samuel couldn't bring himself to insist. After all he had achieved his goal. And it was not as if Mr Nicholls was going anywhere, not with children at home depending upon him.

"Just one question before I leave you Mister Nichols; many children do you have. I counted five at your flat?" The question seemed to completely flummox William. He stared blankly at Samuel for a short time unable to pull the information out of his memory. Then as if he had become struck with the information required he briefly shook his head and answered.

"Five?" his voice was weak. Samuel indicated that it did not matter.

"Please have Mr Nicholls escorted to the station when he is ready" he directed the attendant. "Ask for myself or Senior Detective inspector Edmund Reid. We will continue the questioning." The attendant indicated that he would follow the instructions given. Looking again with some undisguised sympathy at Mr Nicholls he left the man to mourn his late wife.

Chapter 4: The Murders in Whitechapel

By the time that Samuel made it back to the Metropolitan Police Station at Whitechapel the morning briefing was about to begin. He entered the room. This was where the Senior Detective Inspector would present the direction for the day to his staff. New cases would be assigned and updates on existing cases would be discussed. It was all managed ably by Edmund Reid. Although close to retirement he showed no signs of winding-down ready for his Autumnal years. In fact, quite recently he seemed to be more invigorated by his job than he had been for the months previously. The staff in general thought that this was due to the fact that he realised that with retirement so close, he may in fact miss his job and would be unable to settle into a quitter pace of life. Whatever the reason, the morning briefings had become much more professionally run. It was only hoped that Reid's replacement would be at least as good when he finally made an appearance.

The news had already been circulated that Edmund's replacement would be Robert Anderson. He was from another station entirely, but was well thought of by his staff there. He would assume his duties at Whitechapel Criminal Investigation Department in early October. But until then, the man to look to for direction was Edmund Reid.

He cleared his throat indicating that the men should quiet themselves. They did so without any further prompting.

"Another murder last night; do we have a positive identification on the body Mister Gates" Edmund looked to Samuel for an update. Samuel took up the mantle and addressed the crowded room.

"One Mary Ann Nichols, aged forty-three of Durward Street here in Whitechapel. Identified by her husband, one William Nichols; they live in a flat with their five children. The victim was clearly engaged in the activities of a prostitute last night when the attack happened. As you can imagine Mr Nichols is rather overwrought at the moment. I will have the opportunity to ask more question when he arrives at the station in a while." Samuel finished his summation. It garnered the approval of Reid with a nod. Edmund took over from this point.

"Victim was slashed twice on each side of the neck and stabbed multiple times. The most unusual characteristic of this particular murder was the way that the stomach was cut open and the insides withdrawn. A poor attempt was made to put them back again." The crowd murmured with a mixture of revulsion and shock.

"Settle down" warned Reid annoyed at the response from his men.

"Could it be the torso killer again?" One of the men asked, Samuel did not see which. The killer to which the reference was made was still at large. The body of a prostitute was pulled from the Thames River in June of that year, one piece at a time. The as-yet-unfound killer was named the torso killer because that was the first part of the body that was recovered. Then like a macabre life-sized doll, other parts were eventually recovered until a positive identification was made of the hapless female victim.

Reid did not take time to contemplate the question; clearly he had already given the possibility some thought and dismissed it.

"No. The results of the attack are completely different. The torso-killer completely dismembered his victim. Mary Ann Nichols had her throat cut with what looks to be great precision. I have inspected the body as has the police surgeon. He and I are of the opinion that this killer is not as unschooled as the torso killer appears to be. The cuts reminded us both of a surgeon. We are more than likely looking for somebody that has knowledge of anatomy. The torso killer, I am convinced has the training of a man that has worked in an abattoirs."

There was a general low rumbling of discussion between people that were either agreeing with Reid or contemplating alternatives.

"Door-knocking people. Find out where all of the local Doctors and Surgeons were last night. Establish alibies. Those that cannot account for their whereabouts, bring in for further questioning. Samuel Gates will work with on the husband and get any information out of him about his wife's movements last night. The senior clerk has put together a list of the local doctors and surgeons. He has the duty assignments on who will be canvassing them." He waited for the room to absorb his direction and continued.

"We must not overlook the possibility of a visiting doctor, so the passenger ships in port will have to be investigated as well. Once again see the senior clerk for the duty roster on who will be assigned to the docks." Edmund then went on to talk about the next case followed by the next and the next and so on. The meeting went on for about thirty-five minutes. He gathered input from the various officers and detectives about what had been discovered. It was noted carefully by Edmund's secretary, a young police constable that could write with amazing speed and clarity. At the end of the meeting Edmund circled back to the most recent case.

"Bad thing this latest murder; the papers have already got wind of it and you can bet your last penny that you will be reading about it in the evening edition today and all of the papers tomorrow. Murders like this capture the imagination of the public. We do not want that to happen this time if we can help it. An arrest that is what we need! Or, if not, a suspect! That is that it will take to steal the wind from of their sails. Move quickly men. We must assure the press that we have the situation well in-hand. We do not want panic in the streets. Is that understood?" He finished with a question that was clearly rhetorical but the majority of the men felt that they should answer. There was a general 'here-here'.

Chapter 5: The Fairclough Family

The day had been long. Samuel had questioned William Nichols at length about the night that Mary Ann had died. He was not able to offer very much that they had not already guessed. His job did not offer sufficient income to school their five children in the manner to which they aspired for them, so Mary Ann had become a casual prostitute. She was never allowed to bring men home, so she had to find a willing candidate that would provide the abode for their brief and paid liaison. This must have cut-down Mary Ann's opportunities somewhat, but it appeared to be working for them for the last seven years.

William Nicholls himself had been at work the day and was at home with the children putting them to bed when Mary Ann left for her night-time job. Samuel had pondered if William could somehow be the killer. He may have put the children to sleep and then snuck out of the house and murdered his wife. But Samuel did not entertain the thought seriously. There was no motive. Why cut off such a valuable source of income for them both. Why suddenly become jealous after several successful years of having a wife as a part-time prostitute. William hardly seemed the passionately jealous type. Murder is a crime of intense emotion. This was conspicuous by its absence from William Nichols. Nevertheless, men had been dispatched to verify with the Nichols' neighbours that William was indeed home when the murder was being committed.

Samuel felt that he had embarked on a long journey. In spite of what Edmund Reid wanted, the reality was that it may be weeks or even months before the department came up with a suspect. He was hurrying through the streets toward another important appointment has he pondered the days happenings. But this time the meeting that he had to keep was of a personal nature. He was due at dinner with this soon to be father and mother-in-law and of course his beautiful fiancé Florence.

He smiled when he thought of her. She was so full of life and curiosity about the goings-on in the city. And having absolutely no-shame was not afraid to ask him to speak at length about his day at work and all of the unmentionable horrors that he must face on a day-to-day basis. It was very unladylike of course, but Samuel did not mind. In his mind after they became married he may be more likely to divulge the secrets of his day. There would always be the confidential cases that he would be required to keep absolutely secret of course. But Florence was so inquisitive that he would succumb to pillow-talk and tell her what he was able to about his work.

Such a conversation would no doubt be on the cards tonight. Samuel turned into the street and hurried down a few doors to a modest, but still very well-to-do terrace. He mounted the stone steps to the main door and tapped on the ornate brass door-knocker. The door was opened by the live-in maid. She was a mature lady that had lost her husband to a fever many years ago and had been picked-up by the Faircloughs to be their maid. Missus Barnes did the cooking and cleaning. Her old face did not betray and sign of weariness. She always managed to look bright and cheerful no matter what the time of day or task that she was called up on to perform.

"Good evening Missus Barnes" he said and gave her his broadest smile.

"Good evening Mister Gates; right on-time as usual. Please come in dinner will be served in a few minutes. Mister and Missus Fairclough are in the drawing room." She stood aside allowing Samuel entry. He took off his hat as he did so.

"Here let me take your hat and coat. The fire is on inside it will warm you up" the offer sounded comforting. It was not particularly cold, but it was not warm either. The last day of summer certainly held a promise that autumn would be a chilly one indeed.

Samuel handed over his hat and coat thanking Missus Barnes as he did so then moved down the hall to a set of double doors. He knocked quietly before swinging them both open inwards. Inside sat Florence with her parents. As feared, Mister Fairclough had the evening edition of the paper open and was reading it his very attentive wife and daughter. Both were engaged in needle work of some description but had stopped in order to listen to what was being read out.

"Ah my dear boy, come in!" said Mister Fairclough with a smile. "We were just talking about this terrible murder in Buck's row. Are you working on the case? Tell us what you know?" He was clearly invigorated about the possibility of gleaning more news about the murder than the paper had reported. It ran in the family thought Samuel. They were all as bad as one another when it came to pumping him for information about current police investigations.

"I'm afraid that I can't talk about that one Mister Fairclough; it's too new and there are still many leads to follow and alibies to establish before we close in on the killer. But rest-assured that the Metropolitan Police will catch their man and he will swing at the end of a hangman's rope. Besides this is not conversation for the ladies of the house and over one of Missus Barnes' wonderful meals?" He let the question hang in the air hoping that it would circumvent any further inquiring questions from them.

"Nonsense Samuel" retorted Missus Fairclough. "Harrold tell him. The Fairclough women are from sturdy stock. We all have strong constitutions and can handle such things that would turn lesser women pale with fright." Missus Fairclough redressed Samuel for even trying to change the subject. For his part Mister Fairclough laughed loudly.

"That is so my dear Millicent. You see what you are facing Samuel. There is no sense in trying to avoid the conversation. We are all intrigued and simply must know what is going on? What haven't the papers reported that you can tell us?" Harrold was not backing down. Fearing that the entire evening would be devoted to recounting his day at work Samuel sought support from his fiancé.

"Florence help me please. Surely you don't want to talk about these things over our meal together?" He gave Florence his best lost-puppy-dog look hoping to win her over. There was no such luck to be had however.

"Oh no you don't Samuel; I stand beside my Mother and Father whilst I am in this house. Tell us everything!" Florence was not going to even try to take the middle ground and take a conciliatory role. It was clear that Samuel was on his own in not wanting to discuss the latest gruesome murder in London. Resigned to the fact that he would now have to spend the entire meal walking a tight-rope of telling his hosts enough to keep them satisfied that they were hearing more about the case than was available to the public in the papers, and not telling them enough to warrant a dressing-down from Edmund Reid. His boss was very particular about such things. Samuel sighed. At this point Missus Barnes appeared behind him.

"Dinner is served" she announced.

"Excellent" said Millicent. "Come along Samuel, tell us everything that you know". She stood up and Samuel offered her his arm to escort her to the dining table. Harrold offered his to Florence and they followed them from the room.

***

The meal had been typically wonderful food from Missus Barnes. Samuel had managed to impart enough of the case history of the latest and most news-worthy murder in his precinct to satisfy the Fairclough family, and yet still retain enough confidentiality to maintain his professional integrity. He had tried unsuccessfully on the odd occasion to turn the dinner conversation to something other than gruesome murders in Whitechapel, but was soon pushed back onto the main topic of conversation by one of the family.

Eventually though when he thought that enough was enough Samuel pulled out his ace card.

"My parents are looking forward to seeing you all again" he said. Harold was sipping on a fine port as a digestive for his equally as fine meal. And Samuel's announcement got exactly the reaction that he had anticipated.

"How are Margaret and Frederick?" asked Millicent.

"They are both enjoying their Swiss holiday immensely according to their latest letter". Samuel fired his second salvo. He tempted the diners with the promise of a letter from his holidaying parents in far-away Switzerland.

"Don't keep it to yourself then dear boy; what are they doing over there? Eating a lot of fondue I suspect" Harrold was on par with Millicent and Florence in leaning forward with eagerness to hear all about Samuel's parent's adventure on the continent. And so Samuel had finally managed to take control of the conversation and skilfully turned the subject to one that he was more than happy to discuss at length.

This took them to the end of the evening very nicely. Samuel secretly patted himself on the back for his deviousness. There was no more talk of his work on the current murder case for the Metropolitan Police. One incident threatened to overturn his crafty change of conversation. Samuel mentioned that the new head of the CID would be holidaying in Switzerland also just prior to taking up his role replacing Edmund Reid. He realised his mistake however and quickly brought up that his parents were becoming adept at skiing. This as it happened was more than enough to ensure that they stayed on topic of Switzerland and not local murders and murderers.

Eventually though the evening drew to a close and lengthy good-nights were exchanged before Samuel was shown to the door. He held Florence's hands in his for a final good night before departing. As he hailed a handsome cab to take him home Samuel reflected upon the day that had been. This was the thirty-first of August in the year of our Lord 1888; the final day of summer. How long would it be he wondered, before the murder of Mary Ann Nichols would be solved and the murderer was hanging from a rope? He hoped that it would be soon.

At any rate, it was now the weekend and he had two days off work. He needed to relax after such a hectic week. Before he knew, he thought to himself, he would be in the thick of it all again.

Chapter 6: Monday the 3rd of September 1888

The day had been characteristically frenetic in the Criminal Investigation Department of the Metropolitan Police Yard of Whitechapel. Talk in the station was of *the murder* and how *the investigation* was coming along. When the postman called he delivered his bundle of letters to the front desk who then in turn had it taken to the mail room for disbursement to the various detectives, clerks and so on that kept the working of the department running smoothly.

One letter however no matter who read it seemed to be passed from one junior clerk to the next before it made its way to the senior administrator. Reading the contents he shook his head in disbelief before directing his junior to hand it on to Edmund Reid's personal clerk.

When the letter was eventually delivered to the man, like all of the others he read the contents with a mixture of bemusement and disbelief.

"Madam Athalia" he said aloud to himself reading the description of the sender that had been written as part of the many paragraphs

"Psychic and conduit to the deceased?! What a......" he caught himself before uttering a profanity aloud in the station.

"Crazy old woman" he eventually said completing his sentence in a more demure way than he had originally planned. If only he had taken the time to register the date that the letter was written he would have realised that it was detailing a murder that had only been reported in the newspapers after the letter was sent. But instead the clerk mistakenly assumed that the writer had read the newspaper reports on the murder and for reasons known only to her wanted to become a party to the investigation in some way.

He dutifully stamped the letter with a receipt of day and time and then pushed it into a draw unwilling to deal with such superstitious nonsense in his otherwise much too busy day.

Chapter 7: Saturday 8th of September 1888, 5:30am

The murder of Mary Ann Nichols exactly one week earlier was not on the mind of Annie Chapman. Her dire financial situation consumed her thinking. Selling flowers and her beautiful crochet works was not enough to keep the rent paid and food on the table. Maybe if it was only for herself, but not the three children. And now that John, her husband had become ill and was unable to work, what else could she do except supplement her income with casual prostitution?

Annie had had quite a successful night giving men what they wanted in return for what she needed. She could feel the money rattling in her purse hidden beneath her constricting corsetry. It was satisfying in a way that none of her male-liaisons would ever be. That was until she met this fellow. He had taken her arm and they were walking towards his residence. He seemed quite handsome actually. The beard gave him a little bit of a scruffy appearance. It was not to her taste, but overall this man was far and above much more gentleman-like than her usual conquests.

Annie had effectively been awake the entire night and dawn would be approaching soon. She had made just enough money already to see her family through to the next month. But when this man had presented himself to her and made his intentions clear, why would she turn him down? It was not as if she was actually looking forward to another frantic penetration. Her vagina was sore enough already, but Annie was curious about how this man would look when out of his quite fine clothes; certainly much better than any of her patrons so far.

They rounded a corner into Hanbury Street.

"Number twenty-nine" said the man, breaking in on Annie's musings. He indicated a small and bland looking terrace house off in the distance. Suddenly out of the shadows another man appeared. It caught the both of them by surprise.

"Oooh-ay1" said the man in a very thick middle northern accent. He tipped his hat and made his way past them disappearing just as quickly in to the dim light as he had materialised.

"Someone you know?" inquired Annie's customer. He turned to look at her.

"Never seem him before" lied Annie. In fact she had recognised the man as a previous consumer of the wares that she was now selling on the streets of Spitalfields. But there was no need for her latest patron to know that. A part of her act was giving the impression that she was not as common as the full-time prostitutes that littered the back streets of London. Hence the very upright outfit that she wore and demeanour that she carried herself with. The man gave a harrumph accepting her brief explanation without further question.

"This way" he pulled her arm creating a sense of urgency. Annie responded in kind and quickened her pace. It would not do to upset the man so soon prior to the act of sex. They arrived at the house. It looked deserted. Annie barely had time to register that the residence did not look to be in use before the man ushered her to the side gate. He must live in a flat at the rear of the property she thought.

If the lighting on the street was dim, the passageway to the rear of the house was positively black. She could barely make out what was ahead of her. They navigated the narrow alleyway to the back of the property. Mercifully the dark helped to conceal the knife that the man had produced from his clothes.

He turned to her and Annie thought that he was to explain where to next. Instead he just smiled. Annie smiled in return assuming that it was simply the man showing how happy he was to soon have his way with her. But his face seemed frozen somehow, like that of a child's doll. Something else too, she should not be able to see his face given the absence of light, but she could. It took her a moment to register but his features were glowing as if his face was lit from the inside. But that would not be the only bizarre thing that Annie was to witness that night. The most extraordinary thing that Annie Chapman had ever seen in her life happened. The man's face melted away was replaced with a gelatinous shapeless blog still glowing with an eerie light. Annie was horrified she drew in a breath to scream but it was already too late. All Annie saw was a momentary flash as the knife was plunged into her throat. She garbled with pain whilst clutching at the injury, but the man's other had was firmly covering her mouth preventing any release of enough noise to alert anyone as to her plight. Again he thrust the knife at her and it severed her throat on the opposite side.

Annie could feel the blood pouring from her neck. She felt cold. Her body trembled and her knees gave way. She fell to the ground.

Looking up at the man in horror she could see that his face had somehow reformed to that of a proper mans. Again he had that malevolent smile upon his face. Annie's last thoughts were of her family and how she was going to get her takings to them. She did not see the knife that again was thrust deep into her body; this time penetrating her abdomen. Just as in the previous murder, the man cut a long line into his victim's body. It was a much neater cut though, not jagged like before. He enjoyed doing it. Separating the skin he put down the knife and reached in extracting her uterus. He smelled it suspiciously. Seemingly pleased with what he found he opened his mouth to consume it.

Like a boa-constrictor he dislocated his jaw and his mouth opened wide; impossibly wide for any human to do. Pushing Annie's freshly harvested uterus into his mouth he closed his mouth and swallowed. Like a pelican that had just swallowed a large fish the uterus could be seen bulging out the neck of the man before sinking downwards and disappearing into his torso. It was a revolting sight. But there was nobody to see it.

Looking down at the body that was still bleeding over the ground the man gave a dismissive snort and stood up. He removed a cloth from within his jacket and did his best to clean the knife and his hands of any blood. He was only successful up to a point. But it was still dark enough for him to make his escape without arousing suspicion. His features had lost their unearthly glow. Gently laughing at how he had terrorised her, he left Annie Chapman's corpse behind him and disappeared into the darkness.

***

It was only half an hour later when a hapless fellow begrudgingly making his way to a dreary job that he disliked decided to cut through the back of the terrace where Annie Chapmans body lay in order to shave a few minutes off his lengthy journey to his employer. This side access way met with another that would take him to the next block without the need to walk around the entire length of houses if he followed the footpaths and streets.

The sun was on its way to the horizon and the sky was filled with the soft light of pre-dawn. As he made his way down the passageway he could see a woman's feet protruding from around the corner of the rear of the terrace that he was effectively trespassing upon. He stopped. Then gingerly making his way forward he craned his neck to attempt to see around the corner. A woman was lying there in a pool of blood, her innards pulled out and on show. For a moment he thought that he was going to vomit. Instead he shouted for 'HELP!' with all of his might. It was the only thing that he could think of to do.

Chapter 8: Athalia's Second Vision

Madam Alice Athalia was having another troubled sleep. She could see though a mist a glowing face that looked malevolently at her. Horrifyingly it distorted and became something akin to a jellyfish. Alice tried to scream but a knife cut her throat; she clutched it in a vain attempt to stop the bleeding. Another cut this time to the other side. The pain was excruciating. Looking around her for help she could see that she was in a side passageway to a house. There was nobody around. She was alone and completely at the mercy of this hideous creature. Looking down at her body she did not recognise the dress that she was wearing. How odd she thought that such a thought would occur to her at this time. There was the knife again. Absolute horror gripped Alice. It was plunged into her abdomen and dragged from the entry point across the width of her body.

Alice Athalia felt herself die. Yet she was still very much aware of what was happening. She knew beyond a shadow of a doubt that her eyes were shut tightly when she died. Somehow, however she could see through her eyelids to what was happening. There was no more pain. This allowed Alice the peace of mind to ponder very briefly on her situation. How could she be dead and yet still see what was happening? Why was she wearing a dress that she knew that she did not own?

Revulsion filled her when she saw the bearded man lift out the insides of her lower abdomen. But Alice fought the feeling. There were more important things to consider than the disgust that threatened to overcome her. The bearded man; his face was no longer a quivering jelly-like blob. It had become that of an ordinary man. It was not glowing anymore either. In fact she recognised the man's face. She had seen it before. As she pondered the question, a new terror seized her. His jaw dropped making his mouth a huge yawning opening. It was so large that he easily fitted the innards that he had extracted from her into it.

Alice wanted nothing more than to turn away, but she could not. He ate the gizzards and swallowed them. Just at that moment Athalia realised where she had seen this man before. It was in a dream, a recent dream. No, more than that, a nightmare. Athalia recalled the horror of the previous weekend where she had awoken screaming in fright. Burton had come to see what was wrong and ensure that she was alright. It all made sense to her in that moment. This was the same man from that terrible dream.

This must too be a dreadful dream she thought. But by even thinking such a thing to herself she had raised doubts in her own mind. She watched the man wiping his hands and walking away leaving her body behind him with casual inhuman disregard. Alice could see the merest hint of light beginning to fill the sky. She was unsure of how long she lay there unable to talk or move. If this was a dream why hadn't she awoken by now? Question after question went around and around in her head until she thought that she was going to go mad.

There was no sense of time passing except by judging the light. It was now shortly before dawn. She heard a wooden gate unlatch and squeak open from somewhere out of her field of vision. It was shut. Then there were footsteps that approached and stopped. A moments silence then the sound of a man screaming for help woke Athalia from her sleep.

***

Alice's eyes snapped open. She sat up in bed and looked around at the familiarity of her room.

"That was no dream; it was a vision" she said to her otherwise empty room.

"There has been another murder." Athalia breathed in and out and felt her lower abdomen just to reassure herself that she was still intact. It was time to write another letter to the Metropolitan Police Department. They simply had to act to find this killer. She would describe the man in as much detail as she could this time and invite them to her home to discuss the vision in more detail if they so desired.

Alice threw back the warm covers and began to prepare herself for breakfast. She had had a very important letter to write today.

Chapter 9: Saturday the 8th of September 1888, 8:30am

Samuel Gates awoke to the sound of a knocking on the front door of his home. He was effectively living there alone for the time being whilst his parents were on holiday abroad. It was not a fancy house by any means, there was no live-in housekeeper to answer the door for him. He grumbled a little at the thought of his Saturday morning sleep-in being disturbed. Again came the incessant knocking at the door.

"Leave that door knocker alone for pity's sake" he said to himself as he scrambled out of bed and fond his thick dressing-gown. He pulled on his slippers and made his way downstairs whilst tying the cord to his garment and attempted to make himself as presentable as he could under the circumstances. He opened the front door. Standing there were two uniformed policemen. He recognised both of them from his place of work.

"Sorry to disturb you so early in the morning Sir" one of them said. Samuel knew instantly that they men would be carrying bad news.

"What has happened?' he asked wanting to dispense with the platitudes and get to the heart of the matter.

"Another murder Sir" said the other police officer.

"Inspector Reid would like you to report for duty today. We are to escort you to the scene of the murder." The news jolted any thoughts of sleepiness out of Samuel. He nodded compliantly. He was electrified. He wanted to ask more questions but decided that he best comply to the current request as quickly as possible.

"Yes, yes of course. Please come in whilst I get ready". He allowed the two officers inside, pointing the way to the front reception room and asked them to 'make themselves at home' whilst he made his way back upstairs.

***

The two attending Police Officers had given Samuel as much information about the murder as they knew on the journey to Spitalfields. It was ascertained that the wounds inflicted on the victim were the same as those suffered by Mary Ann Nichols. The identity of the woman had been gleaned from the purse. This had been masterfully embroidered with her name and address. Annie Chapman was her name. There would need to be a visitation to that address for absolute confirmation. But at this stage there was no reason think otherwise.

The three of them made their way down Hanbury Street to the house in question. There was a crowd of people already milling around trying to see what was going on.

"Police business, move away" said one of the uniformed officers as they approached. People turned in expectation of something from them, as if an announcement would be made about the goings-on at the rear of the house. They would be disappointed. Instead Samuel and his escort were let into the side gate by the constable guarding the entryway. Left without any more news the crowd resumed their murmuring to each other about what each of them had seen or found out from the others present.

Samuel looked down at the body. It was gruesome. Blood had formed a pool around Annie Chapman's body. The insides of her unmentionable-parts were pulled out through a gash that was cut not just though her body but also through the material of her dress.

"The killer didn't even wait to get her undressed" he said

"Not really the place for it Governor" responded one of the uniformed men.

"I suppose not" agreed Samuel looking around. This was hardly the place for a woman-of-the-night to engage in paid-for sex with a man.

"Have you found anything else at all?" he asked of the men present.

"Nothing Sir, no weapon, nothing"

Samuel was disappointed but not surprised. A killer was hardly likely to leave a calling card. He overcame his disgust at the sight and studied the slashes on Annie's face more carefully.

"Exactly like the ones on the first victim. I wonder why. Why two cuts to both the left hand and right hand side of the throat?" he asked not expecting an answer. One of the men however did oblige with his thoughts.

"Perhaps to stop the victim from crying out?"

"Then why not cut the front of the throat, much more effective than the sides" Samuel countered. Another of the uniformed men offered his theory.

"To bleed the victim to death"

"You are assuming that the murderer lets his victim bleed to death before performing the……surgery?" Samuel asked, wanting to clarify the idea that the constable was expressing.

"I don't know; maybe" came the reply.

"The longer that the murder takes to kill his victim the more chance that somebody will discover what is being done" Samuel offered his counterpoint to the hypothesis.

"No, I think that the entire thing is done as quickly as the killer can. He slashes the throat on both sides knowing that the victim will surely bleed to death given enough time, but then makes this huge….incision, a deadly cut in order to get to the insides of the woman. This results in immediate death. It doesn't make sense."

"If he is a mad man then common sense is not really going to be at the forefront of his mind is it?" stated one of the men. It could have been thought of as a sarcastic response to Samuel's musings but Samuel was beyond such trivialities. There was more going on here than could be easily deduced from the body of the victims.

"Get the body to the mortuary. I want the police surgeon to examine it".

With something more affirmative to do than offer conjecture about the motives and mentality of the murderer, the police organised themselves to do as they were told.

Chapter 10: Police Surgeon Thomas Bond

Much like Samuel, Police Surgeon Thomas Bond's morning had been disrupted by a constable from the CID. He had been ordered to report to work too, so he was present when the body of Annie Chapmans was brought in.

"Over there on the main examining table please" he directed the four men that were carrying the sheathed body. He waited almost eagerly for them to lay her out and proceeded to remove the coverings on her. Upon seeing the neat and quite symmetrical cuts on the victim's throat he mumbled something to himself. One of the men thought that he was being addressed.

"What was that Doctor?" he said expecting a clarification of the unclear words.

"That will be all thank you Constables. I will send along my report when it is ready." Two of them looked disappointed that they would not be allowed to stay for the examination and the other two seemed relieved that they were excused. The four men left the room without any further words.

Thomas reached for the book in which he recorded his findings from examining the deceased. He flipped through the pages until he found the expert drawings that he had made of Mary Ann Nichols wounds. He found what he was looking for and compared them to the ones visible on Annie Chapman. They were identical.

Moving with care he continued to remove the blankets that the body had come wrapped within. When he exposed the main lower abdomen wound he again compared it to the one on the previous victim.

"Not as jagged a cut. Much more precise" he said aloud. "But exactly the same area and size." Because of his training and experience he was not sickened by the sight of the innards of Annie Chapman being exposed. He looked at them and then grabbing some forceps and separating the wound so that he could see inside more clearly, he frowned.

"The Uterus is missing?" he said, somewhat perplexed. He wondered if it had somehow been left on the ground where she was found, but dismissed the thought. Regardless of where the pieces were found, they would have been transported to him. That was standard procedure.

A hand reached over and clasped Thomas on the shoulder. He jumped up and let out a cry of surprise.

"What on earth are you doing?" he said as he realised that it was Samuel Gates that had scared him. "You startled me!" Thomas said with a strong note of rebuke in his voice.

"I spoke your name when I entered the examining room Doctor Bond" explained Samuel with a look offence on his face. Thomas realised that he had simply not heard Samuel because he was concentrating on the examination so deeply.

"My apologies Mister Gates, I was deep in thought" he offered by way of recompense. Then taking the opportunity presented to him he sought clarification on a couple of points.

"I take it that you have been assigned to this case, which is why you are here on a Saturday as well as myself Mister Gates?"

"Yes" Samuel confirmed.

"There were no parts of the body left behind at the murder scene?"

"None that we found Doctor, the area was searched for clues and resulted in nothing" he sounded more than a little forlorn.

"Ah, I see" said Thomas.

"Why, Doctor Bond, is something missing?" inquired Samuel.

"The Victim has had her uterus removed" Bond's finding shocked Gates.

"Are you sure?' he said rather clumsily not immediately able to think of anything else to say under the circumstances.

"Of course I am sure Mister Gates......" it was clear that Bond was about to launch into a scathing rebuke at having his professional observation questioned by a Junior Detective Inspector. Samuel realised the error he had made in asking and sought immediate consolation.

"I do apologise Doctor Bond. I did not mean to doubt your abilities. I was just so taken aback at the assertion. It is somewhat of a surprise don't you think?" Samuel's genuine plea did indeed offer Thomas solace and he let go of the reproach he was in the middle of verbalising.

"Yes, it is" Thomas agreed. "There is more" he said tempting Samuel with his findings so far.

"Please tell me" begged Samuel.

"The two cuts on the throat are exactly the same as those on last Mary Ann Nichols. The cut across the lower abdomen is in the same place and extends a similar width, but it is more clean, the work of a surgeon. Not like the first attempt. The cut was rough, that that of a butcher. But of course, there were no missing organs from the first victim". Doctor Bond concluded his summary.

"Is there enough similarity to acquaint the two murders to the same murderer?" Samuel wasn't sure if he wanted the answer even as he asked the question.

"Undoubtedly" confirmed the doctor.

"That is what I had concluded as well." Samuel said quietly. It was almost a defeated inflection, as if the weight of the corroboration was not one that he wanted to bear.

"Has a date been set for the inquest into the first murder?" Thomas wanted to know.

"I believe that it will be Monday the twenty-fourth of this month" Samuel answered.

"Then there is a lot of work to do before then Mister Gates; if you are to find this killer." Thomas was pointing out the very obvious.

"It's lucky that there are so many of us working on the case then Doctor. We are sure to find something that will point the way to the murderer soon enough" Samuel was just being cocky. He did not believe that they were any closer now to finding out the identity of the murderer of Many Ann Nichols than they were when she was found. He pondered the ramifications.

"More of a surgeon's cut than a butchers, you say?" he said aping the Doctor's former comments about the abdominal cut. Thomas nodded.

"Thank you Doctor Bond. Please send along a full report when you have it."

"I will" assured Thomas. With that Samuel nodded his goodbye and left the doctor to complete his examination of Annie Chapman's remains.

***

It was well after noon by the time that Samuel received the completed report from Doctor Bond. He was one of the few staff that had been called into work on the weekend to take charge of the latest murder. Police Sargent Plymoth was there too. He looked immaculate in his uniform and impossibly groomed moustache. Samuel wondered if he ever wore clothes other than his uniform.

Samuel was reading the report out to the small contingent that were standing around his desk. Apart from the Sargent, there were two other Junior Detective Inspectors and of course Edmund Reid. He was not going to let a little thing like the weekend get in the way of his continuing handling of his role as head of the CID.

Samuel completed the final paragraph of the police surgeon's findings.

"It is incumbent upon my person therefore to conclude without any doubt that the murder of Mary Ann Nichols and that of Annie Chapman were carried out by the same assailant in the same way." Samuel looked around at the men surrounding his desk.

"Well then" said Reid "We have two murders and as yet no definitive suspects. The inquest into the first murder is twenty four days away gentlemen. We need to find that killer. Imagine what the press will write if they get hold of this? We will look indolent and that simply will not do! I will not retire as the head of the Criminal Investigation Department at the end of October as the man that could not get this cased solved! " He glared at his small band of men.

"Am I making myself clear?" He looked at each of them with a stern expression.

'Yes Sir' each of them answered in turn.

"Get to work then. Today is fortuitously Saturday! You are sure to find those surgeons and doctors at home today! Yes, that will do very nicely indeed. Alibies, one and all, spread the search area wider in case he is from outside of the Whitechapel area. Find me suspects that we can question!" Again Edmund Reid's barked orders were met with a chorus of 'Yes Sir'.

Samuel took the lead reaching for the list of doctors and surgeons in the area that had been put together by the clerical staff. He separated the pages in no particular order leaving out the ones that had already been marked-off as having been spoken too.

"There one page each, with about eight per page, both home and doctor's office addresses for everyone that we need to question. It will be difficult, but we should be able to make a good enough go of it today." Even as he spoke he was doubting his own words. It was already after midday. If they started with the reminder of the lists now it would be well into night before they would be finished.

"Do whatever it takes!" Reid barked his final orders before retreating to his office and closing the door loudly. The men all moved as one to leave on their hopeless search.

"What we cannot do today we had better do tomorrow" said one of the other inspectors.

"On a Sunday, the Lord's day?! We shouldn't be working" objected another.

"Do you want to tell Mister Reid that you couldn't finish questioning all possible suspects because you didn't want to work on a Sunday?" asked Samuel. This quelled any further objections. They left the office without speaking further.

***

It was extremely difficult to manage but Samuel managed to locate the either doctors on his list. He had to shuffle from home addresses to gentlemen's clubs in a few cases to catch up with some of them. Only one had the decency to actually be home when he called. By the time he had questioned the last one on his list it was late. He had cornered this particular surgeon out to dinner. His housemaid was very willing to tell him the restaurant that the Doctor and his wife were dining at.

Samuel had been greeted with absolute outrage in every instance. He had tried unsuccessfully in every instance to be as conciliatory as possible. But Doctors and Surgeons were an easily offended lot. The very thought of a police inspector calling into question the virtuousness of them was nothing short of insulting. He had taken pages of notes and put up with angry wives and friends as he followed his procedures and questioned each of them.

He was finishing up with the last of them, and probably the worst. Samuel knew that it would be in no small part due to the fact that he had interrupted what looked to be a splendid dinner at a very fine restaurant. He may well have felt the same if the positions were reversed. But that did not stop Samuel from being deflated at the barrage of indignation that he had to suffer from this man.

"Once again, my apologies for disturbing your dinner Doctor Cannongrove" Samuel knew that he may have sounded anything but sorry at the time but he was so tired and fed up with the monotony and fruitlessness of his day that he no longer cared. For his part the doctor was not going to accept such a meagre apology and Samuel suffered through yet another volley of threats to take this to the highest levels of the Ministry.

"Well do try to have a good night Doctor. Missus Cannongrove" he stood up from the private table hidden conveniently in an alcove of the restaurant. Closing his book full of what he felt were completely worthless notes he walked away hoping that the other remaining diners in the small but stylish restaurant did not take too much notice of him as he departed.

At least he could have tomorrow off work and off the case. That gave him some hope that come Monday he would have a renewed sense of enthusiasm for this dual murder investigation.

Chapter 11: Monday the 10th of September 1888

Samuel arrived at the department at his usual time already knowing that Edmund Reid would be in a foul mood. Samuel had taken the time on Sunday to pick up a copy of the most likely paper to publish the story of Annie Chapman's murder, the Sunday People, a labour party tabloid. His suspicion was correct. Plastered over the front page was an overly emotive headline citing the murder they had all hoped would not be found out by the press. The article was particularly scathing of the police and how the situation was being handled by them. The journalist had even coined a nickname for the killer 'Jack the Ripper' after the way that the bodies had both been ripped open.

That alone would raise all sorts of questions from Reid about how the press found out about the second murder and why they were so quick to attach it to the same as yet unfound murderer as that of Mary Ann Nichols.

Sure enough even as he waked through the door from the rather blustery day that was forming outside, he entered a storm of a different kind.

"Well find out how the *Sunday People* found out about the second murder and more than that find out why they have published that both were perpetrated by the same killer!" Reid could be heard clearly shouting above the usual din of the office.

"Has somebody here spoken with the press?" the hollered question brought the busy office to a temporary halt as everybody looked at everybody else and wondered who would be brave enough to answer Reid and risk provoking him further. Samuel took it upon himself to champion the virtuousness of his fellow employees.

"The press could well have been present in the crowd of people outside the property where Annie Chapman was found sir. And it is no stretch of the imagination that if not, then when they did show up the neighbours would have been only too happy to gossip about what they knew or saw or heard through someone else." Samuel's summation of the possibility silenced the room even further as everybody waited for Reid's reaction.

To their amazement Edmund did not explode with anger at Samuel's proposal. Instead he stroked his chin and looked very much like he was deeply contemplating the possibility. Eventually he nodded and appeared to be appeased.

"Right you are Mister Gates, it is impossible to keep these muck-raking journalists from talking with anyone and everyone that can help them concoct an overblown story for that Sunday travesty." Reid paused and a little life returned to the office. Samuel had closed the distance between the two of them by now. Reid looked as if he had another thought and raised his finger gesturing at Samuel.

"But Mister Gates, how did they join the two murders together…?" Red looked like he was about to get angry again so Samuel nipped it in the bud.

"Definitely stretching the truth for the sake of an inflammatory story sir; how could they possibly have access to Doctor Bond's report, only a handful of us have seen it? And none of us are likely to take the press into our confidence. It would jeopardise the case."

Samuel had effectively headed-off another infuriated outburst from Reid.

"Yes" he said nodding his belief in what Samuel had stated. "Right you are Mister Gates. But you can bet your last half-penny that there will be ramifications from that story; and we will be the ones that have to pay the price for it. Briefing room!" he concluded his mild retort with an early call to the regular morning meeting.

The people involved all made their way toward the room. It filled up quickly. Reid stood at the head of the room waiting for everybody to arrive. Just as he was at the point of bringing the meeting to order three very officious looking men arrived. They stood out from the rest because of their very fine looking clothes. They had a certain air about them too. It was indefinable but somehow represented authority. This was recognised by Reid and he addressed them.

"Can I help you gentlemen?"

"Whom do I have the pleasure of addressing?" the tallest of the three answered.

"Detective Inspector Edmund Reid of the Criminal Investigation Department. And you are…?' he said in a tone of voice indicating that he was not to be trifled with.

"I am Detective Inspector Frederick Abberline. With me I have Detective Inspector Henry Moore and Detective Inspector Walter Andrews. We are from the central office of Scotland Yard and have been dispatched here to assist you with the investigation of the murder of Mary Ann Nichols." There was a stunned silence. All faces turned to Edmund Reid to see his reaction at being invaded from the north by fellow Detective Inspectors.

"I see" he said with measured calm. "Well gentlemen; it seems that you have come just in the nick of time. We appear to have a second murder that is attributable to the same murderer. One Annie Chapman, found Saturday morning mutilated in the same way. I doubt that men of your calibre read it but the Sunday People newspaper….." Reid was interrupted by Frederick Abberline.

"Yes Inspector Reid. We are aware of the recent press and the new murder. And most unfortunately we are aware of the name that is now sure to be associated to the killer, Jack the ripper." Abberline could be seen rolling his eyes as he quoted the reference.

"We have much to talk about. Please join in my office at the conclusion of the morning briefing and we can talk through the details of the case. What has been done and if you will bear with through this meeting; you will find what we are planning to do next." Reid's offer was laid out for the new arrivals.

"Please proceed" agreed Abberline.

What followed was a summary from the men who had canvassed the local doctors over the weekend. Much like Samuel's offering they had nothing concrete to offer. All of the doctors had alibies that were either able to be substantiated by wives, colleagues or other friends of prominence in the community. None of it came as much of a surprise to Reid. He digested the information as if he was expecting it and showed no sign of annoyance at the lack of any leads that could help them. Reid took the time to read out the Police

Surgeon's examination report to everybody so that they were all aware of the findings.

Further investigative works were issued. The ships that had been in port for both of the days were top of the list. A second visit to them just in case the murderer was a doctor or ship's surgeon on a foreign vessel. Reid again wanted the butchers targeted as he felt that the precision of the cuts although more readily attributable to a skilled and well-trained doctor, could still have been the work of a lowly butcher. Perhaps it was one that had a good steady hand and love of his craft.

There was conjecture on why the uterus of Annie Chapman was removed and why it could not be found. The only conclusion that garnered universal support was that the murderer was secretly insane to want to take-off with such a thing. Samuel noticed that during this part of the proceedings there were men that had to whisper to one another about the actual meaning of the word uterus. Slang names used to describe it were whispered in return.

The briefing went on for a long time. Longer than the one after the first murder. Samuel was unsure at this stage if it was being drawn-out by Reid in a show of his leadership skills in front of the Scotland Yard Detective Inspectors. But he dismissed the thought. He had not thought of Reid as petty enough to succumb to the vagaries of vanity. And with his retirement coming up, there was simply no need for Reid to ingratiate himself to Scotland Yard. He was after all, not after a posting there.

Eventually the meeting was closed and people talked amongst themselves as they separated to carry out their assigned tasks.

Samuel had been given the task of a second questioning check on one of the ships in port that had been positively identified as being in port on the dates of both murders. He left to do his job. On the way out he looked over at Reid as he escorted the three Scotland Yard newcomers into his office. He wondered how the introduction of three new bosses would help the outcome of the investigation.

Chapter 12: Tuesday the 11th of September 1888

Monday had been another fruitless day. The mood in the CID was one of trepidation. The three new Inspectors from Scotland Yard had begun to make themselves heard in the morning briefing. More suspects and a wider search area were proposed. A clerk was listening to them and shaking his head at the seemingly impossible workload that the new bosses were proposing. He was grateful to receive the mail to distract him from their barrage of orders.

The first one he opened looked vaguely familiar. There was something about the envelope, the writing the patterning on the envelope and then when he opened it the paper itself. It was all rather fine. He read the contents of the letter to himself

Almost immediately he groaned. Now he remembered. It was this crazy old woman again proportion to have had a vision about the killer and was willing to work with the police to see that the culprit was apprehended.

"The only vision that you have had my dear is of the Sunday papers. Crazy old duffer" he said dismissively. Nobody around him heard or cared what he had mumbled under his breath. He dutifully stamped the letter as received with the time and day and folded it up to join it friend in the top draw of his desk. He had much more important letters to read and distribute to the correct area of the police department. He certainly had no time for this silly old woman claiming to be a psychic and to have some intimate knowledge of the two murders to date.

Chapter 13: The Remainder of the Week

The remainder of the week was a repeat of Tuesday, not just for the clerk that receipted and distributed the mail, but for all of the employees in the CID. Scotland Yard, or the Celtic Three as the men had been calling the new inspectors behind their backs, were working everybody at a frantic pace. Edmund Reid had appeared to take much more of a supporting role than his men would have thought. He did not appear to be put out by the fact that these northern invaders had effectively wrested control of the CID from him. Only Samuel had at a time had the nerve to question Reid about his feelings on the change in command.

"It's good for the investigation Mister Gates. We simply must have that killer brought to justice and swinging from the end of a rope before I retire. And then if the Celtic Three can help me achieve that then I will be offering them all of the support and assistance that I am able."

Assuaged but still a little mystified at the compliance with which Reid was treating the newcomers, Samuel did not approach the subject with Reid again.

***

The other occurrence that was prominent during the unfolding of the week was that fact that the other papers, some of them decent conservative party broadsheets had begun to use the phrase 'Jack the

Ripper'. It was a surprisingly low-brow use of such a tawdry turn of phrase. Yet it was adopted by one, then the next and so on until there were only two newspapers that had not joined in on the journalistic fray.

"It would only be a matter of time" quipped Sargent Plymouth. "Mark my words, by next week there will not be a single paper that is not calling the murder Jack the Ripper!" Time would prove him to be correct.

Chapter 14: The Inquest

The week of Monday the 17th through to Sunday the 23rd of September proved to be equally as frustrating. Not because no suspects had been gathered. The pressuring from the Scotland Yard Inspectors had indeed produced results. There was suspect after suspect hauled into the CID for further questioning. Some two and three times, but still no charges were able to be laid against any one of them. In every instance the alibi was able to the either proven, or sometimes more interestingly, not proven and in those cases it only managed to highlight infidelity by the suspect. There were four suspects out of the twenty that had been gathered, that had to admit to their extra-marital affairs and produce their mistresses in order to win their freedom from the clink.

"Alibi proven; marriage ended!" Once more Police Sargent Plymouth had a way of breaking through the complexity and offering a dry summation, devoid of any sympathy for the former suspects.

The morning briefings swelled with men as more and more people were brought onto the case. There was a certain prestige now associated with working on one or both of the most talked about murders in the city in many years.

"Short memory, the public! What about the torso murderer? Not a word about poor old Elizabeth Jackson. Pieces of her were pulled out of the Thames over the entire month of June until we had enough to put her back together again. Not a word about that in any of the papers now. It's all about Jack the Ripper. When will he strike next?

Who will be the next victim? It's woeful I say. The public are treating this like a circus act to amuse and terrify them."

Nobody disagreed with Police Sargent Plymouth's decrying of the public's thirst for more gruesome news with regard to the two murders in Whitechapel. The week went by and still there was nothing to present in the scheduled inquest for Monday the 24th of September. What would the

***

The day of the inquest was upon the CID. The courtroom where it was to be held was the largest available in Whitechapel. The popularity of the case was recognised by the authorities and catered for in this way. It could easily have been a closed inquest, but the general feeling of those in charge was that this could easily be a cause of consternation from the press and the public.

Samuel arrived at the building. It had columns all around it and the stonework was clearly the work of expert stonemasons. He was with his fellow Junior Detective Inspectors. The senior men on the case had arrived much earlier and were sitting dutifully down the front. The mayhem out the front of the building was unexpected.

"Have you ever seen the like, for a murder inquest?" asked one of Samuel's colleagues. They had not and indicated thus.

"We had best see if we can get a seat inside. I get the feeling that this is going to take quite some time" offered Samuel. With his compatriots in agreement they shoved their way through the crowd and into the courtroom.

The queue for the members of the public to gain access stretched from the main courtroom all the way down the long corridor and almost to the main entrance. The queue itself was being added to with every passing second.

"Quickly, before all the seats are taken" said one of them and they hurried down past the queue only to be intercepted by a familiar voice.

"Samuel!" Samuel and his three friends turned to see who was claiming him.

"Florence? Millicent?" said Samuel somewhat shocked to see his fiancée and future mother-in-law in the queue. In fact he had to take a second look at the both of them. They were always quite snappy dressers, but today they seem to have gone above and beyond the call of the occasion. Both were resplendent in outfits that would have been more in keeping with a night at the opera than an audience gallery viewing at a murder inquest.

"What in heaven's name are you doing here?" he asked of them both. Looking somewhat guilty it was Florence who answered.

"We simply could not resist Samuel. And this is so much better than croquet with the ladies. Is it not Mater?" Florence sought support for their presence from her mother.

"Quite right my dear. And this is where the news is made Samuel. Why wait to read about it in the next day's papers when we can have a front-row-seat.....so to speak." Millicent looked at the queue with some trepidation.

"Is there anything that you can do Samuel, please?" begged Florence.

"Oh yes my dear boy, we simply must attend this inquest. It is in the interest of the ladies that we abandoned today. We promised them a first-hand account of proceedings". Millicent Fairclough gave Samuel a pleading look at least equal to the one that her daughter was throwing at him. Samuel looked beset upon. He glanced over at his colleagues for some support, all three of which offered him only shrugged shoulders of non-committal. Exasperated at being put into such a position he groaned audibly but conceded.

"Come with me; I'll see what I can do" He took Florence's arm, who in turn took her mothers and they walked boldly past the queuing people to the door of the courtroom. It was easy to get past the uniformed constables, as they were from the Metropolitan Police in Whitechapel and recognised the four Junior Detective Inspectors. They dutifully waved them into the room, but made to stop both Florence and Millicent until Samuel confirmed that they were with him.

Inside the upper gallery was all but full, and there were precious few seats on the floor. He saw where the others from his ranking were sitting and indicated to the bailiff to come to him.

"Can you please find seats for these two ladies? I would be very grateful" pleaded Samuel. Seeing that these members of the public must be of importance to the inspector the old man nodded obligingly and reassured Samuel to 'leave it with me'. He showed Florence and Millicent to a back row that was elevated and would offer the women a good view of everything, but that was low-key enough that they would not stand out too much amongst the other police staff.

"Thankyou Samuel" smiled Florence with glee that they achieved their goal for the day.

"I'll see you tonight at Van Dorset's" he said to his fiancé reminding them of the dinner reservations for both his and her family that evening. It would be the first opportunity for both families to dine together once more since Samuel's parents had returned from their holiday in Switzerland. She waved her acknowledgement and Samuel turned to see where his colleagues had got to. They had taken their seats and one of them looked back indicating that he had reserved one for Samuel. He rushed over to take it for fear of missing out in the growing melee.

Eventually the room was overflowing and the presiding Queen's counsel that had forgone ceremony of waiting for everyone to enter and then call upon them to stand upon his entrance, spoke from his chair.

"Enough is enough! Please close the doors we cannot fit in anymore!" The doors were closed to much verbal consternation by those that had not made it inside.

"Clearly this is going to be different to any inquest that I have had the duty to administer in all of my years." Began the QC. "Nevertheless we will proceed with an appropriate degree of demeanour from everybody present. There are certain etiquettes to follow and I will not abandon those simply because the city of London is more interested in this case than any of the others that should perhaps be of greater concern to all good citizens". Some of the crowd were oblivious to the fact that the QC had gently insulted them for just being present.

The inquest began with the reading of the case notes from Detective Inspector Edmund Reid. This was surprising to his men as they had thought that Frederick Abberline was now seen as the one in charge. Perhaps it was a political manoeuvre thought Samuel. Why stand up as the head of an investigation that was going so dismally.

The public attendees were anything but orderly and let out various collective 'oooos" and 'aaaahs' when the more explicit parts of the murder were described. Also unusual was that this was now the inquest for both the deaths of Mary Ann Nichols and Annie Chapman. It was widely felt more expedient to handle both of the inquests at once. So at the conclusion of the details of the first murder, Edmund then had to take the courtroom through the details of the second.

It felt much more like a trial than an inquest into the two murders. Samuel was called to recount what he had found when attending the scene as had all of the other inspectors. Hearing the same story over and over again from slightly different viewpoints was interesting because the presiding QC allowed them to offer conjecture. This was the main difference to a trial. Under those circumstances, such dalliances would not be tolerated. What was clear at the end of the summations from all concerned was that there so many differing viewpoints about how and who committed these heinous crimes.

Thomas Bond then had to present his findings for both of the examinations. His use of medical language was clearly way above some of the public listening but it was captivating nevertheless. His detailed descriptions about the cuts and the way that they were inflicted drew more gasps from the courtroom than anything else.

The number of people that had to speak and the questions from the QC to understand the statements drew-out the proceedings beyond anything that anyone had guessed. Although it was a cold day outside, the number of people in the room soon raised the temperatures and people were fanning themselves with anything they had at hand.

The witnesses that were called that had come forward claiming to have seen either of the women prior to their murder found themselves at the receiving end of particularly gruelling questioning from the QC. Differing descriptions of the man that both were supposedly seen with ranged from a 'perfect gentleman', to a man that had the 'look of a seafarer' and even a 'shabby-looking' fellow 'clearly of no particular upbringing at all.' By the end of the conflicting accounts nobody in the courtroom was any wiser as to a potential firm description of the suspected killer. The entire inquest was a marathon of repetitive stories and contradictory viewpoints from the 'witnesses'.

The final summation from the QC was lengthy and rambling using such typical legalese as 'on the one hand we have…' and 'when we take into consideration'. Samuel had all but dozed off by the time the old man mercifully reached his conclusion.

"Unless there is a significant turn of events to shed further light onto these murders and in some way lead to the successful apprehension and criminal conviction of the perpetrator then I have the unhappy duty to offer that there is no conclusion to this investigation. It will be so noted that it is an as yet unsolved case in both instances. I would beseech the Metropolitan Police Force to do better than they have been doing and work whatever hours are necessary to bring these two murders to a resolution. I note that the newspapers are now littered with satirical drawings indicating the general public's lack of confidence in the Police. As the leaders of the Criminal Investigation Department you will appreciate more than most that such an erosion of trust in the police is to be taken very seriously indeed. And any and all efforts made to reverse that situation." With that the QC rose from his chair. The bailiff shouted out

"All rise for his worship" and without waiting for the mark of respect to be afforded to him he walked out of the room by his private side door. The room erupted in a frenzy of talking that escalated to the point that it was impossible to hear somebody that was close at hand. Samuel tried to look around to see if Florence and Millicent were still there and managed to see the both of them hurrying toward the door. They were clever in making an early exit he thought. It would take a while to empty the room now. He would see them at dinner tonight anyway, and was certain that they would have their own viewpoints on the proceedings to offer him.

Chapter 15: The Palace

"The palace wants this solved! The public are outraged!"

Edmund Reid was giving the morning briefing the day after the inquest. The room was fuller than it had ever been. The Men from Scotland Yard, the ones that everybody assumed had wrested control of the investigation, were standing beside Edmund looking berated just as everybody else was at the harsh words from Reid.

"An erosion of trust in the police is to be taken very seriously indeed. And any and all efforts made to reverse that situation!" Reid read from the findings of yesterday's inquest. There was absolute silence. People either looked at each other or at the floor.

"It all seems so simple then doesn't it. We must reverse the public's feeling that the police are inept and cannot find this murderous maniac!" Reid was shouting, clearly very angry at the findings of the inquest.

"And how are we going to achieve this miracle?" Reid looked around the room. People actively averted his gaze fearful that he was not asking a rhetorical question. And he wasn't.

"Mister Gates. One of our best and brightest! Pray tell us all what it is that the police can do to win back the trust of the public whom we protect from insane killers?"

Samuel was not put-out by the question. Unlike those surrounding him that thought that Reid was looking for ideas that could help the situation, Samuel listened to the question with more care than that. He knew very well that Reid was not asking for a well-resolved solution to implement. He simply wanted to hear the very obvious so that he could continue his reprimanding of the job done so far in uncovering the perpetrator.

"We must find the culprit and bring him to justice Sir!"

"Exactly!............Find the killer……Restore public faith in the Police! How simple. And yet it seems beyond the combined capabilities of everybody in this room! I will not have Her Majesty the Queen send another message to the CID other than one of congratulations for catching Jack the bloody Ripper! Is that clear?"

The men mumbled their acquiesce on the matter rather half-heartedly.

"What was that? I couldn't quite make it out?" Edmund screamed at them all. There followed a chorus of boisterous 'Aye Sir' and 'Yes Sir' from the men.

"That is what I wanted to hear. Now assignments….." Reid went on to parcel out the dreary foot-work of re-questioning those that had already been questioned. Then a new list was produced, one of suspects from previous investigations. And then a third list was produced of cattle drovers. The search now encompassed butchers, slaughterers, doctors, surgeons, medical students, morticians, and now all crewmen on the boats that were positively identified as being docked during both murders. The lists were extensive. But the manpower to ensure that they were processed was strong.

There was a general feeling amongst the men that this was the start of the end for Jack the Ripper. Surely with this renewed sense of urgency, spurred on the by the want of Queen Victoria herself that it would only be a matter of time. Hard work and persistence would pay off and net the wrongdoer. Before long he would be swinging from the end of a rope in front of a grateful crowd of Londoners.

***

Wednesday, Thursday and Friday passed by before anybody knew. The average starting time at the station moved to be very early indeed. More and more men were showing up at 7 o'clock and some earlier still. And the time that people left work for the day stretched backwards to seven, eight and nine at night. There was nobody that was untouched by the sense of urgency that the royal interest in the case had brought. Samuel had become a ghost even in his own home. He left for work before his parents had awoken for the day and crept in just as they were readying themselves for bed.

He had had to send Florence an apologetic letter via his mother for his absenteeism. But thankfully the response had been received that she understood and supported not only him but all of the police force to catch the murderer and end the case once and for all.

Saturday too, saw men at their desks and continuing their rounds questioning suspects. More and more were brought in but still by the setting of the sun on Saturday evening the 29th of September, they had nobody to positively identify as Jack the Ripper.

***

Samuel sat at his desk. The men that had been around him and the suspects that had been brought in for questioning had one-by-one left. He was now alone. He looked up from reading the case notes from Thomas Bond for the umpteenth time.

'What more do I hope to gain from these?' he asked himself silently. He heard a clock strike and looked up at it. It was difficult to see. Most of the lamps in the office had been extinguished by men on their way out. He squinted and could just make out where the hands were pointing.

"Ten pm!" came a loud voice beside him. Samuel all but jumped up in fright. It was Edmund Reid.

"Working late again Mister Reid?" Edmund sounded pleased as he asked the question of Gates.

"Yes Sir. I thought that there may be something in Bond's findings that could help, but…." His voice trailed off not wanting to admit that he had found nothing more that could assist him.

"To catch this killer Samuel, it may be necessary to walk the path of his victims." The unusual assertion from Reid confounded the young man.

"Sir?" he said clearly not understanding the implication.

"Instead of sitting here reading a report, go out and see if you can catch the killer. Lady luck may smile upon you Mister Gates." Edmund seemed unusually friendly whilst making the unusual suggestion. It was a little disconcerting. But in context to his first sentence the proposition now made sense.

"Go to where the….*ladies* would find a willing….liaison and put myself into the position of witness should one of them be the next victim. I am sure to be able to recount more to an inquest than any of the witnesses did in the first inquiry. I may even stumble across the Ripper himself!" Samuel was renewed; enthused with the idea.

"That's the spirit Mister Gates. Happy hunting" smiled Reid and gave Samuel a hearty slap on the back. It was an extraordinary suggestion; for one of the Inspectors to join the regular constables on the streets, questioning prostitutes and searching high low for the murder on the streets that he roamed; but why not? As an Inspector he would have a keener eye for detail that the regular constables patrolling the streets may not possess. It made perfect sense for him to abandon protocol and join the hoi polloi and search at the very scene for the killer amongst the city dwellers. Samuel was still mulling over the positives of the suggestion when Reid bid him farewell.

"Goodnight Samuel. I'll see you at the briefing bright and early on Monday morning" Edmund disappeared into the gloom of the office. Samuel heard a door open and close. He was alone in the station.

"But where to look?" he said aloud to himself. He stood up and walked over to a map of the area that hung on the wall. It was large. He noted a few places where the ladies of the evening would find someone willing to pay for use of their body. But in truth there were so many.

"Not near the docks surely. If it *is* a seaman then he won't want to draw attention to himself". Samuel looked at the area that the first two murders had been committed. He decided for no particular reason to draw a line in pencil from one to the other. He found a pencil on a nearby desk to do just that.

If he were to prescribe a logical area to his search then he must decide upon its borders. He drew a square. Using the length of the line between murder one and two as the top side he completed the other three. A square was the first shape that came to his mind. He looked at the area that it covered within Whitechapel and even outside of it.

"Too large" he said. The more that he looked at it the more that it made sense that the next murder, and he was sure that there would be one, would be removed from the first two. His eye was drawn to the bottom corners of the square. The area around Lower Chapman Street and the goods depot on Aldgate High Street were the bottom two corners of the square on the map. If he confined himself to the quieter areas of both, staying off the main streets and searching for similarly quiet alleyways and streets then he could locate women selling themselves and question them about what they had seen.

It was a good plan. If it netted any worthwhile result then more men could be drafted to assist. He would happily take the lead and direct them to the areas in his search area that he could not cover himself.

With renewed vigour he collected his hefty coat and left the station.

Chapter 16: Sunday 30th of September 1888, 12:30am

Elizabeth Stride walked with her latest client. He was something of a gentleman and had insisted that she take his arm as they walked down the street. Elizabeth looked up and saw the name of the street that they were turning down.

"Dutfield Yard" she said aloud as they turned off Berner Street.

"What of it?" asked the man that she had so successfully picked up, and hoped would pay her a pretty penny for her favours. Not wanting to cause any friction Elizabeth quickly backed away from any potential confrontation.

"I've never been here before, that's all" she said hoping that it would gloss over any discontent in her gentlemen acquaintance.

"Over there" said the man pointing to a darkened area of the small street. Elizabeth struggled to see what he was pointing to. She assumed it was the doorway to his abode. She did not say anything more. Thoughts of exactly why she had never bothered to venture down this tiny street began to occupy Elizabeth's thoughts. It was most likely because she did not know anybody that lived here or indeed anywhere nearby here at all. Her home was quite some distance from here. But that would serve to protect the secrecy that she veiled around her extra-curricular activities to raise more money during the night-time hours. She began to lick her dry lips preparing them for what she assumed would be a hurried onslaught from the man beside her.

It was best to prepare herself for his frantic advances. They were all the same, men. All hot and bothered until they got what they wanted, and then the magical personality change came over them. He would be no different. Within ten or even fifteen minutes he would not be able to get her out of his home quickly enough. But she would not leave without adequate compensation for her services.

She was still thinking about the money that she would earn when she became aware that her gentleman had stopped.

"Are we here?" she asked as she turned toward him. She didn't even see the knife lunge toward her in the dark. It severed her main artery on the left hand side of her throat. The sharpness of the blade and the accuracy and deepness of the cut ensured that Elizabeth never even got to cry out in pain or fear. She was so shocked at the feeling of blood pouring from her throat and in such quantities that she could scarcely comprehend what was happening.

Vainly she clutched at her throat; it was an autonomous action. But the man grabbed both her arms and held them in a grip that was unbelievably tight. Spurts of blood in time with her rapid heartbeat streamed from the open wound. Blackness enveloped Elizabeth Stride. Her death would be nowhere near the trauma of the previous two. She collapsed to the cobbled street. Still jerking and attempting to mutter her shock at what had happened she succumbed to the twilight of that place between life and death.

The man crouched down, his knife at the ready to do even more damage to the woman's body. He leant forward and sniffed at her vagina like a dog sniffing a piece of meat found lying in the street. Then pulling a face of disgust he stood up. Clearly there was something about her body that he did not like. He returned the knife to the place where he had been hiding it, Elizabeth's blood still dripping from the blade.

He looked down at her still twitching form. Then with a gruff grunt of disapproval he turned and walked back the way that he had come. He drew a pocket watch on a chain from his waistcoat. It was barely 12:35am on Sunday morning the 30th of September. He had plenty of night left to find another victim; one that would satisfy his particular craving. He walked down the street. He would make his way toward St James.

Behind him Elizabeth Stride breathed in her last breath of air. Then silence covered her body.

Chapter 17: The Hateful Man of Whitechapel

He was an angry old man. Life had been unkind to him on many levels. He could never have been described as handsome. Not even as a young man. He did not excel at school and fared even worse in the school of life when it came to romance. There is someone for everyone his mother had said whilst she was alive. But he did not believe that at all. For most of his forty years he had searched for someone to call his own. Either a friend in the schoolyard even just one, rather than being bullied by the bigger boys. Later in life he searched for a lover after he began his career as a clerk in the Goods Depot on Aldgate Street in Whitechapel. But he would fail at that too.

And it was his boss that he had come to blame for all of his misfortunes. His boss was a man of Jewish persuasion. It was that that he had decided was the problem that was sabotaging his entire life. For whatever reason, and in reality, there was none to be found, he would blame all Jews for the hand that life had dealt him. Oblivious to the fact that his employer had been a fair and just boss, he simply did not care for any of them.

He was using the gaslights to read the paper as he made his way home from a particularly late night doing an inventory stock-take. It was gruelling work, something more blame all Jewish people for. He was reading an editorial column about Jack the Ripper and the inability of the police force to catch the killer.

"Probably a Jewish Police Commissioner" he mumbled with distain as he agreed with the rather vitriolic column. He turned into Mitre Square. Something caught his eye in the distance. At first he thought that it was a pile of rubbish on the ground. But the more that he looked the more that he was able to ascertain. Surely that was the dress of a woman, splayed out across the cobblestones? He made his way cautiously toward the prone figure. He was close enough now to identify for certain that this was indeed a woman on the ground. There was blood; lots of it. His heat beat increased as he approached slowly.

Then the magnitude of what he had found became clear. This woman had been murdered in a most horrible way. She was cut open and there were parts of her innards that were on show. He felt sick. He closed his eyes tightly hoping that the scene would not be there when he opened them again.

Then as if struck by lightning he concluded that this was the work of Jack the Ripper.

"The Ripper?" he said aloud. He looked around him, there was nobody to be seen. His first instincts were to shout for help, but something stopped him. It was the angst and inner loathing that he had for anyone and everyone that had had a hand in dealing him with such a lowly and unhappy life.

Words that he had just said to himself echoed in his head; 'The Police Commissioner is probably Jewish'. He heard the words repeated in his mind.

"Jack the Ripper is probably Jewish" he said aloud. Hearing his own words somehow gave them gravitas. A plan began to form in his twisted mind. He pondered it briefly and decided that it was for the best. It would help his one-man-fight against the dominance of the Jews in London. It would focus the police onto the very people that he so easily despised for no logical reason.

There was blood over the apron that the woman was wearing. He leant down and unfastened it from her body. Then quickly wrapping it up in itself he scurried away like a rat with a prize. He knew exactly what he was going to do. He knew the address of his boss, the Jew that he hated so much. He would take the blooded apron there and leave it by the tenement Goulston Street, occupied by his boss. He would write something on the walls to acknowledge that the apron was from the latest victim of Jack the Ripper. Above all he would implicate all Jews in the message that he would scrawl on the wall by the bloodied apron.

That would set things right he told himself. It would focus the police force upon the Jewish people of London and above all, bring about public hatred of them all. He could not have asked for a sharper blade for which to inflict his hate-filled rant.

Finally life had been kind to him. He had the means by which to make life difficult for all of those that he blamed for everything that he had suffered throughout his. He was resolute; he would do this and make London a better place for people like himself. There were men and women everywhere that should thank him for what he was about to do.

Chapter 18: Sunday 30th of September 1888, 12:30am

Barely fifteen minutes before the hateful man had found her mutilated body; Catherine Eddowes was pondering her good fortune. She had been unsuccessful with her potential *employers* for the entire evening. But now events had turned in her favour. She had come across quite an attractive man that had made it abundantly clear that he was very interested in her.

He looked like he had a bit of money as well. Christmas had come early for Catherine, or so she thought. They passed a small party of drunk men that looked her up and down like she was a prize pig. Catherine didn't mind, they may one day be future clients. It always paid to be nice to men, no matter how uncouthly they behaved.

He wasn't much of a talker, this one. But that was not unusual. She was happy enough with silence as they walked the cold streets. Fog intermittently rolled in and obscured the vision ahead. The gas lanterns on the side-walks were emitted an eerie muted glow in the foggy conditions.

"This is the place" he said breaking the silence. She looked at him. He was smiling at her. He was ready for a frenetic dose of love-making Catherine thought. They had been walking along Mitre Street and had reached Mitre Square. The gas lamps here could not hope to illuminate all of the area, there were too few of them.

"Across the square" he further instructed. Pulling her arm Catherine allowed herself to be led by him. She had assumed that he lived on the far side of the square. But about half way across and at the darkest place in the square he stopped.

"What is it? Can't see the way?" she asked, thinking that he had become confused in the gloom.

"I can see perfectly in the dark. Better that you" came his quixotic reply.

"Then I don't understand why we are stopping here if you can see where we are going?" she said, confused with the turn of events.

"I just wanted to take some time to look upon the next victim of Jack the Ripper" he said coldly. Catherine froze. Her heart skipped a beat.

"You're having a lend of me surely?" Catherine said, her voice jumping with nervousness. Her question was met with a malevolent smile. It turned Catherine's legs to jelly and she felt her heart sink into the pit of her stomach. She looked around frantically but in vain, there were no people anywhere to be seen.

Catherine drew in a breath and began to scream with all of the might that she could muster. The call rang from her throat carrying the unmistakable sound of absolute terror. A knife sliced through the air and cut the front of her throat, deeply with inhuman ease. The cry ceased.

Catherine clutched her bleeding throat with both hands and vainly tried to run away but the man savagely pushed her to the ground. Trying as best as she could to hold her gushing bloody throat with one hand and right herself with the other she looked up at her attacker, her eyes open so widely with terror it must have hurt.

Fear was overriding the agony that Catherine should have been feeling. All she could think of was the need to escape from this maniac. She was unable to get to her feet, her legs did not want to obey her instructions. The best that Catherine could do was to kick like a child on a sled pushing themselves along like a frog.

The murderer laughed at the sight. He would have happily tormented her for quite some time more, but his need was great. Leaning down and pushing her to the ground so that she was on her back facing him he raised the knife again and then looked at her face to gloat at her expression.

Catherine was unable to make any noise, but the look of absolute fear on her face described her feelings better than any words could. If anybody had been watching they would not have been able to believe what they saw next. With speed that was beyond anything capable of a man he cut open Catherine's stomach with one hand and ripped out her uterus with the other. Her body twitched as he ripped out her innards. Sniffing it, there was a look of satisfaction on his face before he dislocated his jaw and swallowed the uterus whole. Then as it made its way down his throat he caught the scent of something else that pleased him.

He dug around inside Catherine's now motionless body until he found what he thought had attracted him; it was one of her kidneys. He plucked it free from the tangled mess and took a long deep smell. Yes, that was what he wanted. It pleased him very much indeed. This too he ate.

He sat back like a cat that had just swallowed the cream. He was satisfied. He was especially gratified with the way that this woman had squirmed and tried to escape. The terror that she felt was exhilarating for him. As if contemplating something that was really quite trivial, he wondered if she had any appreciation of how good her dread had made him feel. Then dismissing the thought as irrelevant he stood up and put his knife away. He found a handkerchief and began to wipe his hands and face. A sound interrupted his libations. It was the sound of someone running, and it was getting closer.

***

Samuel was less enthusiastic now than he had been when he first left the station on his mission to patrol the streets of Whitechapel. It was cold and he was tired. He had exhausted his two search areas and was now heading outside of the area that he had drawn on the map. It was difficult to see any great distance in the fog that was enshrouding the city streets. He was walking toward St.James for no particular reason. It seemed quieter here than in Whitechapel. But of course it would be. There weren't he extra patrols in this area that were now commonplace in Whitechapel. He was now outside of the borders of the influence of the Metropolitan Police Force and the Criminal Investigation Department that it housed. This area fell beneath the purview of the City of London Police Department. They had graciously offered help with the *problem* in Whitechapel, but had not mobilised their own forces to be more visible overnight as his station had done.

Suddenly, the sound of a woman's short but terrified scream rang out and was almost as immediately cut-off. Samuel jerked his face toward the direction that he heard the sound. His heat beat began to increase. It was somewhere in the distance for sure, but close enough to find. He ran forwards. He was in Mitre Street. This had a square in the middle of it. From the position that he was at in Aldgate High Street it sounded like the scream could have come from there. But there were houses and other buildings either side. The scream could have echoed. Doubt began to creep into his journey. He continued running hoping that he would find what he was looking for and not have to contend with his uncertainty.

Samuel instinctively stopped when he reached the square. There were not enough lamps in the square for him to see properly, and the fog was somehow annoyingly thick here is if it were deliberately obscuring his vision; but he strained his youthful eyes and could make out a man standing somewhere near the centre. He began to run toward him. The figure seemed to jump up and regard him very briefly and then just as quickly ran in the opposite direction.

"Police; stop!" shouted Samuel. The man did not stop, but continued his escape down an alleyway that would lead to Duke Street. Samuel got to the point where the man had been when he spotted him and almost tripped over the lifeless body sprawled out on the cobblestones. He barely had time to take it in. This was it! He had come across Jack the Ripper in the act of mutilating someone. He did not waste another second. With renewed adrenalin he bolted after his quarry. Nothing was going to get in the way of him apprehending this man.

The murderer scurried down the alleyway with Samuel in hot pursuit. The alley was dark, darker than the square that he had left behind. It was only defined by the gas light that could be made out at the far end; more than likely provided by a street lamp on Duke Street. The rest was pitch-black.

Samuel stopped just inside the entrance. He could hear no running footsteps on the cobbled street. The murderer must have stopped to wait for him. But then something else cut through the silence. It was a metal on stone sound of grinding and clanking. At first Samuel couldn't figure out what it was for the like of him. But the final sound of a manhole cover sliding back into its place then revealed itself.

"He's escaping by the sewers" whispered Samuel. There would be no hope of catching him. It would be absolutely black down there. At least on the surface of London there were gas street-lamps to break up the darkness of the September night. But below ground there was nothing. He immediately felt hopelessness. He was so close but now so far from catching Jack the Ripper.

"No, I won't be beaten" he said aloud and ran the length of the alleyway until he emerged in Duke Street. Happenstance put a young Police Constable in his path. Samuel's dramatic appearance caught the youngster off guard and let out a small yelp whilst scrambling to find his truncheon.

"Samuel Gates, Junior Detective Inspector from Whitechapel CID; there's been another murder, in Mitre Square. Go and report it to your superiors and get an investigation team there. I'm pursuing the culprit do you have a lantern?" the flurry of information was difficult for the youngster to comprehend but managed to nod his head and produce a hand-held brass and glass oil lantern. Samuel grabbed it off the Constable and turned to retrace his steps. Looking back as he disappeared into the foggy darkness of the alleyway he shouted back at the dumfounded fellow. Samuel's disembodied voice could be heard through the miasma.

"Go and report it!"

The Police Constable looked this way and that suddenly unsure of where he was and in which direction he needed to go in order to get help. Somehow he chose a direction and went to do as he was told.

Meanwhile Samuel had run down the length of the alley and was searching his pockets for matches. He found them, exactly where he always kept them in his waistcoat front left pocket. Setting down the lantern and opening the glass he struck a match and lit the wick. Throwing away the match he trimmed the wick with the dial. In the previous darkness even this small lamp was now shedding an inordinate amount of light on the surroundings. Samuel looked for the manhole cover and found it a few paces away.

He put the lantern down beside it and grabbed the cover through the small openings with his gloved hands. Giving it an almighty pull he barely managed to lift it an inch, but that was enough. He dragged it sideways revealing the entrance to the sewers. There was a ladder. Swinging his legs into the opening he found a rung to support his weight and began his descent. Before disappearing below street level he reached over and grabbed the small lantern. He made his way downwards.

***

The sewer stank. There was movement below him, not just the putrid water carrying the refuse away but rats as well. The stench was overpowering. But he was not going to let it get in the way of his pursuit. He clambered to the bottom and without thinking jumped into the disgusting mess. It came up to his knees. He looked down one direction of the arching tunnel into the blackness, holding up the lap as best as he could to illuminate the way before him. There was nothing. Then turning he did the same. But this time there were a pair of eyes reflecting the light in the same way that a dog's eyes do. They were at the furthest reach of the capability of the small lamp but they were there.

If he squinted Samuel could just make out the figure of a man. The Ripper turned and scuttled away. The noise of the waters sloshing around broke the creepy silence. Samuel was again in pursuit of his prey. Samuel was not even contemplating how to apprehend his target, all he wanted to do was catch up to him and then he would deal with that. His heart was pounding in his head. The two of them were making equally loud splashing noises as they ran as best they could through the murky water. But the Ripper was faster. He could see that his objective was pulling away from him, and then something else. Samuel couldn't quite make out what it was until he got closer, but the tunnel broke into two.

He was sure that the man had taken the right fork. But just as he arrived at the junction, Samuel heard a distinctive sound from the left. Was it possible that his eyes had played a trick on him in the gloom? He pushed the lamp down the left fork. The noises that he had heard were rats fighting. He barely had time to comprehend the nasty little creatures squeaking and biting at each other.

Samuel took the right fork and ran down about fifty only to be thwarted again. There was another junction. This was a T intersection. But which way had the Ripper taken. He stopped. There was no sound. The Ripper was not running away from him anymore. A horrible thought occurred to Samuel. Was the Ripper waiting for him down one of the tunnels? Was he about to be attacked? He likened the Ripper to a cornered animal. Weren't they supposed to be at their most dangerous when cornered; just like he had done now? Samuel tried to compose himself, but his heartbeat was making that impossible. He stretched out his hand to try and throw light around the corners both left and right. But that only made deeper shadows and darkness at the very point where the Ripper may be waiting for him.

Samuel strained to hear any sign that his quarry may be down one or the other tunnel. All that he could hear was the running of the sewer water and multiple dripping sounds. He inched forward looking right and left but was still defeated by the darkened shadows. He had reached a point where he had to make a decision. Either way held danger. If he chose the wrong direction and the Ripper was waiting to pounce on him from behind, he could become the next victim of the maniacal murderer. He chose to go left. It was the wrong decision.

As he turned the corner and revealed the tunnel ahead it was empty. At that moment he heard movement in the waters behind him and he spun around to see a knife wielding hand hurtling toward him. Samuel used the lantern to intercept the attack and smashed the knife away from the hand of the attacker. The blade must have struck a brass part of the lantern because it did not shatter the glass, but it did temporarily dull the flame to the point of uselessness. Samuel was forced by circumstance to grapple with the killer hand to hand in near darkness. In those precious few seconds that the struggle lasted all that he could think of was to not drop the lantern. It hindered his ability to fight effectively. The knife could be heard clanking against the stone tunnel wall and plopping into the water.

The Ripper's now empty hands enclosed Samuel's throat with a grip that he could barely believe it was so strong. Again the lantern came to Samuel's aid. He brought the bottom end of it down on the head of the man; at least where he assumed the head would be in relation to the arms. It was still so dark he couldn't see the face of his assailant. The lantern almost breathed back into life just as it impacted the head of the man. Immediately the vice-like grip around Samuel's throat was released. Simultaneously there was a yelp from the accoster. Again the lamp dulled making it impossible to see properly.

Samuel was aware that the man had turned and run away from him. He could hear the thrashing of the water. Emboldened by his success at this moment all he wanted to do was catch Jack the

Ripper. Samuel once more gave pursuit. The lamp recovered enough to throw light down the tunnel. Samuel could see the man running in the opposite direction. He was fast. Much faster through the knee-deep water than Samuel would have thought possible.

Samuel ran after him with all of his might; his heat pounding in his head, adrenalin running through his veins. On and on they travelled through the dank tunnels. The Ripper was pulling away from him. But Samuel was determined not to lose his man. Junction after junction revealed itself but in each case Samuel knew which one to take as he could hear his quarry ahead of him, even if he couldn't see him all of the time.

Left and right, and left and right. The chase continued; then a potential disaster. He had reached a three way split in the tunnel, right, straight ahead and left. The tunnels were smaller. He would not be able to stand upright in them. He took the centre one and stooped over made his way up but then stopped. Something was wrong. He could not hear the runner ahead of him. He must have taken the wrong tunnel. The echoing of the splashing had confused him. Still stooped over he turned around and made his way back to the juncture.

When he emerged he had to listen carefully to discern which direction he had to take. It was a fifty-fifty bet now anyway. He knew it wasn't the centre tunnel. It had to be either the right or the left. He put his head into the left tunnel, there was no sound. He did the same with the right. He could just hear the sound of the murderer splashing away from him.

Samuel once more gave pursuit. It was difficult running whilst bending over and holding a lantern ahead to see the way. But he pushed himself onwards. Eventually he became aware that there was no sound of running ahead of him anymore. A flash of dread and anticipation flowed through Samuel. Had the Ripper tired and was catching his breath? Or was he frustrated with a grate or other blocked access? Maybe he was now trapped and Samuel would have to face him in this compromised position?

He slowed down and moved with more caution. He was nervous. Doubt crept into his emotions. The memory of the strength of the Ripper was still fresh in his mind. He could see nothing ahead.

A rat squealed behind him. Samuel spun around out of reflect-action rather than design. If he had not done that he may have seen the tunnel leading directly up. It had come into the circumference that the lantern afforded. But Samuel was looking behind him and walking backwards. The rat revealed itself, it was swimming toward him. Samuel retreated out of disgust backwards and used a foot to kick water at the rat. It took fright and swam in the opposite direction. Keeping an eye on it until it was safely out of range Samuel swung around to face forwards, but he had passed beneath the circular opening that had been above him and was again looking forward.

He walked on, there was nothing but blackness outside of the range of the light. Behind him, a figure clinging impossibly to the side walls of the cylindrical opening that Samuel had not seen dropped downwards landing with a frighteningly loud splash directly behind Samuel.

Samuel had barely a chance to whirl around before the murderer had brought down what felt like two clenched fists onto the back of Samuel's head. There was a flash of light as Samuel cried out from the pain. He lost his footing and fell to his knees beneath the onslaught. Miraculously the lantern did not fall from his hands into the water. If that had happened he would be in total darkness. Samuel's fight-or-flight instinct took over and he chose to fight.

Growling like a wounded animal he leapt to his feet to face his attacker. But the Ripper had paradoxically not pressed home his advantage and had taken-off once more. His head aching tremendously he began his pursuit once more.

He came to the point where he had entered the smaller tunnels. Now he was in a position to stand upright properly once more. He held the lamp up to see where he was. There was a ladder leading directly up at the side of the tunnel. A sound of grating metal against stone could be heard and a trickle of light fell down the access way. The Ripper was escaping to street-level. Hampered by the lantern but still not wanting to drop it Samuel gave chase. As he was about half way up the ladder the manhole cover was slammed shut above him. Samuel clambered upwards until he reached the manhole cover. He pushed against it with one hand but was unable to make it budge at all. He rested the lantern on the highest rung of the ladder and used both hands to push upwards. It was impossible. Was the Ripper standing on the inspection plate preventing him from exiting the sewers? He gave it another shove and managed to move it upwards slightly debunking his misgiving thought.

Unintentionally he knocked the lantern from its place and it fell downwards splashing into the water below. Samuel was in darkness. The only pinpoints of light now came through the drainage holes in the cast-iron cover. This made his plight seem much bleaker. The darkness combined with the thought that he may now be trapped beneath the streets of London gave him the extra strength that he needed to push the manhole cover up enough so that it would be slid across the cobbled street.

With a couple of almighty shoves he was freed from his subterranean maze. Pulling himself up he surveyed the streets. He couldn't immediately identify where he was but he did not care. All that mattered now was to get back on the tail of Jack the Ripper. The alley that he had emerged hand three directions to choose from. He turned and looked down each. There was no sign of his prey.

Desperate to not lose the scent he randomly chose the way behind him and ran down the length until it opened up and revealed what looked to be Camomile Street. It was well lit with gas lamps. Samuel looked up and down its length and could see nobody. He retraced his steps to the displaced manhole cover and chose another direction. This time it ended in a dead end. It must have been the one way that he did not take.

Running back to the starting point once more he took the remaining direction and found that the alley did a crescent and ended up back once more on Camomile Street. Samuel was breathing hard he was absolutely exhausted. He was dejected. He had had Jack the Ripper in his sights but he had got away.

"No" said Samuel aloud and puffing. He doubled over and clasped his knees with his hands trying to get his breath back. After a while he had managed to slow his frantic breathing. He felt better. Not recovered, but able to go on.

He walked onto Camomile Street. It was still annoyingly deserted. Trying to gather his directions Samuel turned toward the way that would lead him back to Mitre Square.

Chapter 19: Police Commissioner Charles Warren

Police Commissioner Charles Warren had left specific instructions with his men that should any news of Jack the Ripper be reported in his jurisdiction to inform him immediately, day or night. And that is exactly what had happened. The young constable that Samuel had briefed so rapidly and borrowed the small lantern from had followed his superior's orders. Arriving at the scene in Mitre Square that he had been told of by Samuel Gates he had blown his whistle to alert all of the other police in earshot. When they had responded he had bravely issued instructions to have the Police Commissioner awakened and notified of the murder. The urgent whistle had attracted more than just police as people came from their houses to see what was happening in their neighbourhood.

The Commissioner lived only a few streets away from Mitre Square, so his arrival at the sight of the murder was fast. Surveying the scene he looked very worried.

"Keep these people back!" he said annoyed at the leering crowd that had formed. He squatted down and studied the devastated body of the woman that was sprawled out before him. It made his stomach wretch with disgust. There was no doubt about it. This was the work of the dreaded Jack the Ripper for sure. But now it was a murder in the purview of the City of London.

"Tell me again exactly what this Inspector said to you?" Charles Warren stood up and addressed the young constable that had attended the scene and sent for him.

"A man Sir. Said his name was Samuel Gates, Junior Detective Inspector Whitechapel; and that there was a murder here in Mitre Square and to report it. He was giving chase to the murderer." The constable's summary was accurate enough.

"Pursing the murderer?" The commissioner said almost in awe.

"Yes Sir" confirmed the young man.

The Police Commissioner secretly hoped that Samuel would be successful and that the terror of Jack the Ripper would end this very night. But he did not want to take any chances.

"Well then, best that we give his Samuel Gates from Whitechapel a helping hand." He said not making himself perfectly clear.

"Sir?' queried the constable.

"Call out every available man that you can find, all of you" he said loudly addressing the four other police that were present.

"Search the area. Look for anything suspicious and report back to me. I will be at the Station" he said referring to London City Police station. There was a chorus of 'Yes Sirs' from the quartet.

"You" he said pointing to the young constable.

"Remain with the body. I will send someone to take the remains away. I want the body removed as quickly as possible. Check the immediate area for any clues and keep these people away. The rest of you get to work!"

They needed no more encouragement and moved off quickly. Police Commissioner Charles Warren was about to leave the scene himself and coordinate from his headquarters when he noticed a rather dishevelled fellow making his way toward the scene. He wasn't sure exactly what had caught his attention but he kept looking at him. The gaze of the Police Commissioner was followed by the young Constable who upon recognising the approaching man quipped

"That's him Sir, Inspector Gates!"

Samuel had heard his name as he approached the growing number of people surrounding the latest victim. He looked up and nodded at the young constable.

"Sorry to not return your lantern Constable; I lost it in the sewer. But it did save me from two attacks from the......." Samuel looked around at every face that had turned toward him. All of a sudden he was reticent to name the villain that he had been chasing.

"Go on say it... Jack the Ripper" said one of the cockney men in the crowd.

"Now now, don't put words in my mouth.." Samuel began but was quickly cut off by the Police Commissioner.

"Mister Gates, forget about the borrowed lantern, we will replace the young Constables lost item. But right now I need you to accompany me to London Police Station. I want to know everything that has happened." Charles' tone was one of authority. Samuel recognised that but sought just a little more information to cement his assumption.

"Whom do I have the honour of addressing Sir?" he asked in the most polite way.

"Police Commissioner Charles Warren of London Police Station, that's who" piped up the young Constable. "This has happened in our jurisdiction......" the youngster was clearly going to state the very obvious so Charles cut him off.

"Thank you Constable. You have your orders. See that they are carried out".

"Yes Sir" he said somewhat admonished and not wanting to disappoint his superior any further.

Samuel knew of Charles Warren but had only ever seen him at functions from afar. It was dark and the Commissioner was not in his usual garb, so Samuel had not immediately recognised him. He tried to make amends for is lack of acknowledgment.

"Good morning Sir. I would be very happy to accompany you to the Station and make a full report"

"Is there anything else that you need to gather from the scene of the crime Mister Gates?" queried the Commissioner.

"Nothing that the attending police cannot skilfully accomplish Sir" Samuel's strategic compliment fell upon fertile ground. Heartened by the accolade the Commissioner smiled and indicated that Samuel should lead the way.

"Let's see if we can find a cab and hasten our journey" Charles suggested.

***

At the London Police Station, a rather grand old building, Samuel was recounting for the umpteenth time the cat-and-mouse chase that had ensued when he had pursued the murderer down into the sewers. Even though it was still dark outside the station felt like it had a full complement of staff in it. Constables on patrol had awoken those not on duty to join in on the search of the surrounding area of Mitre Square. Word had spread from person to person and it seemed that men of every rank in the Police Station had come to work or joined in the search emanating from Mitre Square and were reporting as ordered back to the Police Commissioner.

Every detail of how Samuel had come to be in the area in the first place, to the scream that had lead him to Mitre Square to the pursuit had been recounted over and over. Each time there were different questions from the Commissioner about detail that he may have mentioned in one version of the events but omitted in the next. It felt like he was the star witness in a cross-examination during a trial.

"Tell me again how the......assailant managed to hide in a tunnel above you without you seeing it; if the sewer was so small that you had to crouch down to see, surely you would have noticed it?" Warren was clinical with his dissection of the facts that Samuel was presenting.

"There was a rat Sir, I turned around to shoo it away and walked backwards for a short time, by the time I had turned around the access way must have been above me and I missed it. Much to my near detriment too as that is where the Ripper....."

"We have not yet ascertained that this is the work of the Ripper Mister Gates, please confine yourself to the facts and not conjecture" The Commissioner interjected. Samuel sighed with frustration and regathered his thoughts.

"Yes Sir. That is when the suspect jumped down from the access way to assault me". Samuel was tired. He smelled awful from his time in the sewers, but the Commissioner had not allowed him to clean himself up. First-hand knowledge of the incident made his recounting of the events had elevated Samuel to a status that nobody before had attained during the recent murder investigations in Whitechapel. And now that the City of London was involved the Commissioner was going to make damned sure that the case was put to rest. He was all too aware of the public backlash against the Police in general, because the Whitechapel men could not solve the case. He did not want that to continue because of the lack of proficiency from his men.

He was about to continue when one of the duty uniformed men walked boldly up and looked like he had something important to communicate. It captured the attention of all.

"What is it?" demanded the Commissioner.

"A bloodied apron sir, one that would match the clothing worn by the victim" he stated.

"Found where?" Warren almost stood up in anticipation as he asked for more detail.

"In the doorway of a tennament in Goulston Street. Full of Jewish business owners sir and there is more"

The man tempted them all with further news.

"Well don't keep it to yourself man; spit it out!" ordered the Commissioner somewhat annoyed.

"Graffiti sir, accusing the woman of being a gentile whore that deserved death by holy Jewish hands" he finished his report. There was almost a collective gasp from the gathered men. Then mumblings of men to men each expressing their own interpretation of the events.

"Written in white chalk it was, plain for all to see...." The man was clearly going to elucidate to the point of irritation but the Commissioner would not hear any of it.

"Silence! All of you!" Warren brought an end to the collective conversation and looked at the floor. He rubbed his brow with worry. There was silence for a long time whilst he contemplated the information that had been presented to him. Then as if he had reached a decision he looked at the man that had delivered the information.

"Wash it away. Make sure that it is done before morning. I do not want it seen by the public!" his words were almost harsh and had the tone of not wanting to entertain discussion. Nevertheless there was a murmur from his own men that clearly wanted to know why.

"We will question everyone in the tenement; at a descent hour and not before. But the very thought that Jack the Ripper or whoever this murderer that Mister Gates had been pursuing had either the time to write such nonsense or the inclination does not make any sense to me; nor should it to all of you either!" The Commissioner was animated and had everybody's complete attention.

"Should the public get wind of the suspicion that Jack the Ripper be a Jew it then anti-Semitic tensions will boil over and tear this city apart. There are already gangs that patrol the streets of Whitechapel of their own accord that have lost faith in the ability of the Police to apprehend this fiend. I will not be a party to feeding this mob-mentality. Have it washed away now; see to it personally Sargent!"

The Sargent looked like he had been hit with a fist and stood bolt-upright acknowledging his orders with a very complacent 'Yes Sir!' before leaving to do as he was instructed. As he departed there came a familiar voice through the shocked silence.

"Excellent idea Charles; I would have done exactly the same thing in your position" all faces turned around to see who had entered the conversation. It was Senior Detective Inspector Edmund Reid.

"Edmund?" said Charles somewhat surprised to see his counterpart from Whitechapel in his station.

"Word spreads quickly about another murder by the Ripper, Charles. And I hear too that one of our best and brightest has been helping you with your investigation. So much the better" Edmund's immediate acquiescence that the latest murder was in the hands of the London Police rather than his own precinct was gratifying and gentlemanly all at once. Warren stood up to properly greet his counterpart. They shook hands warmly.

"Good to see you again Edmund"

"And you Charles. Now that you and your men are on the case we are sure to have the breakthrough that the Palace has been demanding of me." Edmund was not only gracious with his praise, it also held a tinge of the need for any and all help with this particular case.

"But I thought that you had Scotland Yard......." began Charles pointing out the additional assistance that had already been garnered for the Ripper case.

"You and I both know Charles that Scotland is Scotland and England is England. And we need an English solution to this problem." Edmund's assertion won the approval of the mainly English men surrounding him. This did not go unnoticed by the Commissioner who sought to back-up the affirmation.

"Right you are Edmund, bravo."

"Now Mister Gates, tell me from the beginning everything that you have seen and heard this night...unless you wish to elucidate me Charles?" asked Reid. Charles shook his head and directed his attention once more toward Samuel.

"Yes Mister Gates, once more from the beginning. What had brought you to the City of London jurisdiction so late in the night? You don't live anywhere nearby" The Commissioner wanted to hear everything yet again. Samuel felt exhausted already but drew breath and began.

"Well it is strange that the Senior Detective is here, because it was *he* that inspired me to study the map of Whitechapel in our station and for me to try my best to suppose where the Ripper would strike next. With a couple of search areas in mind I set out to see what I could see but it all came to nothing. I was walking the long way home somewhat dejected when I heard a scream. It was only by happenstance that I was in the area. If I had taken the direct route to my home I would most certainly not have even been within earshot of the scream. But hear it I did and that is what led me to Mitre

Square. It was dark, but the fog cleared enough so that I could make out the figure of a man crouching down......" and Samuel once more recounted his experience, but with renewed vigour now that his superior was there to hear the summation of events as well.

Chapter 20: Athalia's Third Vision

Madam Athalia awoke. It was Sunday morning. The first day of October; it could have been cold or cloudy or both, but it was pleasant. The sun shone through the crack at the meeting point of the heavy velvet curtains in her bedroom. For just a moment there was something that puzzled her, but just as immediately it was dismissed. Throwing back the covers Alice got out of bed and walked to the curtains to throw them open. The view was exactly as she had expected. There was little movement on the street below. The sun had risen. It looked to be a lovely day.

Something made Alice suddenly feel cold. She saw a man on the street below dressed in dark clothing. It awakened a memory within her. In a moment of time the dreams that she had had during the night came flooding back to her. The murder; no two murders! She had witnessed them both through the eyes of the victims. Every excruciating second once more made itself known to her. Madam Athalia almost doubled over in physical pain at the recollection of the memories.

There was a knock on her bedroom door. It startled Alice.

"Yes?" she said, expecting Burton to enter. She was not disappointed.

"Good morning Madam Athalia. I trust that you slept well? Sunday breakfast is served in the conservatory" Burton finished his morning platitudes and studied Alice's face. He could see that there was something wrong. He knew the look and in light of recent events offered a guess as to what it may be.

"You looked strained this morning Madam. Have you had another vision?" he asked his brow furrowing with concern for the old lady.

"Yes, indeed I have Burton. Two this time. And still no answer to either of my letters to the Police about the first two. This will never do Burton. Something must be done; but what?" Athalia's conundrum was plain to see.

"Perhaps Ma'am, you should detail your visions in writing once more but this time we can pay a visit to the Whitechapel Police and present them in person? It is not as easy to put a personal visit from a renowned Psychic at the bottom of the police's priority list as it would be for a letter." Burton's proposal was weighed-up by Athalia. She made her decision.

"Yes Burton; well spoken. That is exactly what we shall do. I shall write down my latest visions and we shall pay a visit to the Whitechapel police first thing on Monday morning. What an absolutely splendid idea! Thank you so very much dear Burton; always looking out for me" Athalia looked much more settled now.

***

Breakfast in the conservatory was typically wonderful. Although Athalia did not eat very much, she did enjoy what she did eat. And Burton was an accomplished cook. He had prepared a most excellent omelette that amongst the ingredients boasted boneless pieces of baked pheasant and wild mushrooms. Upon finishing her breakfast and making herself ready for the day, Alice had retreated to the library to do as she had planned. She wrote about the two murders that she had seen in her mind extracting as much detail about them as she could, especially about the face of the murderer. She was oblivious to time and had buried herself in the writing chore so deeply that it was almost noon by the time she was finished.

It was then that Alice became aware that all was not right. She felt ill. Every time she thought about breakfast she concentrated on the wild mushrooms in the omelette and pangs of pain erupted in her stomach. She got up from her elaborately carved oak desk and went to the wall pulling the bell cord to summon Burton.

When he arrived he could see that Alice had lost all of the colour in her face.

"Madam Athalia; what has happened?"

"Oh, Burton, I do not feel well at all. Please help me to my bed. I shall be retiring for the remainder of the day. And send for Doctor Stewart; I fear that I am in need of his assistance." Burton raced to the aide of Alice and helped her out of the room and then had to practically carry her up the grand staircase. She was becoming weaker by the minute.

First things first, thought Burton. He would get Madam Athalia settled in her bed and ensure that she had water and a clean chamber pot should it be needed for vomiting. He rightly guessed that it must have been food poisoning. He was cursing himself for not sampling the meal that he had prepared for his long-time employer. But he had made due with toast and tea as was his modest want for breakfast. He also noticed that Madam Athalia was too polite to refer to the breakfast as the only possibility that had made her ill. He was grateful for her demure nature. Then he would find a passing street urchin and pay them to send a message summoning Doctor Stewart who thankfully only lived two blocks away. Their Sunday trip to the Whitechapel Police station would have to wait for another day.

Chapter 21: Monday the 1st of October 1888

Samuel Gates arrived for work on Monday morning to applause from his counterparts and fellow workers. He had spent a good deal of Sunday morning with Police Commissioner Charles Warren and his own Senior Detective Inspector Edmund Reid at the London constabulary going over and over the near-miss of apprehending Jack the Ripper. Warren had ordered his resident police surgeon to perform the examination of the body, of the now identified victim Catherine Eddowes. And then at Reid's suggestion compare notes with Thomas Bond, the Whitechapel surgeon. They had both agreed that the murderer was most probably Jack the Ripper.

Their Sunday wasn't complete though. Word had reached them of another murder under similar circumstances, this time very definitely in the precinct of Whitechapel. Samuel had noted that it was within the search area that he had drawn on the map on Saturday night before venturing out. All three of them had attended the scene in Dutfield Yard. This called for another examination by Thomas Bond and resulted in another conclusion that it was the work of the same man. Samuel had effectively worked weeks now without a proper weekend. But he didn't care. All that mattered was finding the murder and stopping him.

Samuel acknowledged the applause with modesty.

"Thank you all, but I feel that I don't deserve the applause as I was unable to catch the villain. Perhaps you should reserve your accolades for the one that does" this garnered a cheer from the men.

The thought of one of them being the cause for apprehending Jack the Ripper was very pleasing indeed.

"Briefing room gentlemen, there is much to discuss" hollered Sargent Plymouth through his impossibly large and overly groomed moustache. All of the men involved in the case filed into the briefing room. When they had settled Edmund Reid addressed them.

"Two more victims on Saturday night, Sunday morning! The Ripper is getting cocky. Two in one night. Victim number one, Elizabeth Stride born in Sweden, aged 44 married with no children. Cleaner and casual prostitute; body found in Dutfield Yard with the throat cut and the lower abdomen cut open. Not missing any body parts this time. No witnesses. Time of death somewhere around one am Sunday morning." Reid shuffled the papers in his hand and continued.

"Second victim was one Elizabeth Stride born Staffordshire England, aged 46, married with three children. Seasonal worker; hops picker and casual prostitute. Found by our very own Samuel Gates with the Ripper crouching over her at approximately 1:45am in Mitre Square. Keeping in mind that the location of this murder puts it inside the city of London; my esteemed counterpart Police Commissioner Charles Warren will be handling that investigation in collusion with ourselves. The examinations of both have concluded that they were the work of Jack the Ripper." Reid was about to continue with the factual presentation of the case when one of the men interrupted him.

"Tell us about the chase Samuel?"

'YES!' echoed the majority of the men present. Realising that this was just about unavoidable Reid conceded and indicated that Samuel should do just that.

"Please mister Gates, regale us all with your encounter." Samuel had to recount his story again, even though he was sure that it would have been repeated from man to man from the London station and would have certainly made its way around the men in his station. Nevertheless there was nothing like first-hand information when it came to this high-profile case. He detailed the story in a way that had become almost the refined version, giving as many facets of it as he could to his listeners. They were completely spellbound by the story. When he was done he had to face multiple questions from many of the men who needed clarification about this point or that. But eventually Reid had to wrest control of the briefing back.

"Alright everyone, enough questions for now. You can continue your cross-examination of Mister Gates after the briefing. But let me make one thing absolutely clear; do not repeat any of this to the press! And do not repeat it to anyone outside of the constabulary. I do not want this to appear in the latest edition of any of the newspapers. It has already fired them up. All that they need to know is that we were close but unable to capture the Ripper. However it is only a matter of time. That is the official stance that we will be sending to the press. Is that clear?" Reid left no doubt that he would not entertain any questioning of his mandate.

There was a noise of agreement from the men, which seemed to satisfy Reid. The briefing continued with the new assignments to everyone. There was an expectation in the air that it was now a case that could be solved. And that it would only be a matter of time.

***

Samuel had been practically accosted after the morning briefing. Many of the men had their own questions about his experience. He did his best to answer the queries to the fullest of his abilities. There was another meeting scheduled for Samuel with all of the Scotland Yard Inspectors and an artist to try and render the images that Samuel had gathered during his chase. It was understood by all that the circumstances prevented a clear view of the Ripper, but any little detail was welcomed and had to be captured.

It was this short time between finishing off the last of the queries from the men and his next meeting that the mail clerk approached Samuel.

"Excellent work Mister Gates, please let me congratulate you on your near-success" he said as he approached.

"Thank you very much. Hopefully the next time it will be more than a near-success. Do you have some mail for me?" he inquired looking at the clerk.

"Not actually addressed to you Mister Gates, but these" he held up the letters that he had received and put in his draw.

"I didn't know what to do with them until now. But it seems right that you should have a look at them. They are from a crazy old lady claiming to be a psychic and to have had visions of the murders. I know they will amount to nothing, but I would somehow feel better if you had them than having them sit in my draw gathering dust." He said. Samuel was perplexed but grateful.

"Surely, let me see them" he asked. The clerk handed him the letters. He opened the first and looked at the date that was written above it and the date that it had been received by the Police. It was jarring. He looked at the second, once more the date that it was marked with by the author and the date that it had been received at the station.

"But this is incredible?" Samuel said trying to grapple with the revelation.

"If the dates on these letters are correct, then the writer has written to us about the murders before any news was published about either of them?" he was aghast.

"Surely not Inspector Gates. The old fraud had seen the Sunday papers….." began the clerk in defence of his own belief that the letters were all but worthless.

"You are forgetting the time that it would have taken to write and post them and for the letters to arrive here. There is simply no way that the author could have read about the second murder for example and then sent this letter if it was dated then, and arrived then" he indicated the two dates on the letter. The clerk squinted and looked at the dates Samuel was pointing at.

"Well blow me down!" said the clerk realising that Samuel was correct. He had not factored in the time that it would have taken to traverse the postal system to arrive at the station.

"You don't think?" the clerk was about to ask for validation from Samuel when Sargent Plymouth appeared.

"The Inspectors and the artist are waiting for your Junior Detective Inspector" Both Samuel and the clerk looked up.

"Thank you Sargent. Straight away" replied Samuel. He looked at the return address on the letters and said in parting to the clerk. I will pay the mysterious Madam Athalia a visit this afternoon to discuss her letters, fear not. I for one am very interested in what she has to say."

Chapter 22: Samuel Gates and Madam Athalia

It took Samuel the best part of the day to dispatch with his superior's questions about his *encounter* with Jack the Ripper. He did his best to instruct the police artist but in the end the images were simply unusable for any identification purposes because he did not see the Ripper's face. By the time he disentangled himself from the station it was late afternoon. He made his way out of the Whitechapel area and over to the much more salubrious Kensington; more specifically Cromwell Road in Kensington.

The homes in this neighbourhood reflected the wealth of their owners. Samuel noticed that the people walking the street were dressed well and polite to a fault. He lost count of the times that he had to tip his hat and wish somebody a 'good evening' as he made his way toward his destination.

Eventually he reached the address that was marked on the letters that he held in his hand. He studied the imposing residence. It was four stories high and a very fine looking house. It sat well within the street of similar homes.

"Being a fortune-teller must pay good money" he said to himself under his breath. He strode up the external stone stairway and was about to reach for the door knocker when he realised that there was a bell to the right hand side of the door. It was a wrought iron pulley system, and was obviously a more refined way to announce one's arrival rather than the clanging of a simple door knocker. That would be too common in a neighbourhood such as this.

Samuel pulled on the finely cast handle and could hear a bell ringing in the distance. It was a short time before one of the two large doors was opened. Standing there looked quizzically at Samuel was a doorman of some description; actually he looked more like a butler.

"May I help you sir?" asked the thin-faced balding man.

"Junior detective inspector Samuel Gates from the criminal investigation department at the Whitechapel metropolitan police department to see Miss Alice Athalia" even as Samuel completed his explanatory greeting he knew that he had said something wrong. The butler's expression made no mask of hiding the fact that something incorrect had been said.

"*Madam* Athalia unwell and unable to accept visitors this evening" said the butler emphasising the correct way to address the Lady of the house. Samuel tried his best not to look like he thought that the gaff was a small one and somewhat unimportant.

"I am sorry to hear that; nothing serious I hope?" Samuel asked.

"Food poisoning; as you can imagine, considering Madam Athalia's advanced years one must be especially careful with such matters" The butler's explanation was illuminating enough, but it did not get Samuel what he wanted. He reached into his pocket and produced the letters to show the door-keeper.

"I was hoping to discuss in more detail Madam Athalia's letters" Samuel did his best to look forlorn in the hope for a sympathetic response from the man. It did have an effect. The butler looked behind him and to what Samuel could see was a very grand inside staircase, as if he were trying to look up to the next level.

"Madam Athalia was determined to speak with the police regarding her letters" he said. He seemed to be indecisive and Samuel offered a compromise that he hoped would at least get him past the front door.

"Why don't you ask Madam Athalia if she has the strength to see me? I've travelled all the way from Whitechapel specifically to meet with her. There is no harm in asking surely?" Samuel leant forward slightly and gave the butler a small smile. After a few moments of contemplation, the butler decided in Samuel's favour.

"Please come in. I will show you to the drawing library and see if Madam Athalia is well enough to receive you" the butler stepped aside and indicated that Samuel should enter. He did so.

Closing the large door after him, the butler introduced himself.

"My name is Burton Sir. If you would please come this way" Burton indicated that Samuel should follow him to the first of the internal doors. The interior of the house displayed more wealth than the exterior. There were very fine looking paintings on the walls and porcelain sculptures that would no-doubt have cost a small fortune. Overall it wasn't what Samuel was expecting to see in a soothsayer's home. The entire place was practically dripping with money.

"Does Madam Athalia still practice….." Samuel began asking but was answered by Burton so quickly that he didn't have the chance to finish his sentence.

"No longer Sir; Madam Athalia has been retired for some years now."

"Oh"

They reached the door to what Samuel assumed was the library and Burton opened it for him. Inside was more of the same, except this time with imposing shelves full of books along the far wall. Elsewhere were more paintings, sculptures and a large desk by the oversized windows. Whoever sat in the chair behind it would have a wonderful view out to the front of the property. Samuel could imagine not getting any work done at such a desk. The busy, and affluent streetscape would offer too much of a distraction. He was still looking around the room when Burton spoke.

"Please wait here inspector Gates. I will see if Madam Athalia is able to receive you?"

"Thank you Burton" Samuel said. Burton closed the door and Samuel was alone. He walked up to the desk and looked out at the street below. People were walking by. Just as he thought, far too much going on to get any work done here. He walked over to the paintings. He was not very well schooled in the arts but couldn't help but suspect that one or two of them were recognisable; at least the style in which they were painted. Neither held a signature that could be deciphered with ease so the mystery of their origins remained unclear.

Next, Samuel decided to inspect the contents of the rather grand library case of the far wall. He expected there to be books on tarot cards and astrology and he was not disappointed. There were books that looked to be written in Latin only. Others in what could have been one of the Slavic languages. Some appeared to be written in Russian. The ones that Samuel could read the spines of were definitely the genre that he would have expected in such a setting.

Some had the astrological symbols on the spines. Most of them were embossed with gold and silver and other colours. The one thing that they all had in common was that like everything in this household, they looked expensive.

Samuel was intently moving from shelf to shelf reading when the door behind him opened and Burton strode through stopped faced him and announced

"Madam Athalia; junior detective inspector Samuel Gates of Whitechapel metropolitan police department"

Samuel's anticipation grew. He wasn't sure what to expect. A rather frail old lady entered the room. She was cloaked in a very fine looking dressing gown. Her hair was short and there was a complete lack of jewellery on her hands, ears, neck. In fact this lovely little old lady looked nothing like the gypsy fortune teller that he had expected.

"Please forgive my appearance inspector, as Burton would have explained I have suffered a small bout of food poisoning. But I am well on my way to recovery. Thank you for coming to see me. I feel that we have much to discuss"

There was no mistaking the strength of her words, even though they were uttered from an infirm form.

"Now come and join me in the sitting room, I will tell you what I know in the hope that it can help you solve these ghastly murders."

***

The sitting room was more intimidating than the library. Samuel was ushered to a lounge that looked simply too elegant and fine to actually sit upon. But sit upon it they did, closely together. Athalia looking directly into Samuel's eyes as she recounted the visions that had led her to write the letters to the Whitechapel police department. The detail that Athalia went into was far greater than the letters that she had written. The words invoked images in Samuel's head as she spoke. Her knowledge of the clothing that the women were wearing was exact. The geographical understanding of the areas that the women had passed through to get to the streets that they were eventually discovered was unquestionable.

One commonality became abundantly clear. Whenever Athalia had had a vision of a murder, she had seen it through the eyes of the murdered woman. That was both the most exciting and frustrating component of the report for Samuel. On the one hand she had seen the face of Jack the Ripper and was able to describe it in exquisite detail. But on the other hand seeing the murder through the eyes of the victim, she was unable to see where the murderer retreated to after he had committed his heinous crimes.

It was like being given the key to a box full of answers, but not knowing where the box was located. Samuel was convinced with everything that Madam Athalia had said. He was left in absolutely no-doubt that she was the genuine article and that she had truly witnessed these murders from a unique perspective.

Athalia was not just content to describe the events to Samuel. She offered him her analysis of the privileged information to which she was privy. It was dark outside by the time that they finished their analysis of the events.

"You have described the man in amazing detail Madam Athalia, would you be able to repeat all of that to a police artist and have them recreate a likeness for us?" He held high hopes that Athalia would be able to succeed where he had so recently failed. She waved her wrinkled hand dismissively.

"There is no need inspector Gates. I have in the ensuing time sketched the murderer. I will have you know that I am somewhat of an artist as well as a physic" she explained. Looking around for the ever present Burton, who had decided to hover for the entire time probably still concerned for Athalia's well-being, Athalia asked him.

"Burton, fetch me the drawing that I made would you please?"

"Immediately Madam" he replied and exited the room, dutifully closing the door behind him as he left. Samuel could barely contain his excitement.

"This could be the very thing that we need to get this case solve once and for all. I don't know how to thank you for all of your help Madam Athalia?" Samuel was practically gushing with gratitude and enthusiasm for the insights that he now had into the Ripper murders.

"Put an end to these horrible killings Inspector Gates; that is all of the recompense that I ask for" Alice was clearly genuine in her wish to help the police solve these murders. Samuel took a moment to look around him and once more be in quiet awe at the display of wealth in which he was cocooned. It probably wasn't the proper thing to say in the circumstances but it slipped out of Samuel's mouth anyway.

"It certainly doesn't look like you need any financial reward for your services Madam Athalia". The moment that he said it, he regretted it. His words sounded like scorn for the obvious wealth that Alice had accumulated. But Madam Athalia was gracious and unperturbed by the comment.

"Inspector Gates, contacting the dear-departed for my clients has been very good to me over the many years in which I have practiced. However, at this moment I would happily trade this entire house to not have to live through another gruesome murder, as if it were happening to me." Alice looked steadily into Samuel's eyes. He suddenly felt very ashamed of what he had said and was about to offer a retraction when Alice continued.

"For reasons unknown the spirits of the murderer's victims have reached out to me even before they have died to show me the monster that is killing with impunity in our city. I believe, and you must believe too, that it is for a reason. And that reason simply must be for you to capture the beast before he strikes again."

Alice's reasoning although saturated with mysticism still rang-true to Samuel. Burton chose that moment to re-enter the room. He handed the sketch to Madam Athalia who in turn gave it another look and an affirmative nod that it was the man in her visions. She handed it to Gates. He looked at the handsome man that Alice had sketched with artistic flair. It was done in simple pencil on her trademark blue-purple coloured paper.

"He looks like a gentleman" he said. The face did not look like one that belonged to a maniacal killer. Alice objected immediately.

"No Mister Gates, not a gentleman; a monster, make no mistake!" There was silence as he continued to look at the sketch as if hoping it would talk and tell him the whereabouts of the Ripper. His silent reflection was broken by Madam Athalia.

"Well, it is late, and I am fatigued." Samuel practically jumped to his feet, suddenly aware that he must have outstayed his welcome.

"Of course, my apologies Madam Athalia, I have imposed upon far too much of your time."

"Not at all Inspector; thank you for coming, Burton will see you out. And remember, monster; not man. Catch him before he kills again." Alice's words had a tinge of desperation about them. Samuel could easily understand it. He could not imagine what it must be like to witness a murder through the eyes of a victim each time that it happened. Boldly he made a promise in the spur of the moment.

"I will Madam Athalia, I assure you" He rose and shook Alice's hand before allowing Burton to show him out of the sitting room and then to the front door.

"Thank you Burton, Madam Athalia has been a great service to the police and to the people of London" Samuel felt compelled to express his gratitude to the butler for facilitating the meeting.

"Very good Inspector Gates. Good night to you"

"Good night Burton" Samuel responded and walked out of the door that the butler was holding open for him. It was night. He heard the door close behind him but did not look back. Cromwell Road was just as beguiling in the night time as it was during the day. There seemed to be more lanterns here on the streets of Kensington. The magnificent homes looked equally affluent in the glowing gas light as they did in the daytime. He walked down the stairs and had to nod, tip his hat at a couple and wish them a good evening. Thankfully a handsome cab was making its way up Cromwell road toward him. Samuel decided to treat himself to a cab-ride home. It was a long way and it was late. He did not fancy adding the extra time that it would take to walk home to his journey.

He hailed the cab and ignored the miffed look that the cabbie gave him when he stated the intended address. Clearly not good enough for the man, but Samuel didn't care. All that he wanted now was to get a good night's sleep and then go to work tomorrow and tell Inspector Reid about his break-through information about the Ripper case.

Chapter 23: The Headless Torso

Samuel had lain awake after he had finally made it home. He was buzzing with anticipation of how he was going to deliver the news that Madam Athalia had provided him with detailed insight to each of the murders and a clear drawing of the murderer as well. The possible responses were what had kept Samuel awake. He decided that it would either be complete disbelief, which would be most likely given the source of the information, or reluctant acceptance, because of the depth and breadth of the insights offered.

When Samuel had eventually fallen asleep it was early into the following morning. It should have come as no surprise to him that he slept in past the time that he would normally wake up. His parents worried that he had been putting in such long hours did not have the hearts to wake him. But when he did open his eyes and realise that he was running late he made every effort to get to the Whitechapel police station in time for the morning briefing at nine-thirty. He was only partially successful.

By the time that Samuel arrived the briefing on Tuesday morning was in full swing. He entered not quite un-noticed but still with very little disturbance to the meeting. He was happily taking in everything that was being said by the Scotland Yard Inspectors and by Inspector Reid and the others invited to update the group on their investigations. He was biding his time waiting for the opportunity to speak to Reid one-to-one.

However things did not go to plan. There was a kerfuffle outside which distracted those closest to the door and eventually everybody once the door was thrown open and Sargent Plymouth stood there.

"Sorry to disturb your briefing Sirs, but there is a situation!" he stated. Frederick Abberline who had been talking at the time responded as expected.

"What is it Sargent Plymouth?"

"The builders have arrived onsite at the new headquarters being built for us and have discovered a headless body in the basement" Plymouth's announcement was a complete shock for everyone in the room. All were aware of the new headquarters that was under construction for them and meant to replace their current HQ but it was not due to be ready for at least another year. Nobody had expected to hear from the builders, least of all about a murder victim found in the basement. There was a chorus of disbelieving phrases uttered in unison that was interrupted by Inspector Reid.

"Enough, all of you! Groves, Northwood, Wycliffe and Gates go and take charge of the investigation at the new building. When you've gathered all of the evidence that you can get the body to Bond for examination and report back here when you've finished" Reid's orders were barked like a General ordering his troops. The men singled out to undertake the work all acknowledged their assignment except for Gates.

"Sir I have been following another lead that I want to report to you before leaving the station" his hastily pulled together reason for staying was accepted with some grumpiness from Reid.

"Oh very well. Williams, take his place!" Reid directed. Absolved from this latest investigation Samuel was now free to talk with Reid at his convenience. Abberline spoke next.

"Imagine what the press will say when they find out that there is a body in the basement of the new police headquarters for Whitechapel?" it was a thought that none of the Inspectors, nor any of the men present relished.

"Let's hope that they don't find out" said Henry Moore rather unrealistically. Walter Andrews was not willing to entertain such an outlandish notion.

"You know that they will" he said in an admonishing tone to his equal.

***

The remainder of the morning briefing went on and after it was through it was abundantly clear to Samuel that they were not more progressed with the case than they had been last week or the week before. But he held what could be the keys to solving the case. He waited for Reid to not have a plethora of people around him before approaching.

"Sir I have something to report" he said rather simply. As if suddenly remembering Samuel's earlier statement in the briefing Reid raised his finger and waggled it.

"Yes that's right, what is it Mister Gates?"

"Not here sir, in your office if it pleases you?" Samuel's rather clandestine approach to imparting this new information seemed to intrigue Reid. He raised his eyebrows and tilted his head.

"Certainly mister Gates. You know the way". He said indicating the doorway to his office. There were more people gathering ready to impose upon Reid's time but he shooed them away. Edmund followed Samuel into his office and closed the door. Samuel waited for Reid to walk around his large desk and take his seat before sitting himself.

"Well?" queried Reid after he had taken his seat.

"We received letters about the first two murders written by……someone that must have had first-hand information about them. Corroborating the dates that they were written and the dates of the murders and when we received the letters it would have been impossible to be influenced by the newspapers reports of the murders." Samuel paused to see if the news was having an effect upon Reid. It was. Edmund leant forward his eyes narrowed slightly.

"Go on?" he asked.

"I have met with this person and have found out that she has first-hand knowledge of the two recent murders as well. I have gleaned the most intricate detail from her about them; details that the reports were unaware of." Samuel was trying his best to offer credentials before letting Reid know that the information came from a retired psychic.

"Who is this woman? How does she know such *intricate detail* about these murders? Why haven't you brought her in for questioning?" Reid was impatient for clarification.

"The manner in which she has obtained her information is somewhat unconventional Sir and she is very old. I would not want to bring her into the police station for further questioning. When I saw her, last night, she was still recovering from an unfortunate spell of food-poisoning. And it is a long journey from Kensington to Whitechapel for a woman of her advanced years." Samuel's explanations did little to assuage Reid's curiosity.

"Kensington? Unconventional? Advanced years?" he had a look of annoyance on his face. Samuel knew that there was no way to skirt around the qualifications of his source of information; he had to come clean and tell Reid everything.

"Sir what I am about to tell you may not at first seem plausible, but please promise me that you will keep an open mind?" Samuel's sudden impassioned plea wiped the look of Reid's face and he sat back in his chair and regarded Gates. He took a few moments to respond but had clearly made the decision to listen to the junior detective inspector.

"Very well Mister Gates. Tell me what you have learned?"

Over the course of the next hour Samuel told Reid in intricate detail about his meeting with Madam Athalia and the letters that had led him to her. Reid studied the letters whilst listening to Samuel. Samuel could not judge if Reid was incredulous or accepting of that he was telling him. But eventually Samuel had to stop talking and await a verdict from his superior. He was disappointed.

"Samuel, what you have said is going to take me some time to digest. Please go about your duties and I will inform you when I have made a determination of some description about all of the things that you have brought to my attention." Edmund's complete lack of decision about the veracity of the information was frustrating to say the least. Samuel was at first dumbstruck. He sat in the chair as if not sure of what he should do next. Noticing his continuing presence, Reid looked at the door and then back at Gates.

"Yes sir, of course" was all that he could manage to say before rising slowly from the chair and exiting Reid's office.

"Leave the door open" Reid notified as Gates looked about to close the door behind him.

"Yes sir" Somewhat dejected with the lack of buy-in from his boss, Samuel felt at a loose-end. He returned to his desk and sat down unsure of what to do next. He no longer had the letters or sketch from Madam Athalia as Reid had insisted on retaining them. Somebody was speaking behind him. The words filtered their way into Samuel's consciousness. He turned around.

"What did you say about the headless torso?" he inquired of a colleague.

"Thomas Bond's initial findings are that it is most likely the work of the same murderer as Elizabeth Jackson, the one in June that we......" Samuel completed the sentence for his colleague.

"The one that we pulled in pieces out of the Thames; so not the work of the Ripper then?"

"'I'm afraid not Samuel"

Gates could not account for the remainder of the day. He was so down-trodden at not having immediately won-over Reid that he had become despondent and withdrawn. He left work early that day.

***

Samuel's mood did not improve in the evening either. He attended a family dinner at the Fairclough's home accompanied this time by his parents. Thankfully they had much to talk about owing to their Swiss holiday and Samuel was not called upon to talk-shop as he normally would have been. Florence was the only one that brought attention to Samuel's quite demeanour.

"I'm just tired" he said as a generic excuse for his lack of energy. The dinner was wonderful, not that he noticed. The conversation was international, but he didn't follow very much of it. And eventually the evening came to an end and they left. He was grateful to get into his bed and put the day behind him.

Chapter 24: Wednesday the 3rd of October 1888

After a good night's sleep Samuel once more felt invigorated. He arrived at work at 8am. There were the usual early-starters. The frosted door to Reid's Office was shut. Samuel thought that he could hear muffled talking from within and elected to not interrupt. He was at his desk when Sargent Plymouth approached him.

"Mister Gates, please see Inspector Reid in his office if you will?"

It was not a request and Samuel knew it. He hurriedly got up and walked over to the door he knocked once and entered. The Scotland yard inspectors were all inside along with Reid. But there was somebody else too. A man that Samuel did not recognise.

"Samuel, this is Chief Detective Inspector Donald Swanson from Scotland Yard. He will be coordinating the investigation efforts from the Scotland Yard inspectors, all of which you know of course, from now on". The brief introduction over, Reid handed over to the Inspector Frederick Abberline.

"Inspector Reid has told us of your psychic friend that claims to have had commune with the victims in their hour of murder Mister Gates. We have had a very comprehensive briefing from him. We have all read the letters and seen the sketch" Abberline gave Samuel a very steady gaze. Samuel's hopes began to rise. If Reid had confided in the three, now four Scotland Yard inspectors, then he must have believed what he had heard.

"Utter poppy-cock!" Abberline said. Samuel was deflated.

"But sir..." he began, not really knowing how he was going to defend his source of information.

"The Criminal Investigation Department is only concerned with absolute fact Mister Gates and not wild supposition from a Gypsy fortune-teller!"

"Madam Athalia does not tell fortunes Sir. And she is no Gypsy..."

"You may have taken leave of your senses and have absolutely no regard for the tried and true methods of investigation that is practiced by both Scotland Yard and the London Police, but we do and this will simply not be tolerated or entertained in any way Mister Gates do you understand!?"

Abberline was clearly angry at Samuel for bringing the information to light, as well as being an advocate for it. Abberline was holding up the letters and the sketch from Madam Athalia as if they were damning evidence in a trial of Samuel's credibility. Inspector Henry Moore took the letters from Abberline and made his own criticism of Samuel whist waving the papers at him.

"This fraud has back-dated her letters and duped you into believing that she has some sort of second-sight. Clearly these are the ravings of a lonely old woman that is only seeking attention or worse than that, to use the Police and this high-profile investigation for self-aggrandisement!"

Moore's critique was even more acerbic than Abberline's. The three Scotland Yard inspectors seemed to be acting as one. It now fell to Inspector Walter Andrews to continue the unfavourable review of Samuel and Madam Athalia. He had much more of a mocking tone than his compatriots, it stung Samuel.

"Why doesn't Scotland Yard simply hand over all such investigations to the local psychic, we would not have any work to do because all of our cases would be solved by ghostly apparitions and mumbo-jumbo. This ridiculous assertion from you is tantamount to neglect of your duties to this station, to your job, to this investigation and to your superiors! What do you have to say for yourself?"

Samuel could not gather his thoughts quickly enough to respond. The newest addition to the Scotland Yard contingent chose that moment to add his thoughts to the adjudication.

"I am told by Inspector Reid that you are a capable man mister Gates, but you really must admit that you have gone astray in this instance. From the man that nearly caught Jack the Ripper to the man that could easily have become the laughing-stock of the entire station. Think of how you would have been mocked if this information had come to the attention of everyone here. As it is Inspector Reid very sensibly sought the opinions of all of the senior inspectors on this case. Lucky for you that he did or you may have made a complete fool of yourself. Have you told any of your colleagues about this?" Chief Inspector Donald Swanson sounded like he had Samuel's best interests at heart, but his tone said otherwise.

"No Chief Inspector".

"Thank goodness for that. You have been spared embarrassment. Samuel looked over to Reid for any kind of support against the verbal barrage that he was enduring.

"Samuel, on Saturday of this week, Senior Detective Inspector Robert Anderson returns from his holiday in Switzerland. He will be reporting here on Monday morning to begin a five week hand-over from myself. I want to be able to tell him that all of the investigations currently underway are well in-hand. And I am not sure that I could say that if I thought that you were chasing after the, the….ravings of this old woman. Do you understand my point of view?"

Reid's statement sounded like a feeble excuse for not wanting to believe the incredible information that Athalia possessed. He clearly had his own retirement now firmly in his sights and was not willing to entertain any bizarre sources of information about the Ripper case. It appeared to Samuel that all Reid wanted now was a peaceful exit without controversy. And it would have been very controversial indeed if Reid had accepted Athalia's visions as true. Henry Moore spoke once again.

"The press is crying out for results and we have nothing to give them. Now we have to contend the rise of vigilante groups to 'Rid us of the Ripper' as they are saying. Gang mentality Mister Gates; we cannot have a rowdy group of drunken men brandishing clubs chasing after any one that they think is Jack the Ripper. The opportunity for further mayhem and mistaken bashings is enormous. And if that wasn't enough for us all to cope with, the Palace has again written to us Mister Gates. Her majesty Queen Victoria believes that the perpetrator must be a butcher or a slaughterer from a ship docked at the time of the murders. That means that we have to now go back and investigate all of the previously questioned, butchers whether land-based or from visiting ships, cattle drovers that were in the city at the time of the four Ripper murders and once more get alibies from them. Those that are unable to account for their whereabouts during the any of the murders will be brought in for further questioning. This is how we will close our net on Jack the Ripper Mister Gates, not following the superstitious nonsense from an old woman".

Samuel was devastated. Clearly the men in charge had very different pressures to deal with and could not extend their belief to encompass the other-worldly.

"We should think of extending our questioning to their employees as well" suggested the Chief Inspector. This was immediately agreed to by all of the others.

"I'll get back to my questioning of suspects" offered Samuel in a weak voice.

"That won't be necessary, we will find something for you to do" said Reid. It sounded ominous, like Samuel had irrevocably damaged his career by bringing what he had to their attention.

"That will be all Samuel" said Reid. Gates was dismissed. He left the office crestfallen and very much aware that he had gone from golden-boy, the pursuer of the Ripper to a leaper in his own police station.

Chapter 25: Thursday the 4th of October 1888

Samuel had been given menial clerical jobs for the remainder of the date following his smack-down by his superiors. He returned to work the following day only to find more of it piled upon his desk. He attended the morning briefing but sat discretely at the back. The Scotland Yard Chief Inspector was running the briefings from now on, he heard from his colleagues. The man was clearly determined to ensure that Queen Victoria's beliefs were fully investigated and a full report made back to Buckingham palace as quickly as possible. Reid did not speak in the briefing at all. He was now clearly happy to allow the Chief Inspector take the reins and run with the investigation.

Butchers, drovers, and their staff were all questioned. Some were arrested and brought into the station for further questioning. The crew of the boats that were in dock at the time were again brought under scrutiny. Even the possibility of crewmen transferring between the boats was investigated thoroughly. But none of the suspicions that Queen Victoria had put forward had amounted to anything. Everyone felt sorry for the Chief Detective Inspector Donald Swanson. He had announced that he would take the findings to the Palace in person, even if they did not have a favourable outcome and ratify what the Queen had suspected. Nobody wanted to be in his shoes and perform that act of bravery.

The rest of Thursday and Friday passed and produced more suspects. But deep down Samuel knew that none of them was Jack the Ripper. Somehow he had to take matters into his own hands and continue the search for the *real* killer.

Chapter 26: Monday the 8th of October 1888

It was an auspicious day in the Whitechapel police station. Senior Detective Inspector Robert Anderson was due to make his first appearance as the new head of the department. Edmund Reid was at work earlier than normal ensuring that everything was ready for the arrival of his replacement. He fussed over the smallest thing with the staff that were already onsite. He objected to seeing some desks with too many piles of papers on them quoting that it looked like the desk-owner was not processing their work quickly enough. Then he would similarly find fault with desks that looked too clean complaining that the inhabitant looked to be bereft of work to do.

It seemed that nothing was good enough or would satisfy Inspector Reid today. Even though his incessant meddling with everybody's workplace was annoying it was generally felt that Reid should be almost pitied. He had to hand over the most high-profile case in the history of London to his successor without a resolution. That must have been difficult to face.

***

All hands were onsite when Robert Anderson finally made his appearance. There was a gentlemanly round of applause when he entered the station. Reid walked through the applauding men to greet Anderson.

"Welcome back from Switzerland Robert and welcome to your first day as Senior Detective Inspector of the Whitechapel police department." Edmund looked genuinely pleased that he was welcoming his successor. It looked very much like everyone was waiting for Anderson to reply and he did not disappoint. Looking around and addressing everyone he said

"Thankyou Edmund, it will be a privilege to head up the Criminal Investigation Department and the Whitechapel police station. I know that you have done an outstanding job during your tenure. I can only hope to emulate your success whilst I have the reins."

This too garnered a further round of applause. Motioning his thanks to everyone for the courtesy he then finished off his brief welcome speech.

"I am aware of the one case that is foremost in everybody's mind at the moment and let me assure you that I will not let it divert my attention from all of the cases that are running concurrently in the CID. Now let's talk more in your office Edmund, you can tell me everything that has been happening."

"Excellent Robert, absolutely first-rate; this way" replied Reid indicating that Anderson should lead the way to his office. As they walked toward the door Reid could be heard saying

"I have ordered the sign-writer to remove my name at the end of this week and replace it with yours"

"Splendid, thank you Edmund, very considerate of you" they disappeared into Reid's office and the door closed.

***

Anderson had appeared barely more than half an hour before the usual morning briefing. It would be run by Frederick Abberline of Scotland Yard but both Reid and Anderson would certainly be there. The briefing was called and the briefing room filled up. Samuel took his now customary place down the back and out of sight. Reid and Anderson were the last to arrive. Abberline addressed the men.

"The vigilante situation is growing worse. There was an incident last night whereby a man fitting the widely-accepted description of the Ripper was beset upon by a group of men upon hearing what they thought was a cry from the woman. As it turns out, the woman had seen a rat and was crying out in fear of that. Not thinking, because that is what vigilante groups do, they descended upon the hapless fellow with makeshift wooden truncheons. Only the quick wits of the man's wife saved him from further injury when she grabbed hold of one of the truncheons and attacked one of the vigilantes attacking her husband. He is now recovering in London Hospital with various injuries sustained in the, thankfully, brief attack."

Abberline paused for dramatic effect. There was a loud murmur of disapproval from the men. The vigilant problem was a sore-point in the police force. The very fact that there were any vigilantes in London was testament to the fact that the police were simply not making enough progress with the case. Abberline continued.

"It is not difficult to understand how Londoners feel in the prevailing circumstances, but we cannot and will not tolerate this kind of mob-mentality. We are going to address the situation by once more increasing the number of police on the streets. People need to see that we are taking this very seriously and can offer them protection from not just the Ripper, but the torso killer and the plethora of copy-cat killers and would-be killers that is erupting in Whitechapel."

This brought a murmur of approval from the men. The remainder of the briefing was pretty standard. Reid and Anderson did not contribute anything other than what everybody already knew, Reid was briefing Anderson of the next five weeks and then he was retiring. Reid's final day at work would be Friday the 9th of November. There was a party planned in a hall nearby, more details to follow. The Scotland yard four would remain onsite until there was a definitive arrest made in the Ripper case and then business would return to normal. It was something that everyone in the room looked forward to.

Chapter 27: The Ripper

It was a cold and densely-foggy night. The rain was had fallen for most of the day but that had given way to a still and misty night. The dim light that was the day disappeared and gave way to the murky darkness of the night. Madam Athalia sat at her desk and looked out of the window. The street lamps had halos of light around them in the haze. There was nobody walking down Cromwell Road. Everyone had more sense and was safely cocooned inside their well-to-do homes.

Alice brought her attention back to her writing. She wrote a sentence or two and for no particular reason looked up again and to the view outside. For just a moment she thought that she saw someone in the dark regions between the gas lanterns that were trying their best to light the road. Leaning forward and squinting she tried to see but the darkness outside and the reflection of the lights in her library conspired to defeat her.

Shrugging it off she returned to her writing. There was a gentle knock at the door.

"Come in" said Alice. The door opened it was, as expected Burton. He was carrying an ornate silver tray with a fine china cup and saucer on it. There was small spiral of steam emanating from the cup.

"Your hot milk Madam Athalia" he announced as he placed it on the desk beside her.

"Excellent, Burton, thank you" she said praising him.

"Will there be any thing more my Lady?" he inquired his head tilted slightly sideways in anticipation of her reply.

"No thank you Burton. I will retire for the evening very soon"

"Very good Madam; I have placed an extra blanked upon your bed as it is such an cold night"

"Thank you Burton, that was very considerate of you. Good night, I shall not be long before I too retire to my bed."

Athalia would never let such a good deed go without thanks to her faithful butler.

"Good night Madam" he replied and left the room quietly. Alice returned to her work for a while occasionally sipping the warm milk. By the time that she had consumed it she felt a wave of tiredness envelop her. It was her turn now to retire for the evening she thought. With one more look out at the street-scape below, Alice closed the thick curtains in the library before making her way upstairs to her bedroom.

***

Alice had prepared herself for slumber and was patting down her pillows when she noticed a breeze. Turning around she could see that the window was ajar just slightly. It was far too cold a night for that, she thought. Moving over to the curtains she separated them. Then reaching up she pulled down the window and blocked off the offending cold intrusion. Shutting the curtains she had not bothered to secure the latch. Her bedroom was on the first floor and she felt quite secure without the need to lock her windows.

Then after settling herself into her bed she blew out the lamp that had remained on to aide her and was soon fast asleep.

The window that she had not locked slid very slowly upwards again. The precision at which it was moved was amazing. The craftsmanship too aided in that the mechanism was robust and well made. It moved without a sound if done very slowly. Soon it was open more than enough for the intruder to enter Madam Athalia's bedroom. Straightening himself up he slowly walked toward the helpless old woman.

He stopped and looked down at her. She was completely defenceless. Even if she had been holding a kitchen knife, what good would it have done her? Stretching out his hand he almost had it over her mouth when Alice's eyes subliminally alerted to the danger shot open. She gasped in a breath to let out a cry but it was stymied by the brutish hand that covered her mouth. Her eyes opening wider with every passing millisecond Alice could feel her heart in her throat and her panic instinct consuming every part of her reason. The man standing above her was the one in her visions, in her sketch. It was Jack the Ripper.

Desperately she tried to look around the room for something, anything to help her. There was nothing but the familiar surroundings of her bedroom. This was the place that she was going to die, she thought. Her situation was hopeless.

The next thing that she saw was uninterpretable and unbelievable. The Ripper opened his mouth and his throat expanded like that of a bullfrog. It was hideous. Unable to think clearly in the circumstances Alice did her best to scream again but nothing would come out. The Ripper's hand was held so firmly over her mouth and nose it was nearly impossible to breathe. She was being suffocated in her own house, in her own bed.

With a garbled hoick he spat something at her. The speed of it moving through the air made it impossible to identify, but there was the sense of solidity rather than spittle. Whatever it was it impacted the front of her neck. It may have not hurt at all but with her tension so incredibly high it felt like a bunch of sewing needles had slammed into her skin. Again she tried to scream to no avail. She was helpless and held immobile by the most heinous murderer that London had ever seen. Madam Athalia knew that she was doomed.

Chapter 28: Tuesday the 9th of October 1888

Burton knocked once more on the bedroom door of Madam Athalia; still no reply. It was unlike her to be so very late for breakfast. She always ate at the same time every day. He had prepared her meal and when she failed to show thought that he had better give her a gentle reminder.

There was nothing more to it, he simply had to enter. Opening the door he announced himself quietly so as not to startle his employer.

"Good morning Madam Athalia, I am afraid that you have slept-in somewhat this morning."

He could see her on the bed but immediately knew that something was horribly wrong. He could see blood on her pillow. The bedroom window was wide open and the curtains pulled back allowing plentiful light into the room. He threw the door open and raced to the side of her bed. The sight that he beheld was sickening. Madam Athalia was lying in a pool of her own blood, her throat cut on both the right and left sides. Mercifully her eyes were closed, but there was the unmistakable expression of horror upon her still features. She had died a terrible death.

Burton tried to stifle a cry of his own but did not succeed. He looked around him disorientated unsure of what to do.

"Who!" he started to say.

"Who could have done......this?" He was close to tears. He felt nauseous. He was sure that he was going to be sick if he stayed looking upon Madam Athalia's corpse for a second longer. He ran from the room into the hallway and stopped. He collapsed to his knees and began to weep openly.

***

To Samuel it looked like it was going to be another day of being ignored by his superiors and given clerical jobs. His colleagues had noticed his sudden fall from grace but were unsure of the reasons behind it. There were thankfully no rumours that Samuel had to contend with though as clearly the men in charge were very good at keeping secret why he was suddenly so out of favour. Samuel had finished a sandwich that he had brought with him for lunch when he noticed Police Commissioner Charles Warren stride into the station and make directly for Edmund Reid's office. There was a worker busy removing Reid's name from the office door. Apparently he had shown up sooner than expected, but rather than shoo him away he was allowed to get on with the job of removing Reid's name and replacing it with Anderson's.

Charles Warren entered Reid's office without knocking and closed the door loudly behind him attracting some attention. Samuel wondered what had prevoked the Commissioner to visit the CID. Then turning his attention to the menial job that he had been assigned he got on with his uninspiring work. He wasn't sure how long Warren had been in Reid's office when the doorway opened and Charles Warren, Edmund Reid and Robert Anderson appeared at the doorway clearly finalising their goodbyes.

There seemed to be an agreement of some sort reached and the Police Commissioner looking worried but somehow satisfied departed. After another brief exchange between Reid and Anderson the new departmental chief made his way toward Samuel. Samuel watched him approaching with a rising sense of curiosity.

"Chief Inspector Reid would like a word Mister Gates" he said rather simply

"Very good Sir" replied Samuel very compliantly. He hurried over to Reid's office expecting Anderson to follow, but he did not. Instead he went off in another direction. Samuel assumed that Anderson had something else to attend to.

Gates entered Edmund's office not knowing what to expect. The last time he was here he had basically been denigrated by the four Scotland Yard inspectors. That unpleasant experience was still very much in the forefront of Samuel's mind.

"You wanted to see me Sir?' he inquired.

"Come in, close the door behind you and sit down Samuel. I owe you an explanation" Reid's words were strangely comforting in the current situation. Samuel did as he was told. He settled himself into the seat and waited for Edmund to speak.

"I realise that you probably think that I threw you to the wolves about your psychic friend and her *visions*, but please look at it from my point of view. I am about to retire. I have the highest-profile case in the history of London to contend with, the press and the Palace all giving us their opinions on what should be done. So when you came to me with your *story,* I had to take into my confidence the Scotland Yard Inspectors so that I could get a different perspective from each of them. And although you know the eventual outcome; what you don't know is how intently they all listened to the account with great and I think, quite impartial interest. Frederick Abberline seemed to be the most interested out of the four of them. But you must give them their due for taking such a fantastic report into consideration. The outcome was carefully considered before we called for you. In fact I have even recounted it all once again to Robert Anderson, on his first day with us as part of his briefing on the Ripper case. He was even more interested in it than Abberline, if that's possible."

It was an overload of information for Samuel. At first he felt a little angry with himself for feeling that they had all dismissed his insight so readily. Perhaps he had been too hasty with his determination. But it was all history now; why was Reid telling him this? As if reading his mind Edmund continued.

"Your probably wondering why I am telling you all of this?"

Samuel nodded.

"I have rather distressing news for you Samuel, so please prepare yourself for a shock." Samuel visibly stiffened not knowing what to expect.

"Police Commissioner Charles Warren, with whom you are acquainted, has called upon assistance in investigating a case that falls firmly in the jurisdiction of the city of London police. A murder that on the surface could be considered to be similar to the Ripper murders, but this time a well-to-do old lady in a fine house. Charles has requested that Thomas Bond do the examination of the body and I have offered your services to assist in the investigation of the murder."

Reid paused. For a second Samuel was utterly confused. He was steeling himself for a shock but instead seemed to be rewarded with another murder case in the city of London precinct. Reid looked down and was almost squirming in his seat adding to Samuel's confusion.

"Now for the difficult part Samuel; the body of the deceased was found by her Butler this morning. Murdered in her own bed, the first-floor bedroom window wide open; apparently how the murder entered. The front and rear doors were locked from the inside. No idea how the killer managed to climb up to the first floor and enter, but that is beside the point at the moment."

Again Reid paused. He seemed to be stalling for time as if he was avoiding telling Samuel something that he really should know.

"What is it?" Samuel asked in a weak voice.

"You had best go to the residence of the victim and question the butler before checking in with Bond and finding out the results of his examination"

Again Reid seemed to be doing a good job of not telling Samuel the full story.

"The residence is known to you Samuel...........on Cromwell Road"

Samuel froze. The office around him seemed to recede away and fall into blackness. All that he could see was the mouth of Edmund Reid saying the sentence over again; residence known to you Samuel on Cromwell Road".

He shook his head unintentionally. The action brought him back to the present.

"No" he said hoping that he could take away the very thought of who the victim was with one word. Reid had a tortured look upon his face. He met Samuel's gaze.

"I am very sorry Samuel, yes, it is Madam Athalia"

"No, it can't be? It simply cannot be Sir….." Samuel tried to deny the information that was facing him. Reid shut his eyes briefly. He opened them again and looked at Samuel steadily.

"If you would rather not assist in the investigation Samuel I will understand completely. But when Charles told me of the murder and who the victim was I thought that your understanding of the…..deceased would give you an advantage in this investigation".

Reid's offer both appealed and repulsed Samuel at the same time. On the one hand he did not want to have to admit that his newfound friend was dead, but on the on the other he wanted to find whoever had done this horrible thing.

"Yes, yes, please Sir, yes I want to take the case" Samuel heard his own words as if they were being spoken by somebody else.

"Good, I'm glad. I don't want to pressure you but the sooner that you get to the scene of the crime the better." Reid was doing exactly what he said that he did not want to do and was pressing the urgency of the case with Samuel.

"Yes Sir, straight-away Sir." He got up from the chair and left the office. It was crowded outside and Samuel had barely waked past two of his colleagues desks when he ran into Robert Anderson.

"Edmund has briefed you?" he asked in a quite stern tone.

"Yes Sir. I am on my way to Cromwell Road now Sir" he explained.

"Excellent. Let me reiterate that we are hoping that the outcome of this investigation is that it is one of these accursed copy-cat killings. Do you understand?" Anderson's statement made no sense to Samuel.

"Sir?'

"It simply will not do to have the people in a salubrious area like Kensington think that Jack the Ripper could enter any one of their homes and kill them in their sleep. We have enough to worry about without the rich and famous feeling threatened in their ivory towers. Do you understand?" Now Samuel did indeed understand.

"Reid and I are taking quite a chance handing you over to the London city police to assist in this case. Don't let us down boy." Anderson's warning resonated with Gates. He suddenly felt grateful toward his new departmental head.

"I won't let you down sir. Thank you Sir" he started to walk away only to find that Anderson was going in the same direction. There was an awkward moment of silence that Samuel desperately wanted to fill. He had a sudden flash of inspiration.

"I imagine that the celebrations were in full swing whilst you were in Andermatt Switzerland Sir?" he said. This provoked a perplexed response from Anderson

"Celebrations?" he queried.

"I heard somewhere that the final part of your Swiss holiday was spent in the village of Andermatt. Every year at the end of September they have a festival celebrating the founding of the village. It goes for an entire fortnight" Samuel explained.

"Don't have a clue what you're talking about Gates"

Anderson looked annoyed and gave Samuel a disapproving sideways glare.

"Sorry Sir, I must have my facts head over heels" he said hoping to recover from the situation. Mercifully Anderson had reached the desk that he was heading for and Samuel continued toward the front door without his company.

As Samuel left the station he was wracking his brain. He was certain that his parents had told him about their disappointment in not being in Andermatt for the village celebrations that were due to begin in the second half of September. Maybe he got it wrong? Anyway, he had more important things to think about now.

Someone had murdered Madam Athalia and he was tasked it seemed, with ensuring that it was not done at the hands of Jack the Ripper.

Chapter 29: Cromwell Road, Kensington

By the time Samuel reached the grand home of Alice Athalia it was mid-afternoon. There were two uniformed police guarding the front door. Samuel identified himself and they indicated that the inspector was inside. He entered. Even though it was all familiar knowing that Madam Athalia no longer lived here made it somehow feel completely abandoned. Samuel walked down the hall and toward the conservatory where he had been told the inspector would be found. He was there with Burton. The Butler looked in a terrible state he was sitting in a chair facing the beautifully manicured courtyard the inspector was standing over him asking a question.

"And you say that there is nothing missing from Madam Athalia's bedroom?"

"Not that I can immediately identify Sir, no."

Samuel's entrance brought a halt to the questioning. The inspector looked up and Burton turned around in his chair to see who had entered the room. Samuel thought it best to identify himself.

"Junior Detective Inspector Samuel Gates on secondment from the Criminal Investigation Department from Whitechapel." He said by way of introduction. The inspector nodded knowingly and responded.

"Yes, I have been told to expect assistance from Whitechapel. Come in please. My name is James Fenton, Detective Inspector, London city police. You'll be reporting to me for the duration of this murder investigation."

"Very good Sir" Samuel acceded to Fenton's authority without question. After all he was only here by the grace of the Commissioner.

"Burton you look exhausted, have you eaten?" Samuel's sudden and unexpected familiarity with the butler caught Fenton off guard.

"No Inspector Gates, nothing…the shock you see, and since alerting the police I've been answering questions all morning"

"Well it is well into the afternoon now, I think that you should prepare something for yourself whilst the Inspector and I have a chat". The offer sounded very appealing to Burton. He had lost track of time since the shock of finding Alice murdered in her bed. He had not even realised that he was hungry and tired until that very moment.

"Yes, sir. I'll be in the kitchen if you require me for further questioning"

"Thank you Burton" Both of the inspectors watched the bedraggled butler leave the conservatory before conversing further. Samuel looked at the breakfast table that had been set up with what could correctly be assumed was Madam Athalia's breakfast that went untouched.

"You know the butler?" asked Fenton.

"I was consulting with Madam Athalia about the Ripper case only last week. She had visions of the murders and I was following up the lead. The Inspectors in charge of the case felt that her evidence did not hold up to scrutiny. And now bizarrely she has been murdered in a way that has a passing resemblance to the Ripper murders".

It was not what Fenton had expected to hear from the young man. He blinked his dismay at the very thought that the victim had any connection to the Ripper murders at all.

"And after proclaiming her knowledge to the Whitechapel police, she has ended up murdered in her own bed; coincidence?" James waited for Samuel's response. Samuel contemplated the thought but did not reply. Fenton posed another rhetorical question.

"Or a past customer that was unhappy with Madam Athalia's message from a departed loved-one." Fenton was clearly keeping an open mind about the case so Samuel thought that he should do the same. He offered his own alternative.

"Or a simple robbery that went wrong. The thief unwittingly disturbed Madam Athalia whilst searching for valuables and he panicked and killed her?" They contemplated each other.

"In that incidence, it would then all just be happenstance that Madam Athalia was the victim." James was fishing for something. Samuel spoke his mind in reply.

"Any of the scenarios are possible. We have to keep an open mind." The answer clearly delighted Fenton.

"Excellent; exactly what I wanted to hear. We are going to get along just fine. No sense in assuming *anything* until we have enough evidence to support it." He all but gave Samuel a hearty slap on the back. With what seemed to be the test of his pre-determined bias safely out of the way, Fenton began to brief Gates on what he had discovered so far.

"The window on the first floor of the master bedroom was wide open when the butler discovered the body. He had prepared breakfast for his employer and went to rouse her when she failed to show up at her usual time. There are no other permanent staff, but there are cleaners that show up on a weekly basis. They do not have a key and rely upon either the Mistress of the house or the butler to be here to allow them entry. Nothing appears to have been taken. There is no motive for the butler to slay his employer, he is now all but unemployed. However, I don't want to discount the idea completely until I have all of the facts. I am having the deceased solicitors make known to us if there is any bequest to him in her will." James paused to gather his thoughts and continued.

"None of the neighbours saw or heard anything. I have spoken with them on both sides, across the road and here over the fence to the back. The constables are busying themselves with the rest of the street in case anyone up or down the road saw anything or anyone that was suspicious. I imagine that a crazed killer like Jack the Ripper would stand out in a neighbourhood such as this, wouldn't you think Junior Detective Inspector?" Samuel knew that it was a jibe, but thought that he should respond anyway.

"The Ripper must have looked very normal to the four women that he as murdered so far. So maybe he would not have looked out of place here in Kensington at all?" Samuel's refusal to discount the Ripper as a suspect clearly pleased Fenton. It was further affirmation that his new investigative partner was not ruling out any possibility.

"No, maybe not" there was a moment's silence and then Fenton continued his briefing.

"The butler says that Madam Athalia has no enemies; no disgruntled customers that he can think of. She has clearly done very well for herself with her chosen career. She does not have a gambling habit, so there are no debt-collectors chasing her for monies owed. No gentlemen friend that could have been a jilted lover, well not at her age surely, but I had to find out anyway."

Samuel cringed a little at the inference. He had thought of Madam Athalia as a kindly old grandmother figure even though he had only known her briefly. The very thought of her being involved in a jealous lover situation did not even enter his mind. But strangely, it gave him more respect for Fenton, for at least exploring it as a possibility.

"And that brings you up to date. I have of course made the butler tell and retell his version of the events over and over hoping to see a crack in the account. But so far nothing that would make me think that he is lying. Equally there is nothing that is reinforcing my belief that he is telling the truth either."

"He alerted the police?" Samuel sought clarification.

"Yes, found a constable on patrol not far from here, he is one of the men guarding the front door now. You can speak to him if you wish and get his version of events. Burton approached him at about eight o'clock this morning looking quite distraught and informed the constable that his employer was murdered, *her throat cut*, his exact words."

"Is there anything else?" Samuel had the feeling that he had got all of the information that Fenton knew about the case so far.

"We should have the results of the examination by this evening. I believe from recent information that Madam Athalia will be examined by the Whitechapel police surgeon?"

"Yes, Thomas Bond, a good man; excellent at his job" Samuel confirmed.

"Then perhaps you can give me a hand questioning the remaining surrounding households. I would prefer to have first-hand accounts rather than reports from the constables that are doing the rounds now" James's suggestion was an excellent one. Samuel agreed enthusiastically. He looked over his shoulder in the direction of the kitchen.

"Burton won't be going anywhere. We'll leave an officer watching him, just in case he decides to make himself scarce" James was leaving nothing to chance. Gates smiled his appreciation of the plan.

"Let's go then" Fenton indicated that they should leave. They walked down the hallway and past the kitchen. Samuel indicated that he wanted a brief word with Burton. He stood in the open doorway and addressed the man. Burton could be seen sitting at one of the stools clearly the privy of the staff only, it was un-cushioned and looked uncomfortable. He had what looked to be a half-eaten sandwich on a plate in front of him and a half a glass of milk.

"Burton. I will be questioning the neighbours for the remainder of the afternoon and then reporting to London city police to find out the results of the examination. Will you be alright here?" Samuel's question had genuine warmth and concern within it. Burton looked up. He seemed to be miles away but managed a nod and a softly-spoken reply.

"Yes Sir Inspector Gates, thank you"

"Alright then. I'll be back tomorrow" Samuel re-joined James and they continued their way through the impressive hallway toward the front door.

***

Talking with the neighbours was a different experience in the street to talking with residents in Whitechapel. Every door was answered by either a housekeeper or a butler and they had to be circumnavigated to get to the home owners. But the staff too had to be questioned. It was easier to do that with the servants than the wealthy. They had to be mollycoddled with assurances that it was a *terrible event*, and almost certainly a *robbery gone wrong*. Both James and Samuel were acutely aware that they could not alarm anyone about the situation or about any of the avenues of investigation that they were exploring.

Unfortunately one of the homes was owned by a Magistrate who wanted to know everything; not accepting the barrier that it was an ongoing investigation and they couldn't say much about it. He of course knew the Commissioner and would get the information anyway. It was a thinly veiled threat to come-clean with *all* of the information or face the consequences. It was here that both James and Samuel worked out that they had similar ways of dealing with such a sticky situation.

Working in unison, they managed to extricate themselves with assurances that they were meticulously following procedure and would let the Commissioner know of the special interest and thus allow the information to come from the top down rather than from the simple investigating detectives. They picked up on each other's explanation and built upon it. In the end after not really giving away anything, but saying quite a lot, they seemed to satisfy the grumpy old man and were able to get away.

Even though time-consuming and at times harrowing, the questioning turned up nothing. Not a single person recalled seeing anybody or anything out of place on the night in question. The fog and general miserable weather was, no-doubt, the main contributing factor for that. By the time they were finished both James and Samuel were exhausted. But they could not afford themselves the luxury of rest.

"By now the medical examiner's report will be ready" said James

"Then let's get to the mortuary" Samuel said rather sensibly.

"It's a bit late. I know that the Commissioner wanted to read it the moment that it was ready. We should find it at the police station by this hour"

Eager to find out the contents of the report they hastened to the London city police headquarters.

***

James and Samuel entered the London city police head-quarters. It was late and there were fewer people around than there had been an hour ago. Walking with familiarity, James led Samuel through the labyrinth of desks and toward the office of the Commissioner. It was all familiar to Samuel since his time spent here describing his pursuit of the Ripper at the end of the previous month.

"The report will be on the Commissioner's desk" explained James. As they approached the office of Charles Warren he appeared at the doorway along with Thomas Bond. They were finishing up a conversation and it appeared that the Commissioner was saying goodbye to the surgeon. They both looked up at the men approaching them.

"Ah Mister Fenton, and Mister Gates excellent timing; I have had the pleasure of speaking with your notable surgeon from Whitechapel about the results of his examination. Doctor Thomas Bond, Inspector James Fenton. And of course you know young Samuel". Warren's introduction over, Bond acknowledged the men and proceeded to brief them on his findings.

"In short gentlemen, I would have to conclude that this is the work of somebody that would have us believe that the murder was at the hands of Jack the Ripper. For reasons that you will be charged to find out, the killer has made an attempt to mimic the incisions that he must have surely read about in the newspapers, but has failed to cut with the assuredness of indeed the veracity of the Ripper. The wounds you see were not as deep; and whilst one could consider the Ripper's victims to have been savaged with an almost maniacal precision, the wounds suffered by the victim and ultimately leading to her death were a pallid reproduction of those that have become the hallmarks of the Whitechapel murderer."

Bond finished his reprisal of what was no-doubt a much more comprehensive report to the Commissioner. It seemed to please the departmental head enormously.

"So you see gentlemen, we are not facing a new modus-operandi from an existing and still at-large murderer, rather we are confronted with a lunatic that seeks to create mayhem and have us believe that the Ripper will break into the homes of anyone and murder them whilst sleeping. This is obviously the machinations of a truly sick mind!"

Warren's relief although evident, did not disguise the fact that whoever the murderer was in this instance, they were potentially much more dangerous than the Ripper. The sentiment was voiced by James.

"Sir; will this information find its way into the hands of the newspaper reporters? If so it could go a long way toward destroying the plans that this fellow must have had of creating mayhem...." Fenton never got a chance to complete his thoughts.

"The newspaper reporters have already been briefed by me Mister Fenton. Madam Alice Athalia was the victim of an insane ex-lover jilted many years ago and who had allowed his displeasure to fester to a point where he sought out the woman for which he had such strong feelings, and broke into her residence with the specific objective of murdering her". It was complete fantasy, based upon nothing that either Fenton or Gates had yet turned up.

"But how did you....." James was again interrupted.

"The people of Kensington need to feel that this was a one-off incident that is unlikely to ever be repeated. And from tomorrow when the papers print that little story, they will be horrified and indignant of course that such a thing could happen in their neighbourhood; but Mister Fenton, Mister Gates and Doctor Bond, they will continue to feel safe and not at threat from a psychotic murdering imitator".

That appeared to be the end of the discussion.

"That will leave the two of you to turn up the real-culprit, at which time, I will confess that I had miss-led the press with the specific aim of taking the public's focus away from this lunatic's agenda so as to spite him and ensure that his devious plan fell upon fallow ground and did not take root." Warren's epilogue to his plan suddenly made the whole thing make sense. It was a clever ruse on his part. Clearly the only thing that mattered to the Commissioner was ensuring that between now and when the murderer was captured that the press did not have any more fodder for causing discontentment with the people of London. But just in case any of the men listening to his plan had any doubts he solidified his resolve with his parting remarks.

"Let the press have Jack the Ripper to scare people with and help them sell more newspapers. What I am giving you is time, outside of the spotlight of public sentiment, to find whoever is really responsible for this murder. Be sure that you don't squander the opportunity I have devised for you. Happy hunting; keep me informed and good night gentlemen".

With that he gave them all a very self-satisfied grin and departed. The three of them watched him leave; admiration for his Machiavellian manoeuvrings growing within them all.

"I suppose that is why he is the Commissioner" remarked Bond.

"Indeed" replied Fenton.

"Is there anything else that you can tell us that may help?" Gates already had his mind on the task ahead.

"Only that the murderer must have been a very nimble fellow to have climbed up the outside of house to gain entry. Maybe you should look for an acrobat from a travelling circus?" At first Bond's comment seemed a little too glib, but then both men realised that he was being genuine. James and Samuel could see in each other's expressions that they were both actually considering it as a possibility.

"Thank you Doctor Bond" said Samuel.

"Yes; it was good to meet you and thank you very much for your report."

"Good evening gentlemen" with that Bond left the two inspectors to ponder everything that they had heard. There was a moment's silence.

"What next?" asked Samuel.

"Home, food and sleep" replied James. It sounded heavenly after such a frenetic day.

"Excellent thinking" Samuel's relief was evident in his voice. He was ready to call it a day.

"We shall reconvene here tomorrow morning at eight-thirty sharp"

"Done! See you tomorrow" they exchanged good byes and left together. Samuel turning one way to head home and James the other.

***

By the time that Samuel made it home his parents had already begun eating. He could smell the aroma of food wafting down the hall the moment that he opened the front door. It was good to get in from the chilly night. He followed the scent of the food to the dining room.

"My goodness Samuel you certainly are late today" said his mother as he entered.

"Come in and sit down your mother has made the most wonderful Zurchergeschnetzeltes and rosti." The two words were unknown to Samuel and he gave his mother a quizzical look.

"Zurch...." He began to try and repeat what he had heard but was unable.

"A veal and onion and mushroom dish cooked with cream and the rosti is a patty made from shredded potato and then fried; delicious!" ensured his mother.

"Well it certainly does smell wonderful he said as he took his seat and his mother spooned a couple of the golden rosti onto his plate from a serving dish and then ladled some of the main course onto it that he had found so unpronounceable.

"You picked up the recipe from your travels in Switzerland I take it?" he asked as he began to eat his meal.

"Yes I remember this one the best; we discovered it in Andermatt and...."

"Andermatt!" said Samuel talking over the top of his mother. The show of bad manners did not go without a severe look from both of his parents. Realising what he had just done he apologies immediately.

"I am sorry mother, but something that you said reminded me of something today that I thought quite odd."

"Oh, what is it?" asked his mother; both parents now intrigued.

"The new man taking over from inspector Reid had recently returned from Switzerland. I am sure that he said that he was in Andermatt for the final part of his stay before returning to England"

"Well he couldn't have picked a better time, the festival would have been in full swing by then end of September" said his father.

"That is what I thought that you had said, but when I questioned him about it he didn't seem to know anything about it. Don't you think that is strange?" he asked looking from one to the other.

"Yes I do" agreed his mother.

"He must have been walking around with a blind-fold on. And you say that this is the new head-man. Sounds like a buffoon" his father was very dismissive. Samuel looked a little distant as he tried to reason why Robert Anderson would nave not know anything about the village festival.

"They have been doing it for centuries you know; celebrating the founding of this beautiful mountain village" his mother repeated something to him that she had told him weeks ago when they had returned from their own holidaying in Switzerland.

"Yes" said Samuel. Then as if coming to his senses, he realised that he was inadvertently turning the conversation away from the subject that his mother had been telling him about.

"I am sorry mother. You were saying that you discovered this dish in Andermatt?"

Reinvigorated by the reminder his mother continued to tell Samuel of the story of *discovering* the meal in a local restaurant and then ordering it the next three nights running, such was their newfound fondness of it. Samuel enjoyed his meal and the conversation with his parents. He tried not to let thoughts of his case and Madam Athalia's murder intrude upon his thoughts, but it was difficult. They retired to the sitting room to regale Samuel with more memories of their exciting holiday. By the time they all retired for the evening it was raining and cold, perfect weather for sleeping soundly.

Chapter 30: Wednesday the 10th of October 1888

Samuel arrived at the London City Police Headquarters promptly as instructed by his new partner. He found James Fenton's desk with ease. James was reading the morning newspaper as Samuel approached.

"Good reading?" Gates asked. Fenton looked up.

"Nothing that we weren't expecting" responded James.

"Everything just as Commissioner Warren said. And they swallowed it without question" He tossed the paper down so that Samuel could pick it up.

"You have to admire him; the conviction with which he would have presented to the reporters would have given them little recourse to believe otherwise. He almost convinced me" Samuel made the gentle jibe but it was clearly still quite a compliment for the well thought out tactic that the commissioner had employed so that the actual investigation could proceed unimpeded.

"I have an appointment with Bates, Bates and Walden; Madam Athalia's solicitors. I get to see the contents and if there were any bequeathments to Burton or not."

"I think that you are barking up the wrong tree. He was devastated by Athalia's death. But I can see that we need to explore every possibility with an open mind" Samuel was clearly not particularly interested in this avenue of exploration.

"Well, it sounds like it would be a wasted journey for you. And I can tell you anything that I find out. What are you going to do?" asked James.

"I'm going to return to the house and talk some more with Burton. I think that he would have had time to ponder everything by now. He may have remembered something that is important that he didn't think so at the time. It's definitely worth my time and effort". Samuel didn't need to sell it to Fenton.

"I agree. Let's meet back here in the afternoon and we'll compare notes" offered Fenton.

"I'll see you then" confirmed Gates.

***

When Samuel arrived at the house on Cromwell Road there was no longer a constable guarding the door. The home exactly as it had done when Samuel first saw it. He paused to take in the exterior. There was only a frail looking trellis with a vine of some description growing up it. Enough for a man to grab hold of for sure, but not enough to hold his weight. The window to the main bedroom was sufficiently far enough away from the wooden structure to make entering the house via that window just a little too difficult. It was a puzzle to be sure; how did the murderer enter through the window. Someone would have surely noticed a ladder pushed up against the front of the house. The questioning of the neighbours turned up no such evidence of such an occurrence.

Still scratching his head Samuel walked up the outside stairs and rang the doorbell. It was a little while before the door opened. Burton looked at him and opend the door wider.

"Inspector Gates; please come in" he said, seeming still somewhat glum. But it was to be expected under the circumstances. Samuel entered respectfully removing his hat.

"I want to ask you some more questions Burton. I hope you don't mind?" Samuel's caring tone seemed to strike a chord with the old butler.

"Yes Sir of course; why don't we speak in the kitchen" he said. This puzzled Gates a little. He looked at the doorways to both the library and the sitting room on either side of the capacious hallway. Responding to the non-verbal prompting Burton elucidated his reasoning.

"It would seem improper to use the rooms that Madam Athalia did for receiving guests Sir. After all I am only in service of the Lady of the house. The kitchen and the servant's quarters in the basement of the house have always been my dominion. I hope you understand?" Burton looked sad at the very mention of his late employer. Satisfied with the explanation but now feeling even more sorry for Burton, Samuel apologised.

"Of course, Burton, how insensitive of me; I do apologise. Please lead the way" He followed the man to the kitchen where Burton offered him a seat at the servant's table. He sat and waited for Burton to join him.

"May I get you some refreshments Sir?" he offered before moving to take a seat for himself.

"Nothing thank you Burton. Please sit."

"Yes Sir" Burton pulled up his stool and they sat facing each other across the small table.

"I realise that this entire ordeal must have been difficult Burton. And that you have gone over and over the story with Inspector Fenton, but I am hoping that now a little time has passed that you have remembered something that may have slipped your mind. Is there anything that you can recall that you have not told us yet; anything at all no matter how small?"

Burton took in everything that Gates said and could be seen to contemplate it very carefully. He raised his finger when a thought occurred to him.

"There is something that I had not told Inspector Fenton Sir. It was Madam Athalia's movements that he was asking about. Well, apart from her bridge club and rose appreciation society, there was nothing that took Madam Athalia out of the house. Inspector Fenton has the details of both, but I did omit, by accident I assure you, to tell him of Madam Athalia's retreat to her country residence after the second Murder and vision and before the third and fourth. She was only up there for a week. But it had entirely slipped my mind you see. There was no wish on my part to not disclose everything that I knew to the Inspector. I hope you understand Sir?"

Burton was clearly nervous about the admission, fearing that he had inadvertently done something wrong. Samuel moved quickly to reassure him.

"Don't concern yourself please Burton. All that matters now is that you have remembered and let us know" Samuel pulled out his notepad and pencil and looked to Burton for further clarification. Burton took the hint and rattled off the address of the *country* residence.

"Maidenhead road in Windsor Sir; Riparian Manor. It is easy enough to find" Burton gave specific directions describing landmarks and surrounding properties so that locating the house would be achievable. Samuel was a little confused though, he had assumed from the phrase country residence that it would be farther out of Kensington. But maybe that counted as country for the old lady.

"You did not accompany her?' he asked.

"No Sir. The housekeeper Missus Harris takes good care of Madam Athalia when she is in residence at Windsor." Burton's explanation made it sound like something that Queen Victoria would do when not in Buckingham Palace. Samuel supposed that having the English Royal's castle in the neighbourhood called for such pompous phrasing. All of the nearby manor houses probably referred to themselves in the same way he mused. Samuel was still pondering the thought when Burton broke in on his thinking.

"But that is the only thing that I can think of that I did not tell Inspector Fenton about Sir."

"Oh; well that's good Burton. Thank you. As you can imagine there would be all hell to pay if the neighbours thought that this was a random act of violence in a quiet and well-to-do area. So please remember that when you, if you, read the papers today" Samuel thought it best to explain the rationale behind the Commissioners story to Burton. Burton instinctively looked over to the paper that had been delivered but remained folded on the kitchen counter.

"I haven't opened it Sir. I would always wait for Madam Athalia to be finished with it before reading it myself" he explained.

"The Commissioner has concocted a story that may seem at odds with the events as you have experienced them. But it is for a good cause. It will leave Inspector Fenton and myself free to investigate Madam Athalia's murder completely and bring the murderer to justice without being hindered by anxiety and even hysteria from the locals. Do you understand?" Samuel was really hoping that the old man did. Burton blinked at him like a puzzled schoolboy.

"I suppose so Sir. If the Commissioner thinks that it would be best?"

"He does, believe me" Samuel tried to sound just a little evangelical in his support. It was enough to win-over the butler.

"Well that is good enough for me Sir. I shan't say a word in opposition to anything that I read, not to anyone at all Inspector Gates." Burton's tone was one of conviction.

"Excellent. I knew that I could rely on you Burton. Thank you very much"

"Will there be anything else Sir?"

"No thank you Burton. I'll take my leave of you. If you think of anything else...." He began asking, but Burton finished his sentence for him.

"I will be sure to send word to yourself or Inspector Fenton Sir" Samuel was satisfied that he had gained everything that he had hoped from the meeting. He was hopeful that Madam Athalia's other servant would be able to add more to the story. She may hold a vital clue that will help. Samuel said his good byes and exited. For now he had another important appointment to keep.

***

Lunch with Florence and Millicent was pre-arranged a week ago. He had not yet had the opportunity to tell her of his new assignment. Samuel was sure that she would be excited to hear all about it. The Orange Pekoe Team Room had to be booked well in advance as it was so popular. When Samuel arrived at the small but salubrious establishment on the Kensington High Street he surprised both his fiancé and soon-to-be mother-in-law.

A waiter was showing Samuel to the table when they both expressed their appreciation.

"Samuel, we expected to wait much longer for you?" Florence was teasing him but somewhat accurately. He had expected to be late for their appointment if he had had to travel from Whitechapel to Kensington. Millicent joined in.

"Yes Samuel, we ordered a cup of tea anticipating that you would be at least another half an hour?"

"That would be true if I had not already been in the area on my latest case" he said rather mysteriously. It raised the curiosity of both women immediately.

"Quickly Samuel sit down and tell us all about it" prompted Florence. He took his seat and allowed the waiter to place his napkin in his lap and walk off before illuminating the situation.

"Have you read the papers this morning?"

"There is only further conjecture about the next Ripper murder; but nothing other than the usual fascination that all of London has with the case."

"Not the Ripper" said Samuel, heightening their curiosity even further.

"Do tell Samuel! Don't keep us in suspense" begged Florence.

"The psychic….."

"Madam Athalia..No!" Millicent knew the reference immediately.

"Didn't you consult with her at one point about the Ripper murders?" asked Florence.

"We read that it was an insane former lover from years ago that lost his mind, broke into her home killed her in her bed" Millicent's understanding of the Commissioner's concocted story was complete. He tried to answer both women without directly lying to them. Although he had mentioned Madam Athalia to them both; he had not told Florence and Millicent of the in-depth visions that she had shared with him. He wanted to keep a healthy amount of professional privacy of his investigations as any Inspector would.

"Yes I did consult with Madam Athalia at one stage, so it was very distressing to find out that she had been murdered shortly thereafter. But I have been seconded from Whitechapel to the City of London police department to aid in the capture of the murderer. I am working for Commissioner Charles Warren and the head investigator James Fenton. It is all very….."

"Exciting!" said Florence finishing Samuel's sentence for him.

"Well I was going to say, prestigious, but yes it is exciting too" Samuel did not want to miss the opportunity to impress his fiancé. He was successful. They questioned him at length about the case and the secondment and how Edmund Reid felt about it all. As usual Samuel managed to talk a lot about it without saying too much at all. He was in fact covering up the fact that he had somewhat fallen from favour at the CID; and doing a very good job of it too.

The entire lunch was devoted to either the continuing Ripper murder investigation which both Millicent and Florence felt would suffer without Samuel being present, or his new impressive appointment to the City of London police headquarters. Millicent felt that it was a harbinger of things to come, and that she hoped that they would recognise his talent and keep him there. It was an excellent career move thought Missus Fairclough.

Eventually the lunch grew to a close and Samuel had to excuse himself. He was anxious to get back to the station and exchange information with James Fenton.

***

Inspector Fenton was at his desk when Samuel arrived.

"Guess how much the butler is going to receive from Madam Athalia's estate? James asked as Samuel settled himself into a chair.

"How much?" he asked.

"Three hundred guineas!" he said allowing the figure to sink in.

"That's quite a lot for a butler to inherit" Samuel said. James nodded in agreement.

"But he isn't the only one of the bequeathments" James said thinking that he was about to spring a new piece of information on the young inspector. But Samuel would not let James have his moment of glory. He deflated the man with his insight.

"Housekeeper in Windsor, one Hillary Harris?" he asked awaiting confirmation that he was correct and was in fact already in receipt of the new information.

"Oh; you knew. The butler told you did he?"

"Yes he did. Nothing to hide you know! I have the address. Should we arrange to question Missus Harris?" Samuel was being a bit cheeky, knowing that would be at the forefront of Fenton's mind.

"It will take some time to get there. I say that we start first thing in the morning. Meet here at seven o'clock and we will take the train. So Burton Edward Abberline of Edinburgh and Hillary Harris of Portsmouth have both gained three hundred guineas from the death of Madam Athalia. Very interesting; they could live quite comfortably for the rest of their lives on that golden nest egg" James said deliberately tinging his words with a note of suspicion. Samuel chose to ignore the tonal inference. It was another two facts that had come to light that were more immediately interesting.

"Edinburgh you say? I never detected a Scottish accent" noted Samuel.

"I wonder if he is related to Frederick Abberline of Scotland Yard?" he then said following up his first thought.

"Why don't you ask him the next time you speak?" suggested Fenton rather pragmatically. Samuel nodded and made a mental note that it was exactly what he would do.

"What about the bulk of the estate; the house in Kensington and the one in Windsor?" Both would have easily been worth tens of thousands of guineas.

"A younger sister living somewhere in Derbyshire. And by *younger* I mean in her seventies" James responded and scanned his notes looking for the location that he had been given.

"Matlock Bath" he said when he had located the correct section of his notes.

"Never heard of it" confessed Samuel.

"A spa town, for you to take in the healing waters of the natural springs" explained Fenton.

"Well, if that sort of thing appeals to you I suppose" Samuel did not sound like he would give credence to the healing power of spring waters at all.

"What now?" Samuel set aside the thoughts for a time when he could follow them up. He was not more interested in what they were going to be doing for the rest of the day.

"We have Madam Athalia's bridge club to speak to and her Rose appreciation society." James outlined the duties for them for the remainder of the day. It was going to be a busy afternoon.

Chapter 31: Thursday the 11th of October 1888

Samuel dutifully arrived at the London City Police Headquarters precisely on time at seven-thirty in the morning. He could hear that Commissioner Warren was speaking with someone in his office. The door was closed so he could not make out what was being said. James was nowhere to be seen. Samuel had just removed his pocket watch to check the time when the door to Warren's office opened and James Fenton emerged.

"Good morning Samuel" he said when he was close enough to greet his partner without the need to raise his voice.

"There has been a change of plan. I have been asked by the Commissioner to placate the nearby Magistrate, you remember the one, officious fellow?"

"Yes I remember him" replied Samuel.

"Well he has taken umbrage to the story that was printed about Madam Athalia and now has to be taken into our confidence. I am not anticipating that it will be difficult, but I am sure that it will take quite some time to smooth his ruffled feathers."

"I am sure it shall" agreed Samuel.

"If you could please go to Riparian Manor without me and question the housekeeper that would be perfect." Clearly James was more than a little disappointed that his excursion to Windsor had been taken from him.

"I'll be as thorough as if you were there in person" he said, complimenting his partner's investigative abilities. James gave

Samuel a look of mock disbelief in the veracity of the compliment prompting Samuel to jokingly withdraw it.

"Well, at least I will do the best that I can without your fine example to guide me" he said rather cheekily.

"Very droll young Mister Gates; very droll indeed" replied James; but he couldn't help smiling at the reference.

"Well then I had best leave now if I am to catch the next train. Good luck with the Magistrate James, I have the feeling that you'll need it" said Samuel rather sympathetically.

"Thank you Samuel. I am certain that I shall" he responded.

***

Samuel was successful in catching the next Windsor-bound train. He sat at the window in the carriage and watched the scenery go by. All the time though he was thinking about the late Alice Athalia. If only she had not been murdered by a copy-cat killer, Samuel would be able to avail himself of her other-worldly knowledge. His thoughts drifted to his niggling suspicions that her death was simply too coincidental. Just at the point when her insights were made knowledge to the Inspectors in charge at Whitechapel she is suddenly murdered in her own home. Was it just happenstance or were the two events connected. But the obvious question remained, why would anyone in the Whitechapel police want to cause harm to the old Lady. They were all so sure that her visions were completely unimportant.

He tried to shake off the misgivings in his head. There was nothing to support his outlandish theory. He pushed it to the side and concentrated on everything that he did know about the case. The answer had to be there somewhere. And it more than likely had nothing to do with the Ripper murders other than the fact that whoever did it wanted everyone to think that it was perpetrated by the now infamous murderer.

The time that he invested into thinking about all aspects of the nonsensical murder did nothing to bring him closer to a viable theory. Before he knew it the guard was calling out that Windsor was the next stop. The train pulled noisily into the platform in a whoosh of steam and clattering of bells and metal upon metal.

Samuel stepped down to the platform and looked around him for the exit. He followed the crowd assuming that they would know the way; he was correct. It looked for the most part that the people were sightseers and holidaymakers on tour.

When he was outside of the station he opened his notebook to once more review the instructions that Burton had provided. It would be quite a walk from the station. There was a row of cabbies at hand. Samuel decided to treat himself.

***

The handsome cab driver knew the residence that Samuel was looking for so the detailed instructions turned out to be unnecessary. The cabbie dropped Samuel off at the large gates that hung from equally large walls surrounding the property. Through the intricate wrought-iron could be seen a gravel drive leading up to a very imposing residence. This was even more substantial than Madam Athalia's Kensington townhouse. There was no bell, or gatehouse so Samuel assumed that he had to open the gate and proceed otherwise un-announced.

Grappling with the clumsy mechanism Samuel successfully but noisily opened the gate and let himself in. A though occurred to him as he regarded the residence again. If Madam Athalia had been here on the night in question, would the murderer still have sought her out and taken her life?

He walked up the gravel driveway looking around at the immaculately kept gardens to either side of it. This house was going to take more than just one housekeeper to maintain. He must find out everyone that was part of its upkeep. Eventually he arrived at the imposing double doors; there was no bell but a rather ornate and somewhat creepy looking door-knocker. It was cast in the shape of a gargoyle with the ring hanging from its mouth. It was hideous to say the least.

Timidly Samuel knocked on the door three times. He was unsure if he would need to do it louder; the house may be so large that the housekeeper did not hear it? His fears were ungrounded though, the door opened and a very matronly figure looked at him with an air of mild annoyance.

"Under the circumstances this house is in mourning, I am not receiving visitors" she said.

"My name is Samuel Gates; I am a junior inspector with the London City Police" he said by way of explanation. She closed her eyes and nodded before replying.

"Yes of course, I have been expecting the police since I heard the news. Do forgive me? This has been a most distressing time. Please come in Inspector Gates" she dutifully stepped aside to allow him entry.

"Thank you" he said and entered the grand foyer. He tried not to take too much of it in before speaking again.

"It's Missus Hillary Harris, isn't it?" he asked seeking confirmation of her identity.

"Yes, how thoughtless of me. I should have introduced myself. I am afraid that I am not myself today Inspector Gates; you understand I hope?" she was distressed that she was not receiving him in the manner to which she would normally. Samuel was sympathetic.

"I do Missus Harris. Is there somewhere that we can go to talk?" he asked while now taking in the grandeur of the interior of the house, at least the parts that he could see. The paintings hanging on the walls in their golden ornate frames and the fine sculptures alone in the foyer were a sight to behold He couldn't help but comment.

"Madam Athalia certainly had good taste in art" it was a leading question. Samuel hoped that Hillary would open up about how she could afford such things, the house included.

"Gifts from some of the finest homes in England, Wales, Scotland, Ireland and the continent; people came from all over to consult with Madam Athalia and she reaped the rewards of a successful career communing with the loved ones that had passed on". Hillary had a far-away look in her eyes as if remembering all of the clients that she had been seen in the manor.

"Were you in service to Madam Athalia for very long?" he inquired.

"Twenty nine years Inspector Gates; the finest of my life. I have seen crowned Kings and Queens from all over come to Riparian Manor to consult with Madam Athalia, and all of them left satisfied that they had indeed made contact with the ones that they had lost. As you can see; Madam Athalia's clients were very grateful. Everything that you see here, the furniture, paintings, tapestries, sculptures, all gifts from her clientele." Hillary paused. She had a look of absolute sadness upon her face.

"Not for some time now though. Madam Athalia had been retired for some years and rarely saw clients anymore. A few, but none for the last six, no seven months now. And even then, more in the Kensington townhome rather than here. Riparian Manor was her refuge from the city life you see? Madam Athalia came here frequently to relax and escape the frenetic pace of London."

"Let's talk in the kitchen; it's this way" she said indicating the direction that Samuel should take. The tour through the hallways to the kitchen was equally as impressive as the foyer. The kitchen was large, just like the one in Kensington it had a servant's table and chairs. Hillary directed him to there.

"Please sit. May I get you something. I have just boiled some water and was going to make some tea"

"That would be lovely, thank you Missus Harris" he said. He was a bit peckish after his train trip and the offer of a nice hot cup of tea was too good to refuse.

The information that Samuel had already gained was not helping with his investigation though. If Madam Athalia had not seen a client in seven months, then he could almost certainly rule them out as a suspect. If disgruntled in some way; why wait seven months to act. Nevertheless it was an avenue of questioning that he wanted to explore for the sake of completeness.

"How did you hear about Madam Athalia's passing?" he inquired as Hillary busied herself making the tea.

"Word between housekeepers travels faster than the post and faster than the newspapers. At least that is how the saying goes in our circles. And indeed it does. It was the housekeeper from the house next door that told me. She heard it from a staff member that had travelled from Kensington to Windsor that afternoon. Who heard it from one of the servants that the police were questioning in the street when they arrived at Cromwell Road. I assume that you were one of those men inspector?" The chain of news was indeed efficient. And it definitely worked faster than the post or the newspapers.

"Ah, yes, yes I was" he confirmed.

"Then there was that dreadful report in *The Guardian*. I could not believe my eyes when I read it. An ex-lover; absolutely absurd; wherever do they get such ridiculous notions. And who is it that allows them to print such nonsense?" Hillary was becoming angry and Samuel sought to divert her attention from the way that Athalia's death was reported.

"I have worked on the Ripper case Missus Harris and I agree that the press seem to invent their stories rather than rely upon fact." He hoped that the reference would be enough to distract Hillary's minor tirade. He was correct.

"The Ripper case, really? How terrifying for you. But what brings you to investigate the murder of Madam Athalia? Surely the police need all of the help on the Ripper case that they can get?"

"Yes of course they do, but there is more to police work than just the Ripper case Missus Harris. And I feel that we need to get to the bottom of this as quickly as possible." Samuel thought to deflect the conversation away from the high-profile case for fear of it tainting his questioning of the housekeeper.

"Do you know if Madam Athalia left you anything in her last will and testament?" he asked and watched closely for a reaction of any kind. He was disappointed.

"No Inspector, I am sorry, but I do not know" she answered looking quite vexed at the query.

"Do you know when Madam Athalia receives guests in the townhouse in Kensington?"

"Oh my word yes. Burton and I keep both of the diaries for Madam Athalia up to date whenever we get together. I know all of the comings and goings in the city and he knows all of the clients that we receive here in Windsor. But as I said before Inspector it has been some months since Madam Athalia saw any clients." Hillary reiterated her earlier answer to the similar question.

"May I see the diary please?" he said thinking that it was odd that he did not see one in the library in the townhouse. Nor did Burton offer it for either himself or Inspector Fenton to view.

"I suppose that it would be alright under the circumstances. If it will help your investigation? Madam Athalia was a stickler for the privacy of her clientele Inspector. She most certainly would never have approved of such a thing. But now….." Hillary's voice trailed off.

"I'll fetch it from the library, right after I pour us both a nice hot cup of tea. I have a tin of shortbread biscuits here that I have made. Will you have one?" she said whilst moving to fetch a cup and saucer for them both. The thought of a home-baked shortbread made Samuel's mouth salivate.

"If you don't think that I'm imposing?" he said rather politely.

"Not at all; they were Madam Athalia's favourite; loved my shortbread biscuits" Hillary busied herself bringing together the tea, milk, pot, sugar, plates and biscuits delivering them to the table. She poured two cups of tea through a silver strainer to filter out the tealeaves. The aroma filled the kitchen. When Hillary opened the tin the wonderful smell of freshly brewed tea was replaced with the alluring bouquet of shortbreads. He insisted that Hillary take one first and then he helped himself to one too.

"Now you just sit there and I'll fetch the diary" Hillary said before departing. Samuel sipped the tea, it somehow tasted better than a normal cup of tea should. He wondered if that was because he was so hungry or because it was served through a silver strainer. That was sure to tinge the tea with an air of exclusivity. The shortbread was a delight. He had to hold himself back from eating it all in a couple of bites.

Eventually Hillary returned with the diary and set it down on the edge of the table just out of Samuel's reach.

"After you've finished your tea you may read the diary Inspector. It wouldn't do to have tea-stains on the pages" it was a sensible precaution. Samuel acknowledged that he would do as he was told. But until then he had more questions to ask and he wasn't so concerned about getting tea stains on his own notepad.

"Was Madam Athalia a member of a bridge club or rose appreciation society here in Windsor as was the case in London?" He wanted to ascertain if there were more people that he should be questioning.

"Oh, no Inspector; whilst in residence in Windsor, Madam Athalia liked to keep to herself as much as possible. All such socialising was restricted to her time in London". Hillary's answer was not what Samuel had hoped for. It appeared that when here Madam Athalia did not go anywhere or see anyone except the occasional client, and even that was rare nowadays.

"So how did Madam Athalia occupy herself whilst residing in Riparian Manor?" he asked an motioned to the large house in surrounding them.

"Madam Athalia liked to simply relax, take in the garden and the river view. But the last time that Madam Athalia was here, there was none of that." Hillary stopped short. She seemed to have not given Samuel the full insight to which she was clearly privy.

"What do you mean?" he asked leaning forward, curious about the forthcoming answer.

"Madam Athalia was writing almost all of the time whilst in residence during her last visitation. The library door was closed and every time that I interrupted with a call to lunch or dinner, I could see pages and pages of writing that had been done. It was most unusual."

"What was she writing?" Samuel's enthusiasm for finding the answer and led to an unintentional grammatical error. Hillary visibly stiffened and even drew in air sharply through her nostrils so that it could be heard.

"*She* is the cat's mother, Inspector Gates!" Hillary's tone was indignant that the pronoun had been used to describe Madam Athalia. Quickly realising the mistake Samuel hastily apologised and withdrew the reference.

"My apologies Missus Harris; what was Madam Athalia writing so fervently about; do you know?" Samuel's genuine apology was accepted with an approving nod from the housekeeper and Hillary continued with her answer.

"I'm afraid not. But I know where all of the pages are, if you need access to those as well?" Hillary was being frustratingly ignorant of standard police procedure. He had to remind himself that not everybody has to deal with murder investigations in their day-to-day lives.

"That would be very helpful indeed Missus Harris" he finished his shortbread and downed the last of his cup of tea so that he could gain access to the diary without inciting the ire of the fastidious housekeeper.

"Well then, I shall fetch those as well. Here is the diary Inspector. I shan't be long" Hillary handed Samuel the diary and he flicked to the last entry to read it first. Just as described, the last of the clientele that had visited was back in June. He didn't recognise the name but made a note of it and the day of the consultation. He then worked backwards and read name after name date after date. Also as expected, Madam Athalia's clients were few and far between in her retirement years.

As he was reading Hillary returned with a large leather compendium. It had leather lace-up straps which held it closed. She set it down in front of him. He put the diary aside and fumbled with the leather straps. Untangling them he opened it up. There were pages and pages of writing.

At first he did not know where to begin so he lifted the pages out one by one and gave a cursory examination. As he was doing this, it must have been the fifth page a single line of perfectly expressed running-writing caught his eye. It said:

The one that almost caught the Ripper will be the one that finally captures him. Samuel froze as he read the words. He felt his heart skip a beat. This must be another of Athalia's visions. But this time it was about him. It simply had to be. The one that almost caught Jack the Ripper will be the one that eventually captures him. He looked up at Hillary who by this time was cleaning away the tea service.

"Madam Athalia was writing about her visions?" he said, in a rhetorical way, unsure himself if he needed an answer, but desperately hoping for the validation of his thinking.

"Oh that doesn't surprise me at all Inspector Gates. Madam Athalia often wrote about the visions that came to her in her sleep. Is that what they are do you think?" Hillary looked over at him. Samuel shook his head and then nodded.

"I think so; maybe?" he answered rather quixotically. Hillary failed to notice the timbre of hope and desperation in his voice and went about her cleaning of the cups, plates, saucers and the silver tea strainer.

Samuel read like a man obsessed. He tried firstly though to place the papers back into the order in which he had found them. He did not want to disturb any continuity that Athalia may have had whilst transcribing her otherworldly visions. The more that he read however the more desperate he became. It simply did not make sense. It was not in any logical order. It was incredibly frustrating. Although the writing was flawless it was nothing but a bunch of disjointed scrawling. Passages and paragraphs did not seem to have any coalescence into a cohesive linear narrative.

Samuel could feel the irritation within him increasing. He wanted this so much to be the guide for him to fulfil the vision that Athalia had had of him. But it was failing to deliver any useful information as immediately as the one line that had stood out so dramatically to him. He was going to need time.

"Missus Harris, is there somewhere that I can sit and read through all of these in peace and quiet" Samuel regretted the question immediately upon asking it. It cast a shadow of the Housekeeper who had no qualms about showing her indignation.

"Making too much noise for you am I?" Hillary gave Samuel her stern look once more.

"No, no no, not at all Missus Harris, but these writings are so intricate that I will have to study them at some length if I am to draw out the true meaning of Madam Athalia's words." The explanation found favour with the housekeeper.

"Well, that's different. In that case of course Inspector. Please feel free to use the library. I'll show you where it is. Maybe being in the same surroundings in which the visions were written will help. Do you think?" Hillary motioned for Samuel to lead the way back down the hall.

"I hope so Missus Harris, I really do hope so" he replied.

Chapter 32: Visions in Words

Samuel's mind continued to race even as Hillary settled him into the library and took her leave of him. By his reckoning, if Burton was correct about the last time that Madam Athalia was here, they had not yet met. So he was not entangled in her thoughts; which gave him even more hope that the visions that Athalia was writing about were indeed him.

He read everything picking out the parts that he could make the most sense of. There were frustratingly few references to *the one that almost caught the Ripper*, but he persevered and pieced together every reference to *the one* that he could find. When all of the bits of information were pulled together it described 'an ambitious man in the throes of love' and 'a meticulous man with fair hair'. Both references could easily have described Samuel's engagement to Florence. The mention of his hair colour was not open to interpretation, it was accurate.

The pride and anxiety that built-up in Samuel as he sought to verify that he was indeed the man in Athalia's visions that would eventually capture the Ripper was elating. He read through the scrawling's again. Most of them meant absolutely nothing. But then he began to see a pattern about the location where the next murder would be. That is what he concentrated on for the next few hours. He was only interrupted by Missus Harris with a sandwich and glass of milk for his lunch.

There were quite a few references to 'grinding grain into flour' which were puzzling. They seemed to have no connection with anything, but it was mentioned so many times that he took note of it in his notebook. The only thing that he could think of was a mill or windmill. He could not immediately think of a windmill or mill street in Whitechapel. But he wanted to consult a map before concluding that once and for all.

Missus Harris was standing over him at one point to collect the now empty glass and plate.

"Oh Missus Harris, I didn't hear you come in. Do you have a map of London somewhere here by any chance?" he asked. The housekeeper looked around the library and tapped her finger on her mouth whilst trying to remember something.

"Yes, yes we do; it's right over here" she said walking over to a shelf and finding a book that she had in mind. It was leather bound and very large. Opening it and turning pages she cried out with glee.

"Here! A map of London for the inquisitive Inspector" she proclaimed. Placing it down in front of him, Samuel could see that it was but one map, it seemed to be of Mayfair. He turned the page; there was another illustrated map this time of Leicester Square. He kept flicking through the pages until he located a map of Whitechapel. Samuel absent-mindedly gave his thanks and Hillary left him once again to his studies.

Scanning the street names he came across nothing that resembled mill or windmill. Disappointed he returned to the bewildering writings of the old Psychic. There were a few sections about the judgement of the killer. Not just the judgement for the murderer himself, but also the judgement of the murderer on the place of residence of the next victim. It was stated in a few different ways across about three disjointed passages.

"What constitutes a judgement?" he said, realising that there was nobody in the room but himself. He thought of other words that would describe such an action. It simply had to have something to do with a court of law. The reference rang a bell in Samuel's memory. He once again looked at the map of Whitechapel. There it was; Miller's Court. It was the name of a street! Not a windmill, but a miller and then joined with the reference to the judgement in a court of law it suddenly made sense.Samuel had found the street where he believed the next murder would happen; Millers Court in Whitechapel.

Next up he concentrated on pulling together any references to numbers. What he wanted now was a number in Millers Court or a date for the next murder to be perpetrated. One passage gave him hope that he had found a vital clue. It stated that the next murder would be 'farther away from Saint Claire of Assisi day but before Saint Bibiara day. He wracked his brain for the dates of the obscure references. If only his Grandmother were still alive he thought? She knew all of the festival days of the saints.

There was something about the first reference, though; it seemed more familiar than the second. A pondered it for a time. He could almost hear somebody talking about it, and the voice in his head was familiar. That was it! Sargent Plymouth was talking, it was something that he had said months and months ago, at the beginning of the Ripper murders. He had made a reference to the first murder having taken place just after the feast day of Saint Claire of Assisi. That was the 11th of August.

If he could locate the exact date of the second feast day then he would have a timeline to work within. Frustrated he stood up and stretched his aching legs. His shoulders were stiff too. Samuel began to pace up and down the length of the library. He stopped a few times at main set of shelves looking blankly at the books before him. It must have been the fifth time before he started taking in some of the titles written on the spines. More about the occult and other things that he fully expected to see in a Psychic's library. But then something else; a copy of the Bible? It was out of place amongst these other heretical works.

Taking it he flipped through to the index and scanned it. His eyes came to rest upon the very thing that he had been seeking. Toward the back of the book amongst the various appendices and annexures was a listing of all of the feast days. He hurriedly found the page and then the very reference that he had sought. The feast day of Saint Bibiara was the 2nd of December. Quickly replacing the Bible where he had found it he hurried back to the next to make a note.

The next murder would be before the 2nd of December. Another nonsensical passage that he had read suddenly made perfect sense. 'After the bonfires of Guy Fawkes have gone, add to that the number of arms that we earthly humans were born of Zeus with and the day of running blood and judgement will be seen'

If Samuel's memory of Greek mythology was correct, then Zeus created mankind with four arms and four legs. But then, feeling threatened by his own create he split it into to forming both men and women that are two halves of the one person.

Guy Fawkes Night was the 5th of November plus four means that the date of the next murder would be Friday the 9th of November. Samuel jumped up from his chair with a shout of glee.

He wanted to tell James Fenton what he had found; but then just as quickly dismissed the thought. No matter how excited he was about the discovery he had made, Fenton was a logical man that would not take to such things as visions written by the very victim of a murder that they were investigating.

He forced himself to sit down and continue with his work. There may yet be more information hidden in the baffling passages. The references to the victim all expounded about how unlucky she would be to fall into the hands of the mad-man that would take her life. 'Unlucky in life, and unlucky death from the unlucky in the residence of her choice'.

It occurred to Samuel that the number 13 was always considered unlucky. It was superstitious of course and not founded in anything. But he was working with superstition made reality. So why not simply prescribe the unlucky number to this passage?

"The victim will be murdered at 13 Millers Court on Friday the 9th of November. Except that I will be there to succeed where I previously failed; I will save the victim and capture Jack the Ripper!"

Samuel was so enraptured by the thought that he did not even realise that he was speaking it aloud. The door opened and Hillary entered.

"I am sorry Inspector were you saying something?" she inquired. Samuel shook his head.

"It was nothing Missus Harris" he said brushing aside the proclamation that he had just vowed to himself.

"I didn't want to disturb you Sir, but the light is fading and I was wondering when you will be returning to London, and indeed if there are any more questions that I can answer for you?" The housekeepers intervention brought Samuel right back into the present. He gathered up his notebook and began to put Athalia's works back into the compendium.

"No, not right now Missus Harris; I need to get back to London and consult with my partner. You are not planning to go anywhere…" he began to ask.

"Where would I go Inspector; the servant's quarters are my home here. I have nowhere else" It was really quite touching. Samuel didn't believe for a minute that the matronly old housekeeper had anything to do with Madam Athalia's murder.

"I should be going" he said and gathered up his belongings. Missus Harris escorted him to the door. A thought occurred to Samuel that he wanted to know.

"Do you know Madam Athalia's sister at all?"

"I know of Madam Athalia's sister, but I am afraid that I do not know her at all. There has been no journey from Derbyshire to London for a visit, or vice versa; not in all of the time that I have served here".

"How curious; I wonder if they were estranged?" Samuel mused.

"I really couldn't say Inspector" was the reply.

"Well, thank you very much for your hospitality Missus Harris. If there is anything else either myself or my colleague Inspector James Fenton shall return"

"Very good Sir. Have a safe journey home" she said with true warmness.

"Goodbye" he smiled at her. He left and walked down the gravel driveway his mind still filled with the thought that he was the only person that had pre-knowledge of where and when the Ripper was to strike next. It would be like throwing darts at a dart-board from only arm's-length away. He was sure to strike the target at dead-centre.

***

The train journey back to London was similarly filled with visions in his head of him apprehending the Ripper. He knew what the man looked like from Athalia's sketch. He knew the address; the date there simply was no way to fail. The thought was intoxicating, but he could not tell anybody about it. He began to plan ways to get police to be in the area of Millers Court on Friday the 9th, but then began to doubt his own plans. What if the increased police presence were to frighten-off the murderer?

Maybe what he had to do was to simply show up as if he was not expecting to be there and capture the man single handed? But that worried him as well. He would almost certainly need backup. Suddenly the knowledge that he held became a logical trap that he had to navigate. Visions of the future do not come with precise instructions on how to use them. The more that he thought about it the more frustrating it became. No-one would believe how he had come by the information. But he needed people to support him in his bid to stop the maniac. There simply had to be a way, and he only had a certain amount of time to find it.

Chapter 33: Friday the 12th of October 1888

"What else did you find out?"

The question broke into Samuel's consciousness.

"I'm sorry?" he said, unsure as to what the meaning of the question was. James Fenton sighed loudly. He had been questioning his partner about the trip to Windsor and his questioning of housekeeper Hillary Harris. But Samuel had seemed very distracted and quite non-communicative about his interrogation of the woman.

"You said that she knew nothing of the bequeathments to either herself or Burton. But what else did you ask her?" James was openly displaying his frustration at how difficult it was to extract information from Samuel. Picking up on the naked display Samuel shifted in his seat and forced himself to come back to the present. He flicked through his notepad.

"She is the cat's mother Inspector Fenton" said Samuel imitating the offence at the bad grammar.

"Eh?" responded Fenton confused by the reference.

"It doesn't matter" replied Gates dismissing the rebuke that had fallen upon ignorant ears. He scanned his notes. Apart from spending a lot of time trying to interpret the writings of Madam Athalia, he had managed to question Hillary very little indeed. That was a fact that he did not want to share with Fenton.

"Has never met the Sister from Matlock Bath; not sure what the story is there? That is in spite of being in service at the Windsor Manor for the last nine years. Maybe both were just too old and frail to travel to and from Derbyshire by that stage, or maybe some kind of falling-out? Anyway, I looked through the diary, which is kept synchronised with the one in Kensington. Madam Athalia's last client was a Mister Christian Umberton of Park Lane here in London; but that was some time ago in June. The visitation prior to that was January of this year by a Missus Sarah Princelett of Salcombe and before that November of last year by Mister Matthew Durham of Hertford. It appears that Madam Athalia was as retired as she had claimed and rarely saw clients anymore. I have the addresses of each. Unlike here in London, Madam Athalia was not a member of any card-players club or Rose appreciation society or the like. Relaxation, peace and quiet seemed to be the only thing that was done whilst in Riparian Manor. Oh yes and that the grapevine of housekeepers and butlers works faster than the telegraph, postal service or newspapers" Samuel finished his summary hoping that it seemed like a thorough examination of the housekeepers knowledge.

"Telegraph?" said James giving Samuel a sideways look of curiosity.

"The housekeeper found out about the murder before it was printed in the papers. A gossip-chain of servants from London to Windsor you know" he answered placing his finger against his nose.

"Ah ha; I see" said James, not really seeing at all.

"Well let me tell you what I have found out whilst you've been hob-knobbing with the hoity-toity in Windsor." He was making a small joke.

"Do tell?" answered Samuel in his best imitation of an aristocratic accent.

"No money missing from the old woman's account; we already know that nothing was stolen from the house even though there are some quite valuable pieces there. In short we are no closer to finding this copy-cat killer than we were at the start of this investigation." The summation was not really what either of them wanted to hear. It would not do for this murder to go unsolved. It had the attention of the senior people from both Whitechapel and London police headquarters.

"That is somewhat depressing" admitted Samuel.

"Yes it is. We should question the chap that lives in London and find out his whereabouts on the night of the murder. Apart from that we are clutching at straws I'm afraid." James outlined their next move.

"Well let's get to it then; no sense in hanging around here waiting for the crime to solve itself" Samuel said standing up from his chair.

"Right you are" responded James. They left the station with a faint hope that they would get the break in the case that they needed to identify the killer soon.

***

Samuel allowed James to take the lead in the investigation for the remainder of the day. He was busy pondering how he was going to deal with the information that he was keeping to himself about the next murder. The day passed uneventfully. The very old man that had been the last to see Madam Athalia for her professional services was too infirm to have climbed in through the window. He was mortified at the news of her passing when he read about it in the papers. Moreover he was in hospital with a bout weak-chest during the entire week of the murder. He was ruled out as a potential suspect.

Samuel and James went their separate ways to try and reinvigorate themselves with a restful weekend. Both had hopes that the new week would bring with it some vital new clue that would help them solve the case.

Chapter 34: Monday the 15th of October 1888

Samuel had spent most of the weekend with Florence. He had tried to not talk about the case because it was not going as well as he had hoped. Florence had managed in her own inimitable way to extract enough information from him to satisfy her curiosity of all things investigative. The weekend flew past and then it was Monday morning again. Samuel showed up for work at the London city police station with a plan to enable.

***

"I have an idea about how to stop this copy-cat killer from striking again!" Samuel announced as he sat at the desk opposite James Fenton.

"Oh? And what would that be?" asked James curious about the grandiose proclamation.

"If the Ripper is caught, then there would be no fuel to add to the fire of the copy-cat killer. He has murdered Madam Athalia for whatever reason, but sought to disguise the killing as one that would be attributable to someone else. He is clearly a nervous man that wants someone else to hang for his ill-doings. But what if we take away the scape-goat?" Samuel leaned forward looking very much like he was expecting an answer.

"I don't know; what?" replied James

"He would be out on a limb. Capture Jack the Ripper and you take away the copy-cat killers cover. He would be identified as the Kensington murderer or some other glib name that the press would come up with. And I bet you your last half-penny that the very thought of not being able to hide behind Jack the Ripper would take the wind out of his sails completely. He would be too scared to murder again!" Samuel slapped his hand on the table to finalise his point.

James contemplated it in the way that Samuel had become accustomed to. Samuel liked that about Fenton. He never immediately dismissed anything. But rather he pondered it and looked at it from different angles to see if it had any value. The extra time that Fenton seemed to be taking digesting this thought was encouraging for Gates.

"I do see your point Samuel. That is rather clever except for one small point" James looked as if he was about to state the very obvious so Samuel intercepted the remark before it was made.

"Someone has to first capture Jack the Ripper. Yes I know. That is where I come in." Samuel's intriguing comment brought a look of captivation from James.

"How so?"

"You are an excellent investigator James and can carry on with this murder investigation without me. And as surely as night follows day, I am certain with time that you will solve the mystery. But the Ripper case is dragging on back in Whitechapel and they need all of the help that they can get. You know that I was taken off the case so that I could come here and work with you?" he said verifying James's understanding of why Samuel was seconded to the London HQ.

"Yes, I know" confirmed Fenton.

"But if I can return to Whitechapel and help to get the Ripper case closed, then that would help you and your investigation enormously. You would have a murderer that would be too afraid, I hope, to commit another murder, and you could close in on him and make your arrest" Samuel finished what he desperately hoped was a flattering and logical-enough plan to get James to recommend Samuel's return to Whitechapel. At first Fenton did not look like he was going to buy any of it. But Samuel could see the idea had some appeal to the intelligent investigator. He regarded Samuel in the way that he would a prized informant; weighing up the information that he had been given and trying to come to a conclusion on how to act upon it.

Eventually he nodded.

"I like the way that you think Samuel, I really do. And I am assuming that you want me to recommend that you have done all that you can do on the Athalia investigation and should be released to return to Whitechapel?"

"It would sound better coming from you" confirmed Gates. Fenton sensed accurately that there was more to the scheme than Samuel was letting-on but he did not push for the real reasons. He was satisfied that the scheme would work with the Commissioner. Samuel would get his return to the Ripper case, and he would get the Athalia case all to himself. It was definitely a win-win situation.

"The Commissioner is away this morning, but I will have a word with him this afternoon, with the intention of having you return to your posting first thing tomorrow morning. How's that?" James smiled.

"Perfect. Thank you Inspector Fenton" said Samuel with true gratitude in his voice.

"My pleasure Junior Inspector Gates" replied James.

Samuel gave himself a pat on the back. He had enabled the first stage of his plan to get back to Whitechapel and on to the Ripper case once more. He hoped that is week absent would have softened Reid's and Anderson's attitude toward him. If he returned under the auspice of Commissioner Warren releasing him from the Athalia case then they were unlikely to refuse. He was sure of that. But would they allow him back on to the Ripper case. He desperately hoped so. He knew that there had been no more progress with the case in his absence. The newspapers were being brutal in their derisive opinion of how the Ripper case was being handled. But just in case that they did not, there was always the torso murderer case that he could take up.

Providing that he was stationed back in Whitechapel he could be close to 13 Millers Court and the scene of the Ripper murder predicted in Athalia's writings to happen next month. That was the most important place for him to be.

And there were some other things too that needed to be fleshed out. Was there a link between Burton Abberline from Edinburgh and Frederick Abberline? Samuel didn't know. But ever since he discovered the similar surnames, he had thought that the two men had similar appearances. They could be brothers? And also, Senior Detective Inspector Robert Anderson; how could he have been in Andermatt Switzerland and not known about the village festival? Samuel did not know if any of these peculiar pieces of information were connected with each other or with the Ripper case or with the murder of Madam Athalia. But they all bore further investigation. Of that fact Samuel was absolutely certain.

Chapter 35: Tuesday the 16th of October 1888

Samuel's plan had worked perfectly. Commissioner Warren had apparently spoken with Robert Anderson and let him know that the Athalia case had been investigated to the full extent that was possible. In no small way with the able help of Samuel Gates, but that it was time for him to return to Whitechapel. And Anderson had agreed. Samuel all but snuck into the Whitechapel Police Headquarters on the Tuesday morning to attend the briefing. Anderson was speaking.

"And of course the press, as usual, are blaming the incompetence of the police. The days have dragged into weeks and the weeks into months. We have made arrests but in each case it has not eventuated in revealing Jack the bloody Ripper! What more can be done? I thought that I was taking over an effective Police station, one that got cases solved; was I wrong in thinking that!?" he was very animated, waving his hands in frustration. And it was an exaggeration too. It had been only one month and sixteen days since the first of the Ripper murders. So the 'months' that Anderson was referring to was a good two weeks away yet. And they may very well get the break that they needed to solve the case in the next two weeks.

Samuel looked around him trying to gauge the expressions of his colleagues. He could see that they were more than a little frustrated at the berating that they were receiving.

"What have you to say Senior Detective Inspector Abberline?" nobody it seemed was immune from the critique of the newly appointed head of the station. For his part Abberline made no attempt to hide his disapproval of the way that Anderson was behaving. Giving Anderson a glare that would turn most men to stone he strode up to the man and let out a loud harrumph before turning to the crowd and addressing them.

"The collateral damage that is being done by this murderer is the reputation of the Whitechapel police and indirectly all of the police in London city. Whilst he remains at large the press are having a field day with the inability of the authorities to apprehend the criminal. Your predecessor had wisely increased the visibility of the constables on the street and my advice to you Senior Detective Inspector would be to redouble the numbers."

Abberline's scathing tone was lost only on Anderson. The crowd observing the verbal smack-down were transfixed. He continued with similar vitriol.

"If the public feel safe then the rantings of the press will hold no weight. That is the best course of action. All that remains is for it to be facilitated."

Abberline's seniority in Scotland Yard and his position as the man in charge of this particular case put him in a position to get away with such brutal honesty. His candour won much favour with the gathered men that resulted in a hearty *hear; hear* from a number of them. He could of course not order such a thing as he was not in charge of the overall HQ, just the Ripper investigation.

Anderson for his part seemed oblivious to the critical tone that Abberline had taken with him. He looked at the ceiling as if contemplating the suggestion and after a while began to nod a little.

"I can see that such a thing would help turn the tide of public opinion back in our favour. The Whitechapel Police go the extra mile to ensure that the citizens of London are safe. I like it. Yes, that is exactly what we shall do; excellent suggestion Inspector Abberline; excellent indeed."

There was a collective rolling of eyes. It meant more duty rosters and extra shifts for everyone concerned.

"I may even put some of the detectives back into uniform to bolster numbers" Anderson's extrapolation on the idea elicited a murmured groan from the men. And that set the tone for the remainder of the briefing. There was little to report by way of progress in the case. Anderson seemed more concerned with the reputation of the Police than in assisting the Ripper case investigation itself.

Samuel watched and listened with growing concern. He could see that Anderson was very much a politician rather than a policeman at heart. If he was to get help from his new superior he would have to find a way to appeal to that side of his personality. Edmund Reid was nowhere to be seen. Samuel wondered where he could be.

***

Samuel was given more appropriate duties for the remainder of the week. Questioning more suspects that had appeared on a growing list of suspects that had to be interrogated and their movements cross-referenced with the time and location of all of the Ripper murders; it was engaging work. But at the end of the week there was still nothing to show. Samuel had seen Edmund Reid sporadically. They had managed a few brief chats, but it appeared that Reid was more involved with arranging for his own retirement than he was in doing any detective work or helping further the various investigations that the station was encumbered with.

It was depressing. Samuel had come to rely upon the enthusiasm of Edmund Reid throughout his time serving as a Junior Detective Inspector beneath him. And now, knowing that he knew, Samuel had to engage with someone senior in the department if he hoped to elicit help to thwart the forthcoming murder next month. Samuel felt alone. He did not have anyone to turn to.

Chapter 36: Sunday the 21st of October 1888

It was a gathering of both families yet again. This time the Gates' and the Fairclough's had booked Sunday lunch at Wilton's in Ryder Street. The weather was brisk, with definite touches of the forthcoming winter in the wind. But the sun was shining and inside the glass conservatory section of the seafood restaurant it was just lovely.

"The scuttlebutt is that the restaurant will be moving to larger premises on Duke Street early next year" Florence shared her titbit of information for the dining party.

"No!?" exclaimed Samuel's mother, clutching her pearl necklace in mild shock at the news.

"Yes" affirmed Florence. Millicent took up the trail of information.

"Of course you know that it is no longer in the hands of the Wilton family since the tragic passing of the owner earlier this year. It is the new owner that has proposed the move. More room means more patrons and no-doubt more profits."

"Well regardless of where it is located and how many people they can squeeze into it, Winton's still has the best oysters in the city; in my opinion." Harrold Fairclough made his view known to the table. This produced a round of agreeing phrases from all.

"Now tell us all about your week Samuel" Florence clearly wanted to change the lunchtime conversation to matters of Police work. They had ordered and were waiting for their meals so it was a perfect opportunity for the inquisitive bride-to-be to satisfy her appetite for investigative matters. Samuel knew that this would be a subject that he would have to content with sooner or later so he decided to let loose with whatever information he could share and hope that it was enough to pass his fiancés inspection. All eyes turned to him in anticipation of his reply.

"The secondment to London City Police went well. The Commissioner spoke highly of me and my partner and I did all that we could on the matter, but we reached a point where we thought that the remainder of the investigation could be concluded by just one inspector so I was returned to Whitechapel to continue my work on the Ripper case."

It was a tactical phrase that Samuel had introduced. He knew it to be an emotive talking point for many Londoners and it would nicely distract attention away from any further probing questions about the Athalia murder case; which was exactly what he wanted.

"Oh yes Samuel, please tell us everything that has been happening in the investigation; we are all eager to know!" Florence affirmed that she had fallen for Samuel's little ploy. He happily obliged.

"More suspects questioned. More cross references done on their whereabouts at the time of each murder and unfortunately nothing that leads us to the actual killer. I know that it isn't what the newspapers want to hear, but believe me there are many men working tirelessly to find the Ripper and see him hang from the end of a rope. It is, believe me, only a matter of time."

"Dear Samuel; we all know that you are working so hard on this dreadful case. Please don't think that everyone is as ungrateful as the press would have you believe" It was Samuel's mother leaping to his aide. He reached over the table and held her hand.

"Thank you Mater, it is very much appreciated"

The general sentiment from everyone was the same. Samuel had managed to illicit sympathy for the plight of the Police in the trying circumstances in which they found themselves with one short speech. Something that Robert Anderson seemed to be incapable of entirely.

"And there is more help that the police could avail themselves of you know my boy" chipped in Samuel's father.

"The vigilantes?" he said seeking confirmation that he was on the right train of thought as his parent.

"Exactly! Don't think of them as a bunch of unorganised rough-necks. They consist of everyday citizens just like us Samuel. They are concerned with their own safety and that of others as well. A noble calling and not the gang-mentality that it sounds like when the word vigilante is applied to them" Samuel's father went on to speak at length about how honourable a cause it was for them to follow. But Samuel did not hear much of it. He looked for all the world like he was riveted to every word that fell from his father's mouth. But he had receded into his own thoughts.

They were a perfect backup plan for him. If he was unable to convince Edmund Reid to help him with the thwarting of the next murder, then he had a pseudo-police force to draw upon. He had given it some thought before but had just as soon dismissed it. And maybe that was because he had thought of the vigilantes as a rabble rather than a clutch of concerned citizens. The way in which his father was painting them now made them seem like a very viable alternative indeed. Samuel turned his attention back to the lunchtime conversation.

"And that is my half-penny's worth" said Frederick Gates, concluding his rather lengthy appraisal and support of the various vigilante groups that had sprung up in the shadow of the Ripper murders.

"Well spoken" said Harrold Fairclough. It appeared that both Frederick and Harrold saw eye-to-eye on just about everything. Both Millicent and Margaret added their support for the assertion as well. It was then that two waiters came up to the table carrying four plates of food. Now the lunchtime conversation was sure to turn to the very tasty dishes that each of them had ordered. Samuel relaxed a little. He felt like he could now enjoy the remainder of the afternoon.

Chapter 37: Monday to Friday

The working week began as did all of the previous ones in Samuel's career as a Junior Detective Inspector for Whitechapel Metropolitan Police Headquarters. It ended in the same way. More work was done. More suspects identified but still nothing to convict anyone. There was little progress to be celebrated. Edmund Reid had been more visible during the week, but still not as involved as he had been. It appeared that the handover to Robert Anderson was all but complete. Now it was simply a matter of time before Reid took his leave permanently from the station.

***

Samuel saw an opportunity to speak with Edmund Reid alone and seized it. Edmund was still co-sharing the office where Anderson had set up, but the new boss had made the journey to Fleet Street to see if he could salvage the image of the Whitechapel station.

"May I come in Sir?" he said as he knocked on the partially open door.

"Samuel, of course please take a seat. What can I do for you?" his very personable tone reflective of his newfound relaxed attitude of late; all due to his forthcoming retirement, of course.

"I wanted to talk to you about the Ripper case." He introduced the subject tentatively.

"Shouldn't you be speaking with Inspector Abberline? After all he has overall control of the Ripper investigation." Reid was stating the very obvious, but it did not deter Gates at all. The reference to Abberline sparked a memory in Samuel. He saw an opportunity to briefly change the subject and find out what he could about the Scotland Yard Senior Detective Inspector.

"Do you know much about him Sir? From Edinburgh I assume, coming from Scotland Yard and all?"

"Abberline? No his family is from East Kilbride south of Glasgow. He simply works in Edinburgh. Why do you ask?" Reid looked vexed at the unusual question. The information however ruled-out any relationship between Burton Abberline of Edinburgh and Frederick Abberline of East Kilbride. Shaking off the trail of thought Samuel recomposed himself to face the hurdle that he had come to jump. He sat opposite Reid and put forward his best laid plan that he hoped would succeed.

"I once sat in this office and told you of the visions of Madam Athalia and how she seemed to know what the Ripper was doing whilst it was happening many miles from her. I also know that you don't believe that the late Madam Alice Athalia had any such insight....."

"Not true" interrupted Reid. The admission confused Samuel.

"But you said..."

"I thought it best to run the idea past the men charged with the investigation and bowed to their judgement in the matter. That doesn't mean for a minute that I am not a believer that there are more things in heaven and earth than are dreamt of in anybody's philosophy." He paraphrased Shakespeare's words from Hamlet. Samuel was taken aback. This was not the response that he had planned upon overcoming with his pre-prepared argument.

"Oh. I see. Well that changes things considerably" he said stumbling now for words and how to reposition his plea for help.

"I get the feeling that you have something to say, or to ask me Samuel. I think that it is better that you just say it rather than try to butter me up first". Reid's minor ultimatum was actually very welcomed now by Gates as he could dispense with the ruse.

"I found in Madam Athalia's writings that make me believe that I know the date and location of the next murder that will be committed by Jack the Ripper. And I intend to be there when it happens. But I need help. I need men to assist me this time so that he does not get away." Samuel stopped and tried to judge how his words had affected Edmund. For his part, Reid was silent for a very long time, in fact an uncomfortably long time. When he did speak it was not what Samuel had expected to hear from someone that believed in a wider worldly philosophy as he had just admitted to.

"No. that is never going to happen Samuel; not in a month of Sunday's"

Samuel was devastated, he was about to object when Reid raised his hand motioning for him to be silent.

"What I will do is support your plan to patrol the city streets with a couple of constables, just as you were doing the first time that you came across the murderer and almost apprehended him. That is a plan that will not need to overcome the objections of men that do not have a superstitious bone in their bodies." Reid looked very pleased with himself.

Samuel saw the logic in the alternative plan that Reid was proposing. In this way he would not have to admit to prior-knowledge of the murder and convince unbelievers that he had an insight that they did not. It was perfect. It would not seem unusual or untoward in any way.

"That is genius Mister Reid" said Samuel with a smile that stretched from ear to ear.

"That is knowing how to work with Scotland Yard and their very literal interpretation of everything that is happening around them Mister Gates" responded Reid with a similar mischievous grin. He continued.

"You shall have your team, consisting of only two; I hasten to add, at your disposal to take them wherever and whenever you wish. Make me proud before my retirement party Samuel and catch this blighter!"

"I will" he said as he stood up invigorated by the news. Then a thought occurred to him. He had not taken Reid into his confidence about the date and place of the next murder.

"Don't you want to know…." he began to ask. But Reid shooed him away.

"Not for my ears Mister Reid, if you never tell me, then I never have to share that information with your new superior. Let's keep it that way shall we?" His wilful ignorance was a small price to pay for getting the help that he so desperately wanted. Samuel thanked Reid profusely as he left the office.

He walked back to his desk and sat down in a state of mild-euphoria. He now had the man-power that he needed to ensure that the Ripper was apprehended this time. He could feel the victory in his hands even though it was still two weeks away. This time there would be no escape for the Ripper. And true Madam Athalia's writings predicting the future, Samuel Gates would be the man to bring him to justice.

Chapter 38: Millers Court

Since deciphering Athalia's premonition, Samuel had been to 13 Millers Court many times. But this time was different. He was there on official police business. The two constables that had been assigned to him were like puppy dogs following him blindly around from place to place. They seemed able enough, but quite young for Samuel's liking. Nevertheless, they would be adequate when the time came, he hoped.

Samuel had a growing feeling of anticipation with each passing day. To the rest of his colleagues he looked engaged and busy with the two young constables that Reid had for some unknown reason assigned to him. But he was oblivious to their vexed outlooks of him. He had a mission now to fulfil before the date of the next murder. He wanted to interview all of the inhabitants of 13 Millers Court to see if he could identify which of them would be the most likely victim. This was the task that completely engaged him for the week.

Chapter 39: Monday the 5th of November 1888

Samuel had a growing feeling of anticipation with each passing day. To the rest of his colleagues he looked engaged and busy with the two young constables that Reid had for some unknown reason assigned to him. But he was oblivious to their vexed outlooks of him. He had a mission now to fulfil before the date of the next murder. He wanted to interview all of the inhabitants of 13 Millers Court to see if he could identify which of them would be the most likely victim. This was the task that he was engaged with for the week.

"Tell us again why we are here sir?" asked one of the constables. Samuel was suitable cagey with his response.

"I am just trying to cover all possibilities constable. This is representative of the accommodation that most of the victims would have lived in. I want to interview all of the residents to see what they know about the murders. What they have heard from their friends. How safe they believe that they are. Are the increased foot patrols putting their minds at ease in these unnerving times? Things of that nature. Does that clarify your understanding constable?"

It did not, but the youngster did not want to be seen to be questioning his superior so he nodded enthusiastically and gave a small salute of acknowledgement.

"Right then, the two of you are charged with getting a list together of all of the inhabitants. Who lives in each room. Knock on doors and find begin to compile that list for me. I will do the actual interviewing starting here with number 1. The two of you go to each of the other apartments and get to it" he was forceful and unreservedly eager and it was somehow contagious. They hurried away to obtain the information that Samuel was after.

Samuel watched his two charges go to the next door and knock before he himself did so on the door of apartment number one. A woman answered drying her hands on a tea towel. Samuel had clearly caught her in the act of washing up crockery in the sink. He assumed that she was cleaning up after breakfast. She gave Samuel a suspicious glare that came across as quite unfriendly. The woman was about fifty maybe older.

"I am Junior Detective Inspector Samuel Gates from the Whitechapel Criminal Investigation Department. I am here to talk to you about anything that you would like to talk about with regards to your personal security." He concluded his spurious greeting and awaited a response.

For her part the woman replaced her frown with a look of perplexed astonishment.

"You're 'here to what?" she asked.

"Talk to you about anything at all madam. I know that the papers will have you believe that we are living in a dangerous city. Is there anything that makes you particularly afraid……" that was all of the encouragement that the old woman needed. Understanding now that she had a willing participant to listen to all of her woes she seized the opportunity and launched into a tirade of pent up opinions of just about everything.

"Safe. You call this safe? Living in a town with a murderer around every corner waiting to cut out your gizzards. You must be joking Inspector?" The woman lectured him at length about the shady inhabitants of the neighbourhood and about how she never felt really safe until her husband was home at night from his job in the local timber yard. Samuel let all of it wash over him. He was solely concerned with sizing up the woman to see if she fitted the profile of the other Ripper victims. He had for the most part already made that decision when she first answered the door, but her propensity for complaining ruled her out of any hope of being a casual prostitute to earn extra money. Samuel didn't believe that there would be anyone willing to pay for her services if they had to listen to her monotonous voice in order to negotiate a rate for sexual favours.

He allowed Missus Barnesworth, as he discovered her name was, to drone on and on because her complaining eventually turned to some of her close neighbours. Samuel had his pad and pencil at the ready to take down names. This was exactly the sort of information that he wanted to know. He hoped that between the constables, himself and the willing blabbermouth Missus Barnesworth he would amalgamate a complete list of the inhabitants of 13 Millers Court.

Missus Barnsworth ranted on for so long that the two constables had returned form the door knocking on the remaining eleven apartments and she was still in full verbal flight about the state of the nation in general. Samuel used the arrival of his junior constables to extract himself from the conversation. He interrupted the old woman's complaining about the local Member of Parliament.

"I'm sorry to stop you Missus Barnsworth, but I see that my constables need my attention. It has been an absolute pleasure talking with you and I will be sure to pass on your views about the honourable member to my superiors to see what they can do about his abject laziness. Good day!" He tipped his hat and motioned for the two constables to regroup with him outside the front door to the apartment block.

The followed him out into the street. It was busy with people going this way that that.

"What did you find out?" he asked.

"We have managed to get the names of most of the other inhabitants. Even if most of them are not home at the moment. The only two that we are missing are the most recent tenants to move in, in numbers six and eight."

Samuel flicked through his notebook.

"I have them. Misses Barnesworth, bless her, keeps a very close eye on the comings and goings in the apartment. Name for apartment six is Blackwall and for apartment eight is Coverley" The constables updated their notes accordingly. They now had a complete list of the occupants.

"So who is home that we can talk to now?" Samuel asked.

"Apartments two, three, seven and twelve. They were able to supply us with all of the others barring the two that you filled in now Sir, thank you".

Samuel wasn't looking as one of the constables spoke.

"Then let's start with apartment number two......?" he left the sentence hanging waiting for one of the constables to complete it for him.

"Mister and Missus Skinner" responded one of them.

"Excellent"

A large part of the day was devoted to meeting the occupants that were able to be interviewed immediately. In each instance Samuel masqueraded his interest in the same way that he had with Missus Barnesworth. It was a ruse for sure, but one that worked time and again. Once prompted the men and women of 13 Millers court were a chatty bunch. All very willing to put forward their views on one another and the state of the neighbourhood and the city in general.

Samuel and the constables learnt that the main topic of conversation when the occupants got together or passed one another for a brief chat was Jack the Ripper. Samuel blamed the propensity of the newspapers for overblowing the story in the first place. But he could see how it felt like a local problem to Whitechapel only and how it would pervade the people's thoughts and feelings on a daily basis.

After meeting the occupants that were home at the time Samuel had no doubts that none of them so far were a good candidate for the next victim. He was looking for women that looked like the victims. Women that were struggling to make ends meet and would turn to casual prostitution to earn some extra money. The occupants that he had spoken with over the course of the morning were older men and women. None of them struck Samuel as likely candidates. He would have to wait for the evening when more of the tenants were home to continue his investigation.

In the meantime, the final interview of the people at home during the day was turning out to be very interesting indeed. An elderly gentleman in apartment number twelve was lecturing Samuel about the failure of the police to apprehend the Ripper. He sounded like he was repeating the vitriolic rantings of The Evening Standard.

"We don't have to settle for it either. I know one of the heads of the safety committee in the local area. None of them live here of course. But just say the word to him and I can get his entire volunteer force here in two shakes of a lamb's tail".

The inference struck Samuel. This must be one of the vigilante leaders. Samuel wanted to know more but also didn't want to scare-off the lead; he made his next move like a chess master.

"Sounds like the kind of man that would see a few things in his line of *volunteer* work. Perhaps we should get him to help us out a little. There is nothing like the voice of experience to help guide the police department to find the wrong doers".

Samuel hoped that his little ploy to gain more information about this vigilante leader would be hidden well enough in the compliment and admission that the police needed his help. He was correct.

"Well, I suppose that there is no harm in telling you where to find him. If you want to get his help as you say?"

"Precisely Mister Carter; it would be a great help to us. I would be in your debt" Samuel continued to butter-up the old man. Mister Carter scratched his chin as if deciding and then apparently reached his decision, in Samuel's favour".

"Alright then I'll tell you. He can be found at Cox's square, number ten. But he won't be home yet. He is a signalman at the railway, always does the early shift so he should be home by three this afternoon. Go to his house then. Gary Hill; you'll be sure to catch him" Mister Carter was unaware that he was making a double-entendre about *catching* the man at home. Under the circumstances it was likely that Gary Hill could be arrested for being a vigilante leader. Senior Detective Inspector Robert Anderson was adamant that if any of the vigilantes were identified that they be run into the station for either a charge of mischief or impersonating an authority figure in a time of crisis, or any other charge that would stick before a magistrate. He was not of the belief that they were helping the situation at all.

"Thank you very much Mister Carter. I'll be sure to avail myself of Gary Hill's expertise in due course. But for now we have more work to do in order to keep our citizens safe; please excuse us. Have a good day" Samuel's cheery farewell resonated with Mister Carter who somehow felt that he had contributed to the well-being of everyone by offloading his opinions to the Junior Detective Inspector and giving him the information that he had.

"Alright then. Have a good day yourselves the three of you" he waved a cheery goodbye as the three police employees retreated. When they had make it safely again to the downstairs front entrance of the building they regrouped for a quick debrief.

"Well it appears that I have more work ahead of me this evening when more of the tenants are home. Hand me the complete list would you?" Samuel announced. The constable did so and Samuel tucked it into his coat pocket.

"But for now we have some alibies to confirm. Let's see if we can do that before lunchtime shall we?" Samuel was referring to the parcel of work that he had been divvied out in the morning meeting.

The work that he had delayed so that he could begin to meet the tenants of 13 Millers Court.

Happy to follow Samuel wherever he went the two constables agreed with him and they waked away from the block of apartments.

***

Samuel had carried out his work during the day methodically and carefully. He had managed, with the help of his constables, to get through the work that he was allocated and returned to the station for more. That too, he and his constables had acquitted with aplomb. But now it was close to six in the evening. His daytime work was over and his constables had gone home. Samuel however, had made his way back to 13 Millers Court to try and catch at home the tenants that he had not yet met.

His first door-knock resulted in meeting a young woman that seemed to thrive quite comfortably on the wage of a housemaid. He was suspicious of her immediately. She was about thirty years old and very pretty. Definitely a candidate. Her name was Candice Gould. He spoke with her at length using the same feeble excuse that had worked on all of the other tenants so far. Candice was happy to talk to Samuel about her fears of walking the streets alone at night, a dead-giveaway that she was a casual prostitute.

Samuel made copious notes about Candice, who assumed that he was taking note of her points of view about this and that. But Samuel was thanking his lucky stars that he had found her. If she wasn't the one that the Ripper would be attracted to then he would eat his hat.

Samuel thanked Candice for her input and proceeded to the next apartment on his list. This one was occupied by a married couple perhaps in their fifties. Too respectable and honest looking to fit the bill thought Samuel. They had various holy icons scattered around their home, he could see them from the door. God fearing people, concluded Samuel and the wife was not a likely victim for the Ripper.

The next apartment on his list was occupied by a gentleman that worked in an accounting firm in Mayfair. Samuel kept his conversation with him brief as he was actually a waste of time for the detective, but did not want to seem like he was not devoting enough time to him.

The next apartment was expecting Samuel. The man living there had been speaking to Missus Barnesworth and was ready to tell Samuel exactly what he thought of the state of affairs in the city. Like the previous visitation Samuel gave him as little and as much time as he thought would seem acceptable in the situation.

The next apartment revealed a young Irish lass in her mid-twenties. She had moved over from Ireland to be a Nanny but was between jobs at the moment. This was a definite strike in Samuel's book. Mary Jane Kelly was her name and she too was a prime candidate to be a Ripper victim. Like Candice, Samuel spent a long time chatting with her to find out as much about the young lady as he could.

After he had finished with Mary Jane Kelly, the next apartment that he door-knocked revealed yet another potential. A rather striking woman in her late twenties or maybe early thirties. She claimed to be employed by an antiques dealership in Kensington. Samuel took down the details so that he could confirm them later. As much as he did not want it to be so, he did suspect that she too may be a part-time prostitute. Primrose Pennyfarthing was her name. Even that sounded like it belonged in an antiques shop he thought. Just as with Candice and Mary Jane, Samuel took down lots of notes about Primrose. She was definitely a third very likely candidate to be the Ripper's next intended victim.

Much to his dismay the next apartment revealed a fourth candidate. Judy Bellwether. Approximately thirty years of age and very cagy about her line of work. The more that he inquired the more furtive she was about it. And when pushed hard would only admit that it involved work at the riverside fish markets. But Samuel thought that her admission was metaphorically fishy as she did not smell of fish at all.

He continued his door-knocking and interviewing the remaining residents. Some were expecting him as the word had got about within the apartment block. Others were surprised to have a Whitechapel Inspector knock on their doors whilst they were trying to either prepare or eat their evening meals. All up Samuel thought that it was a resounding success. He had clearly identified four of the tenants that could easily fall prey to the murderous lunatic roaming the local streets. With his notes safely tucked into his overcoat he headed home for his own well-earned evening meal. It was cold, he would be glad to get home and into the warmth of his parent's home.

As he walked in the direction of home, he felt a growing concern with the role that he was soon to play. If Madam Athalia's notes were to be believed, and he firmly did so, then he was about to play a central part in solving the most high-profile crimes that had plagued London over the past months. He began to wonder if the two junior constables would be enough. If they each watched one of the possible victims, then there was still one left over that would not have a guard.

Samuel contemplated going back to Edmund Reid for more help but just as quickly dismissed the thought. It was Edmund's retirement party at this Friday night. He would only have that on his mind. But he still needed help. What was he to do?

Then a name sprang into his mind he actually said it aloud as he walked the cobbled streets.

"Gary Hill"

He stopped in his tracks. Contemplating the idea from as many angles as he could. And suddenly it made perfect sense to him. He would go to meet this man and draft him into the ambush that he was about to spring upon Jack the Ripper. That would fill the deficit in man-power. Although he was shivering from the cold and wanted desperately to be home, he was spurred on by the thought of what he was about to do. There were so many ways that this could unfold. He had gone over it in his mind a thousand times; it was dizzying. He turned and walked in the direction of Gary Hills residence in Cox's Square.

Chapter 40: Enlisting Help from the Vigilantes

When he reached the address he could see from the light on in the front room that there was somebody home. This was quite a nice little enclave. Neat and well looked after terrace houses on every side of the square. He found the one that he was looking for knocked on the door and waited.

Eventually a regal looking man opened the door and looked Samuel up and down in a disapproving manner.

"May I help you, young man?" He said with a rather aristocratic manner. This was not what Samuel was expecting from the purported leader of a vigilante gang. He was caught somewhat off guard. Gary Hill was wearing a velvet smoking jacket and looked for all-the-world like the lord of a manor presiding over his estate.

"I apologise for calling upon you so late Mister Hill, but I was given your name by Mister Carter of Millers Court. I believe that you are acquainted with him?"

"What of it? Who are you?" Gary said somewhat defensively.

"I am Junior Detective Inspector Samuel Gates of Whitechapel Criminal Investigation Department. I am working on the Ripper case and would very much like to talk to you about it if you have the time".

Samuel's credentials earned him an open door from Mister Hill. He stood aside and motioned with his head that Samuel should come in.

“Thank you” he replied to the silent invitation. He walked past Gary and into the typically narrow hallway. There was the usual steep staircase about half way down the hall, but it was the front room that Gary was gesturing to.

“Please come into the front room” he said. Samuel walked through the open doorway and Gary followed shutting the door behind him. There was a coal burning fireplace on one wall. The room was comfortably warm. It was furnished with a two seater lounge and two single upholstered chairs each of which was accompanied by small side table.

“Please sit down Inspector Gates” offered Gary politely. So far the whole experience had not been what Samuel was expecting. Samuel took a seat on the lounge. It was very comfortable. Along with the fire he could see himself dozing off if the circumstances were different. There was an awkward silence. Samuel broke it by elaborating upon his earlier statement.

“I was given your name by Mister Carter who intimated that you may be able to assist the Police in the situation that we find ourselves in.” Samuel awaited a response.

“A rampant murderer roaming our streets with impunity and the police apparently unable to find him.” It was less than a complimentary summation of the state of affairs but Samuel did not allow it to taint his response. He did not want to come across as overly protective of the reputation of the Police in this particular moment.

“We at the CID are looking at this case in every possible light. There are a great deal of men involved. I like to think of myself as one of the Inspectors that can think outside of the square, if you take my meaning?"

"I do not. You will need to explain yourself, if you don't mind?" countered Hill. Thinking carefully before speaking Samuel tried his best to come across as a member of the police force that works differently to the way that was so far resulting in no arrest and apparently no progress in the case.

"My methods are more holistic Mister Hill. I like to get all of the viewpoints that I can possibly gather. Because you never know when someone, just like yourself will come up with a theory that could break the case once and for all. That is why I am here this evening sir; to get your thoughts on what more needs to be done to apprehend this monster".

Samuel waited whilst Hill contemplated his words.

"More men in the streets to hopefully be there when he next strikes. More eyes looking for anything suspicious. That is what needs to be done Inspector Gates." Hill's viewpoint was nothing new. But it was a segue to exactly why Samuel was here.

"I am glad that you said that Mister Hill. I believe the same thing. But as you know we only have so many police to avail ourselves of. I am thinking that it may be time to draft-in some *additional* help from the concerned citizens of the local area." Samuel's rhetoric clearly resonated with Gary. He jumped at the opportunity that Samuel was seemingly presenting.

"Now that is a very intriguing thought Inspector Gates. One that I would be at the forefront of supporting, if you have the backing of your superiors of course?" Gary was clearly enthused.

“That is good news Mister Hill. I can see that my journey was not wasted. And to answer your question, I have a free-hand from my superiors to contribute to this case as I see fit. It is the outcome of an arrest and a hanging that they are more concerned with rather than the trivial details about which police officer or Inspector actually solves the case. If you take my meaning?”

“I do Inspector Gates. I do indeed” replied Hill. Gary took a little time to mull over what had been said so far. Samuel allowed him the time to collect his thoughts. It was Gary that spoke next, his words still masquerading behind a veneer of plausible deniability.

“If I were to have access to others that feel as you do……as *we* do, then I am sure that a man in your position could make good use of such valuable contributors; to helping solve the Ripper case.”

This was exactly that Samuel had hoped for. All he had to do was stretch out his hand and scoop up all of the additional men that he needed to allow his trap to be sprung. This time it was Samuel’s turn to contemplate matters. He did not want too many men in and around the apartment block on the night in question. So he thought that it was better to ask for a small amount of help. Just enough to cover the front and rear of the building and the one outstanding potential target.

His decision made, Samuel now had to convince Gary that the deployment of the men would not be in vain. But how was he to disguise his need for three men at a particular location at a specific time. He thought quickly.

"I have been trying to find the most likely candidates that the Ripper would be attracted to, and I believe that I have done just that." The very assertion was nothing short of fascinating for Gary.

"Oh? And what have you concluded?" he asked trying unconvincingly to cover up his interest.

"As you can imagine I have interviewed many people over the course of the last few months and you may not know it, but when the last victim was taken, I was nearby and gave chase…"

"That was you?!" asked Gary incredulously "I had read about an inspector that had given chase through the sewers but the man was never named".

"My superiors decided for operational purposes not to feed the press with any more details than they can gather for themselves. We don't want to inadvertently inform the murderer himself how close we are to him; do we?"

"No, no; of course not. Please continue Inspector" said Hill trying to encourage more of the story out of Gates.

"Well my point is this. I believe that I have an insight into the mind of this horrible individual. And it is with this insight that I have determined some likely candidates that I believe should be watched very closely. I have access to uniformed constables of course, but it is the everyday man-in-the-street that is not going to attract attention that I would prefer to assist me in this endeavour". Samuel practically patted himself on the back for his clever reasoning. It sounded well founded, and that was all that mattered right at the moment. Providing he could convince Gary Hill that was all that he needed to do. Rope-in the leader and his supporters would follow.

Gary Hill was clearly enamoured with the very thought. It showed on his aristocratic features.

"Let us stop this verbal charade shall we Inspector Gates." Gary's unusual directness was at this point of the conversation very welcomed by Samuel.

"Yes indeed, please let us both speak plainly so that there is absolutely no misunderstanding" Samuel replied; verifying that he wanted the same thing.

"You need men to help you in your endeavour to protect a selection of women that you feel, one of which, may very well be the next victim of the Ripper. And you want me to supply those men because they will not stand-out in the role that you would have them perform for you. Passive observers, unless the killer strikes, in which case........what Inspector Gates?" Hill was being very forthright.

"In which case, I will be near at hand, as will two uniformed constables to step in and take over from that point. No danger to your men; just the satisfaction of knowing that they helped trap Jack the Ripper." Samuel made the terms of involvement of the vigilantes crystal-clear.

"All they would have to do is blow a police whistle to attract my attention. I will of course supply the whistles. Three men. One watching he back of a particular apartment block, one watching the front, and one keeping track of a young lady as she goes about her business of......well, you understand, I'm sure. My two constables will each be assigned to two other young ladies, and I will be keeping track of one personally." Samuel waited for a response.

Gary could see some obvious holes in the plan"

“If each of the women that is being observed leaves the apartment block and wonders the streets….”

“They are to be furtively followed. The likelihood is that they will bring the Ripper back to the premises in question. I don’t foresee that the murderer will do anything whilst there are people around, he has in the past chosen very quiet places or was at least on his way back to the boudoir of the victim. In the case of the four ladies that I have in mind to watch over and protect, they would certainly bring back their gentlemen to their abode. Each lives alone. It would be too tempting for the Ripper to pass up.” Samuel quickly smothered the doubt from Hill. He wanted to give Hill the impression that he had thought of every contingency.

And so the conversation continued for quite some time. Hill coming up with an objection of varying magnitude and Gates quickly dousing it with is impeccable reasoning. Eventually Hill was silenced. He was convinced that Inspector Gates had exactly want it took to catch the most wanted killer in the history of the London.

“You shall have your men Inspector Gates. Just let me know where and when. I will send word to you of their names. We can arrange a face-to-face meeting prior to the beginning of your observance operation and I can even cycle them with replacements should the length of your campaign extend beyond your perceived timeframes”. Gary made his commitment to help Samuel in the enabling of his plan.

“We begin Friday evening. Why don’t we meet here beforehand, if that is acceptable? We can walk over to our target building from here, it won't take long. Shall we say five pm?" Samuel waited for Gary's acknowledgement.

"Very good Inspector Gates. I will see you on Friday evening at five pm. I will be here as will two other men. I am sure that you won't object if I take an active role in proceedings?" he asked.

"Not at all Mister Hill. I am glad to have a man of your calibre on my side. Until Friday then." he stood up and they shook hands heartily as if they were longstanding friends. There was further talk between them as Gary showed Samuel to the front door. With a final farewell Samuel began his journey through the dark cold streets to his home, more assured than ever that victory was almost within his grasp.

Chapter 41: Thursday the 8th of November 1888

Samuel could barely fall to sleep on the night of Wednesday, but eventually he did. When he awoke it was early on Thursday morning. His head was spinning with how he was going to pull everything together for tomorrow night. He was certain of some things, like not letting the two constables in on the secret that he had drafted vigilantes to help him in his plan. But he was still unsure of other things. What if all of the four potential targets went different ways to pick up their next paying customer? Then all four of them would have to follow their charges away from the apartment block and the extra men that Samuel had ordered for the block. He could think of a hundred different scenarios that would result in disaster. But did his best to quash them.

Above his fears, he absolutely believed in the visions that Madam Athalia had written down that he had found and interpreted. He was as sure as any man could be that the Ripper would soon be in his grasp and that the four women of 13 Millers Court, one of which was sure to be the next victim, would be saved by his intervention. That was the overriding thought that kept Samuel from falling into a spiral of self-doubt and disastrous potential outcomes.

He showed up for work enthusiastic and bubbly. He almost didn't see Edmund Reid as his former boss motioned to him after the morning meeting. Edmund had to practically get into Samuel's way to illicit attention. When he did Samuel looked up somewhat perplexed.

“You are the only hold-out Samuel” said Reid without introducing the subject about which he was speaking. It sounded like Samuel should know what Reid was referring to.

“I’m sorry” he responded genuinely perplexed.

“RSVP’s for my farewell soiree at the school hall on Friday night Samuel. You are the only one that has not responded to the invitation. Sargent Plymouth has been chasing you hasn’t he? Do you have something else on?” Reid’s explanation brought clarity to the subject matter. Samuel arched his head backwards as he realised that he had indeed forgotten to respond that he would not be in attendance of the party. He would be otherwise engaged in his furtive operation to capture Jack the Ripper.

“What time was it again?” he asked trying to buy some time whilst he thought up an air-tight excuse for not attending his former superior’s retirement party.

“From 8pm onwards” said Reid looking hopefully at the young man. As Samuel looked at the face of Edmund he found that he could not bring himself to invent an excuse to not attend.

“I will do my best to be there. I have some surveillance work to do with my two constables earlier on and then again maybe after the party as well. But I will do my best to attend for sure” he said. The response brought a huge smile from Edmund. He had become so relaxed over the last week in the lead up to his exit from the CID. Smiling was a much more common feature upon his face than Samuel had ever recalled before.

“I am glad. I’ll let Sargent Plymouth know so that can complete the guest list. Shall we see Florence as well?” he further inquired. Samuel nodded.

“Excellent. I’m looking forward to seeing her again. Have a good day Samuel” Reid gave Gates a hearty slap on the back and strode away. Samuel felt a little guilty for saying what he had. He really couldn’t spare the time from his operation to attend the gathering. But he took some solace that when he was credited with apprehending Jack the Ripper that Edmund would forgive him for not being there. He may not even notice in the throng of other people and their partners that would be attending.

Putting the thought aside he now had to contend with briefing his two constables on the extra work that they would have to put in tomorrow night. They were certainly not on the guest list so there would be no need to extract them from the party. He already had his speech in mind. He would deliver it whilst they were out of the station. He did not want anyone else to hear. All they had to do was to continue to do what they were doing, follow his orders without question.

Another thought occurred to Samuel. He promised the vigilantes police whistles. He went to see about appropriating a number of them to fit the bill.

***

Samuel’s two constables were suitably malleable. The very thought that they would be used in a covert operation on Friday night that may help solve the Ripper case was too tempting to pass up. They were not just compliant; they were both positively enthused by the idea. The stage was set. Samuel would give the two men their final briefing at 4pm on Friday before they left the station for the evening. He would then allow them to go and get some supper before meeting them at 13 Millers Court. He would then go and brief the vigilantes at Gary Hills house at 5pm and the operation could begin properly at 6pm. It wold be dark by then. Samuel hoped for clear weather and not the persisting rain that had plagued them for the past week. He knew that it was going to be a long night, but Samuel was prepared mentally and physically. All he wanted now was to get his plan in motion so that it could be done. It was all that he could think about.

But as is the case with situations that occupy so much of one's thoughts, there was the potential for expecting one thing so much as to the exclusion of anything else.

Chapter 42: The Face of Jack the Ripper

Samuel awoke with a fright. It was Thursday night, the night before he was to carry out his carefully laid plan. He was unsure if he would be able to sleep he was so nervous about everything that he had yet to do like briefing his constables and the vigilantes in separate session, he was unsure if he would even fall asleep. But he had and he had slept precariously as if there was someone calling his name beckoning him to awaken. Samuel had woken up with such force that he doubted now that he would become drowsy again any time soon.

The sound of the clock in the hallway downstairs alerted him to the fact that it was midnight. He counted each chime up to twelve. Breathing a sigh of surrender that he was now very much awake, he got out of his comfortable bed. There was nothing to it; he would have to do something to occupy his mind for a while until he was able to sleep once more. He resolved to get dressed and sneak out of the house so as not to disturb his parents, and go to 13 Millers court. Just being there he had decided would give him comfort enough to maybe grant him the mercy of some more sleep before morning.

He parted the heavy curtains in his room and gazed out of the window. It was a clear night. He could tell that it was cold, but it was not raining. Then Samuel had an additional thought. The ride on his bicycle to Millers Court and back would hopefully tire him out and further assist him in sleeping for the remainder of the night. With his plan now firmly set in his mind he got out of his pyjamas and into his clothes as quietly as he could.

When he was ready he opened the door of his room and peered into the gloomy hallway. He could hear the snoring of his father coming from the main bedroom. Creeping carefully down the steep stairs he made his way through the downstairs hall to the back door with the ease that comes from familiarity over many years living in the same house. He went into the rear courtyard to get his bicycle and then brought it skilfully though the hall to the front door without bumping into anything. He stopped at the coat rack and put on his heavy coat. Pulling the door quietly behind him he heard the lock latch and he placed the bike into position to mount it. But first he lit the small brass oil lamp that was on the handlebars. It may have been a clear night, but the moon was nowhere to be seen. He would need the light that the portable lamp would provide to aid his journey across Whitechapel to his destination.

With the lamp lit, he pushed off and quietly rattled along the streets. As one would expect there was nobody to be seen in any direction. He could have been the only person in the entire city for all he knew. The occasional light from a window here and there was the only reminder that there were others in his state of consciousness.

***

When Samuel reached his destination he felt a calmness descend upon him. Just being there was indeed the exact therapy that he needed. He stopped about then yards from the building and regarded it in the gaslight glow. There was one of the windows that was open and light was protruding from it. A front window on the upper floor. That was the residence of Mary Jane Kelly he thought to himself. She was probably entertaining a gentleman caller.

Samuel remounted his bike and closed the distance between him and the building. When he reached the front door he got a strange feeling that something was wrong. It was that voice again. The one that had prevented him from having a deep sleep. The voice in his head that prevented him from staying asleep. It was as if it was trying desperately to tell him something very important, but he could not hear what it was. As if the words were being swept away in the wind.

Placing his bicycle against the gas lamp that was outside of the building he looked up and regarded the open and light window of Mary Jane Kelly once more. For just an instant he thought that there was a cry. But it was so short and so weak he was not sure if he had imagined it or not.

He looked at the front door of the building. There was something strange about it. Peering at it more carefully he could now see that the door was slightly ajar. The sound of Big Ben striking the half hour jolted Samuel like he was dropped into freezing water.

A myriad of nearly simultaneous thoughts tore through his thinking. He was too close to the problem. He had not considered an obvious fact. Today was Friday the 9th of November. Why did he assume that the murder would take place on Friday night and not the early hours of the morning? He was there without his constables and his vigilantes. The Ripper could easily be in the building right this very moment. What was he to do?

All of Samuel's logical thinking deserted him in that instant. He ran up to the front door and threw it open and ran down the hallway to the stairway that was in the mid-point of the passage. He couldn't even remember running up the stairs. He would have taken three or even four at a time. He felt completely disconnected from his legs as they carried him to the front door of Mary Jane Kelly's tiny apartment.

He didn't have to worry about how to enter her abode; the door was unlocked. It led straight into the main reception room. It was empty. A table lamp lighting it with a soft yellow glow. Beyond the reception room was the bedroom. The door was open and he ran through it.

The scene was sickening. The body of Mary Jane Kelly was on her bed a man crouching over it. There was a copious amount of blood staining the sheets. A bizarre sound was emanating from his mouth. Samuel's sudden entrance disturbed the man and he both straightened up and spun around at the same time. Samuel knew that he was face-to-face with Jack the Ripper.

Samuel was almost paralysed with both fright and indecision. Time seemed to stand still giving Samuel the opportunity to study the face of the most wanted man in the history of London. He was well dressed. Somewhat handsome. He had a beard and a hat that made him look like he was the captain of a ship.

"You're; you're" stuttered Samuel trying to regain his composure and think of the right thing to say at his unbelievable moment in his life. The man was not moving. He did not look alarmed he simply regarded Samuel as he attempted to speak.

"You are under arrest" Samuel finally managed to get out. There was silence from the man. Samuel couldn't help himself he looked down at the body of Mary Jane. She was eviscerated. It was hideous. Worse than any of the other murders that this monster had committed. The gaping hole had been cut from her throat running all of the way down the length of her torso to her hips.

Samuel knew enough biology to realise that there were a number of organs missing. He could barely fathom what he was seeing. There was no heart, no stomach. Samuel felt a sudden wave of sickness come over him. He had to breathe quickly and look away from the scene straight back into the unwavering eyes of the murderer.

"What!" he said between sharply drawn in and out breaths.

"What have you done with the heart; the stomach?" Samuel was very close to throwing up.

The Ripper did nothing but continue to regard Samuel with a look that could have been one of detached aloofness or maybe emotional indifference. Samuel took a moment to look around the room. There was no sign of the missing organs. Where were they? What had this monster done with them? Silence filled the room taking up all of the remaining space that wasn't occupied by the disembowelled body of Mary Jane. It was an unbelievable torture for Samuel. He had questions. He had the very man within his reach that the whole city wanted to see swing from a hangman's rope. But infuriatingly the Ripper was saying absolutely nothing. He continued to regard Samuel in excruciating silence.

The blood was pumping up into Samuel's head. His heart was racing so fast that he thought that it may explode from his chest. He felt weak, like he was about to faint. Still nothing from the murderer, not a sound. The frustration along with the absurdity of not being able to get the man to speak or otherwise acknowledge him or the situation that he was found in welled up in Samuel until it erupted in anger.

"Say something!" shouted Samuel shaking with the rush of adrenalin still pumping through his system.

"My name is Benjamin Brigges, Captain of the merchant brigantine Mary Celeste; at your service sir."

The silence was broken. The words came from Jack the Ripper. He had a cultured voice. It was a gentlemanly greeting from one well-to-do fellow to another. The stark contradiction between the words spoken by the murderer and the setting in which they were spoken was surreal. Samuel was taken completely off-guard. He had no response for the man. All he could think of to say was;

"What?"

"I said that my name is Captain Benjamin Brigges of the Mary Celeste."

Samuel shook his head violently as he tried desperately to reconcile what the man had said against what he had clearly done. A ship thought Samuel? It explained why this lunatic had not been caught before. He must have been escaping out to sea between murders. But even that did not ring true. All of the port records had been scoured from top to bottom. All ships that had been in port during the murders were found and the crews questioned. What this man was saying did not make any sense.

"A ship's captain?" said Samuel still trying to grapple with the situation.

It was then that Samuel noticed that there was a drip of something coming from the man's beard. He had dark hair and dark clothes but the more that Samuel looked the more that he could see that Benjamin Brigges' clothes were saturated with blood. His beard too, it was literally dripping with blood.

A horrible thought occurred to Samuel. He had lost all censorship between his thinking and his speaking so he just blurted it out as he thought it.

"Did….did…you…eat... the missing organs?"

Brigges put his finger to the side of his nose as if indicating that Samuel had said something that was a secret. Everything began to close in on Brigges at that moment. Without realising what he was doing he doubled over in a combination of horror and revulsion. And that was the moment that Brigges took to make his escape. He ran toward the window and dived through it as though he were a seasoned Olympic swimmer. Samuel barely had the chance to straighten up and take in the scene as he watched Brigges' disappear head-first through the open window. It was unbelievable.

Shaking himself out of his stupor, Samuel raced to the open window and looked out expecting to see the body of Brigges sprawled over the cobblestones below. Instead, incredibly, he saw Brigges standing on the street, bathed in the full light of the gas lamp staring back up at him with a scornful look upon his face.

Samuel had to shake his head to ensure that he wasn't dreaming. By all rights the man should have sustained major injuries or at the very least not been able to be in an upright position. But he was. Samuel almost growled with anxiety and shock and disbelief that the man that he was so sure that he would be responsible for capturing was about to escape. Gates actually contemplated in that second following Brigges through the window. But he dismissed the ideas just as quickly and raced back through the doorways and into the hallway toward the stairs.

By the time that he had made it through the front door of the apartment block and onto the street where Brigges had been standing, the brigand was nowhere to be seen. Samuel almost screamed with frustration, but a sound stopped him. It was familiar. It was the sound of metal scraping against stone. Brigges was entering the sewers again in order to make his escape.

Samuel looked over at his bike. The small brass oil lamp that had lit his way was still shining light. All he had to do was unclip it and take it with him to illuminate his way in the blackness of the London sewer tunnels. He fumbled with the lamp to free it from the handlebars and when successful ran in the direction of the sound that he had heard. He was vaguely aware of noise behind him from the apartment block. The fracas must have aroused the curiosity of any of the neighbours that were still in residence. Somewhere in the back of Samuel's mind he hoped that it would lead to the discovery of the body of Mary Jane Kelly so that the police would be called.

But right now there was no time to think of anything else except capturing Jack the Ripper. Racing down the street he almost passed over the manhole cover that Brigges must have used to make his escape from street-level. Backing up he looked around for something, anything that he could use to help him lift the heavy disc. There was nothing. It was lucky that he was wearing his black leather gloves to stave off the cold. The holes in the cover were big enough for him to get a grip. With an unexpected show of strength, he managed to wrench it from its place and push it aside.

Chapter 43: The Pursuit

Shining his torch downwards he located the rungs of the ladder that would take him down in to the underworld of London. It was an eerie feeling of déjà vu. He had done this before and failed to capture the murderer. But as he descended the ladder Samuel had no doubt in his mind that he would succeed. He did not know how, but he absolutely knew that he would end this murder's rampage though the city of London and be heralded as the hero that brought Jack the Ripper to justice.

Hurrying fearlessly down the ladder he ended up ankle-deep in putrid water. Unlike the last time there was no-doubt about where Brigges was. He was running away noisily from Samuel's position. Gates gave chase. This was not the hide-and-seek pursuit that he had enacted before with his prey. This was a pursuit pure and simple. Samuel ran and ran all the time he could hear Brigges annoying ahead of him. He could not seem to close the distance between them. The tunnels turned left and right and right and left. He had absolutely no idea how far he had run or in which direction he had been going. The chase exhausted Samuel it had gone on for longer than he could clearly contemplate. Had it been a few minutes or had it been ten to twenty minutes? He no longer had the objectivity to discern

***

There were points of the chase where he had to stop and almost double over in exhaustion. But the sound of Jack the Ripper, Captain

Benjamin Brigges seemingly just ahead of him, and out of the range of his lap, spurred Samuel on, and on and on.

Time had lost all meaning for Samuel. He was beyond the point of exhaustion. Fatigue wracked every part of his legs and arms and lungs. Tiredness enveloped him like a curse. He could not give in to the feelings. More than the overtiredness that he felt was the need to live up to the vision that he had interpreted from Madam Athalia's writings. It forced him past the point of pain and into a new reality. Samuel moved past his barriers of surrender and willed himself to continue running, pursuing his quarry. Nothing, not even his own weakness would stop him from fulfilling his destiny.

***

Again he heard the sound of a manhole cover being slid out of its position. It was still somewhat distant, but close enough to spur him onwards. Forcing himself to move forward despite his aching legs he saw that it was becoming a little easier to see. There was another source of light emanating from somewhere. He rounded a corner and it revealed itself to him. A ladder leading up and a manhole cover left open. A gas lap must have been just above and was shining its light down into the sewer. This is where Brigges had exited. Samuel was excited. He anticipated the end of his pursuit. Soon he would have his prize. He ran to the base of the ladder and looked up.

There was indeed a gas street lamp lighting up the surrounds. It was painful to climb but he ignored the plight of his muscles and did so anyway. Soon he was back up on street level in a dead end alleyway in a part of London that he had never seen before. Without the slightest knowledge of where he was Samuel clambered up and onto the cobblestoned street.

There was a building on both sides of him. They were tall. Warehouses of some sort by the look of them. Featureless brick buildings of immense size. The one to his right had a doorway that was still ajar. The one to his left had no visible entrance. It was clear where the Ripper had entered. Samuel followed gingerly. With his miniature oil lamp still in hand he pushed open the heavy seasoned-oak door and peered inside.

Chapter 44: Riverside

Samuel wasn't sure what he expected to see; nevertheless, he couldn't help but feel a little disappointed at the what he found. It was a corridor with a few doors dotted along it. The passageway was dark. Had it not been for his lamp it would have been in complete blackness. There was no sign of his quarry. He had to be here somewhere it was only a matter of finding him.

Samuel crept inside cautiously. He chose one of the doors at random and tried to gain access. Annoyingly, the door was locked. He studied the lock. It appeared to be fastened by a large brass padlock and latch. Whatever was behind here was valuable. Although his curiosity was piqued, Samuel did not have time to wonder at the contents that were being so ably protected. Logic told him that Brigges couldn't be in there because the door was secured from this side. Samuel moved away at on to the next door. It had a similar lock and latch. Moving to the next he found the same thing. Brigges must have come down this hallway. Again and again he found locked doors. Nothing unusual given the location he thought. Obviously the stock that was behind the doors was sensibly under lock and key.

Even inside this large structure he could smell the Thames. He had to be near the river and in a place where boats unloaded their cargo. Perhaps Brigges ship, whatever he had called it, was moored nearby, pondered Samuel as he continued his journey down the dark corridor.

Eventually he arrived at a door that looked a little different to the others. This did not have an external latch. It looked more like a doorway that would lead into an office or the like. Brigges could easily be waiting just behind it. Samuel grabbed the brass handle and turned the knob. The door was not locked. He opened it a crack and shone his lamp inside. The light revealed very little. Then he backed off and looked at the other side of the door, where the hinges were. He strained to see if Brigges was hiding behind the door ready to pounce upon him. He could see a filing cabinet of some description.

Satisfied that he was not about to be ambushed Samuel pushed open the door all the way and shone his light inside.

It was indeed an office. A desk with lamp, not lit. Various filing cabinets and more than that, intriguingly, another doorway leading to who knows what. It was then that he heard the sound.

Samuel froze with a mixture of fear and anticipation. He had worked himself up into such a state about capturing Jack the Ripper, that he wasn't behaving in a way that would be considered normal anymore. Faced with the same situation most people would have run for help, but Samuel was convinced that he had fate on his side. He would prevail no matter what. So he chose to investigate the source of the sound.

It was coming from behind the other doorway. He couldn't ascertain what it was that he had heard, but if he had to put some sort of description to it, he would have said that it was a sneeze. It sounded muffled.

If it was the Ripper, then he had inadvertently given his position away. The cat and mouse game was turning in Samuel's favour, he thought to himself.

Samuel crept forward to the door and gently grasped the brass handle. Turning the knob, he unlatched the door as quietly as he could and opened it a small amount to allow himself to see what was on the other side. Although the room was dark he could tell that it was big. Perhaps one of the many storage rooms for the cargo that this build would have held coming from the visiting merchant's ships docked close by.

Something immediately caught his eye. It was a large cage to the side of the room. It was huge. Samuel guessed that it must have been used to bring live game from Africa or some other exotic location back to England, perhaps to take up residence in a zoo or a private country estate. He peered into the darkness of the cage. There was something moving within its confined space. Whatever it was, was standing upright and moving on two legs. The light was too dim to make out clearly enough detail to satisfy his need to survey the scene before entering. A decision had to be made.

Samuel swung open the doorway and scanned the room for any other signs of movement. There was none other than that in the cage. Samuel shone his small lantern in the direction of the cage to illuminate it as best as he could.

To his absolute amazement he could now see that it was a woman in the cage. The figure was clearly alarmed by the sudden appearance of Samuel and let out a small cry of fear covering up her face with her hands. Trying to adjust his senses to what he had found

Samuel walked cautiously over toward the cage. Inside the female figure could be seen trembling with fear. Samuel took a few fleeing seconds to survey the rest of the room. There were indeed cargo boxes of various shapes and sizes littered here and there.

“Don’t be afraid” He said as he approached the cage.

“I am Junior Detective Inspector........” he did not get the chance to finish his sentence before a jubilant and unexpected voice shrieked back at him.

“Samuel Gates? Is that you!?”

Samuel was gobsmacked. He walked up to the cage bars and peered at the woman who had now taken her hands away from her face revealing herself to him. In that instant he was confounded. He couldn’t believe what he was seeing with his own eyes. Standing right in front of him, caged like a wild animal was a dead woman. He tried to form words in his mouth and managed to stammer only this.

“Madam Athalia?”

Chapter 45: The Many Faces of Jack the Ripper

"Madam Athalia?" was all that he could get out in the second attempt at addressing the captive old woman. There followed a moment whilst the two of them regarded each other as if they disbelieved what each was seeing. But neither could quite bring themselves to believe the situation that they found themselves in.

"I cannot believe it. Madam Athalia ? But you.....you are....you're...." Samuel hesitated to even say the words.

"Samuel, I cannot tell you how happy I am to see you. I have been imprisoned here for weeks. That vile creature gives me only bread and water to eat and only allows me to use the lavatory once a day. It has been a horrific torture." Then she stopped so suddenly mid-sentence that it was jarring. She squinted at him and looked at if she may have made a mistake in identifying the young man.

"It is me Madam Athalia" said Samuel trying to get Athalia to begin talking again. Samuel had to know how she had come to be here?

"Give me your hand" she said sternly.

"I'm sorry?" he replied befuddled at the request and at the harshness with which it was delivered.

"Your hand, give it to me I must be sure that you are not him!"

"Not who? Jack the Ripper? You can see that I am not." He replied none the wiser as to why Athalia would ask him such an odd question.

"You know that I can tell when it is you. I refuse to play games with a monster such as you. Give me your hand or you will have convinced me that you are simply masquerading as a former acquaintance of mine?"

Samuel could make no sense of what Athalia was talking about, but the insistence in her voice left him in no doubt that he should comply. He extended his hand. She grabbed it with both of hers. Her grip was unusually strong for such an old lady. He hoped that his would satisfy her.

Athalia closed her eyes and frowned with concentration. She began to nod a little at first and then more resolutely. She held his hands now more like an old friend during a greeting. She smiled broadly and let out a palpable sigh of relief.

"It is you; thank goodness. Samuel I cannot tell you how overjoyed I am to see you again. How did you find me?"

Again Samuel seemed to be at a loss as to exactly what Athalia was talking about.

"What do you mean it *is* me. Who else could it be. Don't you recognise me?"

"I have to be careful Samuel, that abomination can change its form and appear as anyone that it likes. But he…it, knows that I can tell when it is hiding in the shape of someone else. It is not a human being Samuel. It is an impossible creature from……." Athalia stopped when she realised that Samuel was looking at her as if she was absolutely insane.

"Samuel, I realise, believe me I do, that you must think that I have lost my sanity. And indeed I feel that it has been stretched to its breaking point whilst I have been imprisoned here. But Jack the Ripper, or Captain Benjamin Brigges or whatever he calls himself or is known to everyone as, is not what you think".

Samuel visibly reacted to the name of Brigges.

"I see that you know that name Samuel?"

"Yes, he as introduced himself to me. Is that his name?" Samuel asked.

"No, no, whoever Captain Benjamin Brigges is, or rather was, is gone, the creature has simply taken his place and is telling people that is who he is. This is a long story Samuel, perhaps you could indulge me by finding a way to release me from this cage and I will more than happily tell you everything that I know about the beast".

It seemed to be the logical thing to do. There was still a plethora of questions that Samuel wanted to ask Madam Athalia, chief of which was why she wasn't dead and who was it that he saw examined by Police surgeon Thomas Bond. But just for the moment he pushed all of those questions aside and thought about how to release Athalia from the cage. There was a cage door but it had a huge brass padlock on it. He looked around for something to perhaps hit it with, or a crowbar to try and lever it off. But the room was dark. He shone his lamp around and saw a desk not too far from the cage. There was an oil lamp on it.

Samuel walked over to it and putting his small lamp down produced his matches and went through the usual ceremony of lighting the lamp. He trimmed the wick and the lamp produced a much greater amount of light revealing more of the room. Now much more of the room was revealed

“That’s much better” said Athalia.

Samuel looked around for anything that could help him in his endeavour to free the old psychic. He walked around the room from wooden crate to wooden crate and looked for anything. He could find nothing. He returned to the desk to rummage through the draws in the hope of finding the key that would release the padlock.

“Do you know if he kept the key in here anywhere?” he asked as he rifled through of the three draws in turn.

“I don’t know” replied Athalia.

“Didn’t you see what he did with the key when he locked the cage door? Did he take it with him?”

“I don’t know Samuel, I’m sorry” Athalia’s reply annoyed Samuel. She was not being helpful at all. Surely she saw what her captor had done after imprisoning her. He pushed the point.

“Why don’t you know Madam Athalia. Surely you saw……”

“I am not even sure how I got here Samuel” Athalia’s insistence stopped Samuel from probing further. Instead he changed the subject as he continued to more immediate matters.

“Have you seen Brigges tonight? I chased him here”

“What? Oh no that means that he is somewhere close by! Oh please hurry Samuel I have no wish to be devoured by that horrible thing” Athalia pleaded. The reference struck Samuel. He stopped what he was doing and returned to the cage.

“Devoured?” he said with partial incredulousness and part dread.

“That is what it does Samuel, it feasts on humans, either the entire body or just parts that it finds….pleasing” Athalia closed her eyes tightly as she finished her sentence. It was as if she was picturing herself being eaten by the creature that she described.

"Tell me more about Brigges. What is he exactly? Where does he come from? Why is he murdering women?" He simply had to know. Athalia looked nervously behind him as if expecting Brigges to walk in at any minute. Athalia looked like she was about to argue the point but then as if recognising the burning need in Samuel to have this information resigned herself to telling him what he wanted to know in lieu of attempting to release her from captivity.

"I will tell you what I know. Now that I have met the creature it has all become very clear to me now. The fragments of visions that I had during each of the murders were I believe the living spirits of the victims reaching through the ether to connect with someone with my abilities. The past, present and future mean nothing to our spiritual selves you know?" Athalia's explanation was at risk of becoming a lecture about spirituality. Samuel brought her back onto the main subject.

"Please Madam Athalia, Brigges?"

"I am getting to that Samuel. He is not very talkative when he is with me, but when he is I can sense how many lives he, it has.....appropriated. Captain Benjamin Brigges is just one of those. Whoever that was would be long gone; digested by the monster. This creature has assumed his identity. Do you see? We will never know who the real Brigges was because all we have is this imposter that has taken its place." Athalia's explanation did little to lift the veil of mystery that Samuel wanted so desperately to uncover.

“What sort of creature can do that? Eat people and then masquerade as them?” Samuel was still very doubtful of the idea even though he respected the old lady and her otherworldly abilities.

“I have seen a vision of its true form; it is some kind of impossible sea creature, a jellyfish, larger than any that has been yet discovered, and one that has somehow become sentient. It is aware of what it can do and has lived a life devouring people and taking their place. It has lived in cities other than London. This is only its current amusement. I have seen visions of cities on the continent; other lives it has lived. Oh Samuel please get me out of here I don’t want to face it again.” Athalia had clearly given Samuel all that she was going to do without fretting her continuing captivity.

Samuel conceded.

“I will look in the adjoining room and see if the key is there, or maybe a crowbar or something like that.”

“Don’t leave me here Samuel, I beg you” Athalia was alarmed at the thought of losing sight of her would-be rescuer. Samuel did his best to allay her fear.

“I promise that I will not leave this warehouse without you. It is well past midnight and we are on the docks. There will simply not be anyone about at this time of the night to help me anyway. I will only be in the next room; believe me!” Samuel did his best to look earnest. It worked. Athalia let out an audible sigh.

“I do Samuel; but please don’t be gone long”

“I won’t” he smiled hand clasped her hand before moving away to go back into the smaller adjoining room. When there he noisily opened and closed every desk draw and filing cabinet draw that he could find. Hoping to find a set of keys that may work in the lock and also to give Madam Athalia assurance that he was indeed still nearby. When he was finished he turned his attention to the various shelves. There was nothing that he could use. Annoyed at the fruitless search he returned to the main room. He shook his head to Athalia indicating that he had not found what he was looking for.

"I'll look around here some more" he said comfortingly and went first to the table to retrieve his small lamp to aid his search. He looked around the wooden crates and identified that the far wall away from Athalia's cage held what looked to be the main sliding doors that would more than likely lead out to the docks. Like the cage however it was locked, but this time it appeared to be locked from the outside. There was no way he was going to be able to exit the warehouse that way.

He continued to search and came up with exactly what the occasion called for. There was a crowbar that had been thrown down in-between two of the larger crates. If he had not had his lamp he would have surely missed it in the darkened crevasse.

Perhaps someone had dropped it and was unable to retrieve it. The two crates that it was between where huge. He would not have a hope in moving either of them. And the gap was not big enough for him to wriggle into. Frustratingly the crowbar was just out of arms reach. He almost swore aloud when he realised. It was tantalisingly close but still out of reach.

"What is it?" he could hear from Athalia in the distance. He elected to return to her and tell her about his find. He raced up to the cage. Athalia looked at him her face full of hope.

“I have found a crowbar, I can use it to get you out of here”

“That’s wonderful”

“But it is just out of reach in-between two large crates, I have to find something to help me retrieve it, like a stick or a broom” he was looking around whilst he was speaking for anything that would be able to be used to reach his goal.

“What about your belt? Could you snare it with your buckle?” Athalia’s common sense suggestion came as almost a slap in the face for Samuel.

“Of course I can! Why didn’t I think of that?” he said scalding himself aloud.

“I’ll be right back” he darted off to the crates and shining his light into the dark narrow passage between the two crates estimated that if he could capture the end of the crowbar with the buckle he could drag it out of its resting place.

Samuel removed his belt and flicked it at the crowbar, buckle-first. It did not reach its mark. He tried unsuccessfully a few more times.

“What’s happening Samuel?” called out Athalia.

“Almost got it that time” he lied. He tried again and again without luck. He was getting very frustrated and angrily flicked it once more this time hitting the mark exactly where he needed to.

“Yes!” he said aloud. He gently pulled it back towards him bringing the ensnared crowbar with it. It was not within the reach of his arm. Leaning down he grasped the crowbar and pulled it up. He had it.

Making his way back to Athalia he lay the crowbar on the ground whilst he put his belt back on. It was then that he noticed that Athalia's cage had no bottom to it. This must be the type that they drop over an animal that has taken the bate left out for it.

"Well done Samuel" Athalia's congratulations interrupted his musings about exactly how the cage was used. Samuel finished adjusting his belt and picked up the crowbar and moved over to the small cage door padlock. He inserted the crowbar and pushed down on it with all of his might.

"Move back" he said through strained teeth. Athalia did as she was instructed. The force that it was taking to break this brass padlock was perhaps a little more than he had within him. He was determined to prevail. Mustering his strength once more he pushed with renewed vigour. To his horror the iron crowbar snapped in half loudly throwing Samuel off balance in the process. One half of the crow bar clattered noisily on the floor the other half remained in the brass padlock that looked resolutely unharmed by the attack. Samuel was lucky not to have injured himself in the process.

Athalia was concerned.

"Are you alright?"

"Yes" nodded Samuel. He looked more closely at the padlock. He retrieved his small lamp and shone it on the device. He had indeed managed to bend the locking mechanism a little. Perhaps a more sustained attack was all that it would take he thought.

"I've made an impression, but now with only half of a crowbar to work with I fear that I may not be able to get the leverage that I need to finish the job" he was not thinking how his logical summation of the situation would affect the caged Athalia.

"What, no, that is terrible" her voice was laden with angst. Realising his mistake Samuel did his best to back-track.

"I will continue to try Madam Athalia, but it may take longer than I had planned" he smiled hoping that it would be comforting for the old lady. He was correct.

"Alright then. I have been here so long now, what is another thirty minutes or so in the grand scheme of things" Athalia seemed to have inadvertently put a time-limit on Samuel's would-be success. He did not want to upset her any further by arguing the point. Instead he positioned himself and began again to prise the padlock from its housing.

***

It took another forty minutes of pushing and resting before he finally succeeded. In that time Samuel questioned Athalia more about the creature and how it had come to be in the first place. Alice told him as much as she was able. Then with a loud metallic crack, the padlock was broken

"Well done Samuel, thank you so very much indeed" gushed Athalia as he opened the door giving the old woman her freedom once more. Samuel was exhausted. He smiled and they embraced. When they separated he outlined the next part of their escape plan.

“Not to try and get out of here. I think that I know the way, but his warehouse is a labyrinth. Let’s go”.

Taking her hand, he led her back the way that he had entered the room.

Chapter 46: The Imposter

Samuel did not have the firm grasp of the exact way that he had traversed the corridors that he had first thought. It only took a wrong turn here and there before he realised that they were lost. Shining his small lamp before them Samuel stopped in the middle of a very long hallway.

"What's wrong?" asked Alice.

"I don't recognise this hall, not at all" he said slipping unconsciously into rhyme. He looked perplexed up and down the space in the hope that he would see something, anything that he remembered from his initial journey into the warehouse.

"I heard something" said Athalia in an urgent whisper. She simultaneously squeezed his hand.

"Where? From which direction?" he asked looking back at her with concern.

"I think it was behind us" she said, her tone laden with near panic.

"Then our choice has been made for us. We shall go forward" he responded. They hastened down the hallway to the darkened end. As predicted there was yet another door. Without a free hand to open the door Samuel relied upon Alice. He motioned with his lamp for her to do the honours. She looked at him in an alarmed manner.

"Don't worry, I will go first" he assured the old lady. There was a sound behind them as he finished speaking. They both spun around to see what it was. Shining his torch down the long narrow passage neither of them could see anything.

Convinced that anything behind the door would be better than where they were presently Athalia turned around opened the door and motioned for Samuel to make good on his promise and go through first. He did so, still holding her hand tightly.

There was a familiarity about the room in which they found themselves. But for the like of him Samuel could not quite put his finger on exactly what it was. Wooden crates, a desk with an oil lamp, unlit. A darkened high cathedral-like ceiling too cavernous for his little lamp to illuminate. They stepped forward.

A squealing noise; a movement all around them and a calamitous crash made them both hit the ground in abject terror. They were unable to determine what had just happened. Athalia screamed with fright. Laughter filled the air. A man's laughter.

They both looked up but could not see anything. Then the familiar sound of a match being struck caught both of their attentions. The oil lamp on the table was being lit.

It revealed a scene that chilled both of their hearts to the core. They were in the exact room that they had escaped from. Now both of them were imprisoned in the cage that Samuel had taken so long to free Athalia from. But how? They struggled to take in what had happened.

The cage must have been lifted up by a rope and pulley system hidden in the darkness above. As they came through the door, one that had been previously blocked by Athalia's cage it had been released and dropped over them trapping them inside.

Samuel's first thought now that he had taken in the dire situation was the cage door. To his dismay a replacement lock had been put into place scuttling any idea of using it as a means of escape. Athalia and Samuel were ensnared. As one they looked over at the man that had lit the lamp on the nearby table. It was Captain Benjamin Brigges.

He was clearly amused at the look that they both had on their faces because he began to laugh once more. It was a cruel laugh, mocking their helplessness and fear.

Athalia began to cry. The despair evident on her features. Samuel helped Alice to her feet and held the frail old woman close to him to comfort her as best as he could. Brigges began to applaud as he walked close to the cage to inspect his captives.

"Very well done Samuel, you have been more amusing to me than just about anyone else. I thank you" he stood close to the bars looking from one to the other.

"What do you want?" responded Samuel defiantly. Brigges thought for a moment and tilted his head.

"What I want is to operate you as a puppeteer operates a marionette. And you have performed better than any other that I have manipulated Junior Detective Inspector Samuel Gates. You have indeed been a willing pawn in the game that I have laid before you." Brigges tone was dripping with contempt.

"What's that supposed to mean?" he spat back at Brigges.

"It means my dear boy that everything that has transpired as happened because I wished it to be so. I wanted you to come to this warehouse and find the supposedly deceased Madam Athalia so that

I could then reveal to you how you came to be in this situation, and why you are here." Brigges sardonic answer inflamed Samuel. Nothing was going as he had expected it to. And now Brigges was intimating that he was somehow behind the entire thing. It did not make any sense. Samuel was angry and it showed.

"You look puzzled" said Brigges contemptuously.

"Or is that Anger? No. Of course; it's both. Perhaps I should explain from the beginning"

Brigges put his hands behind his back and began to pace up and down the long side of the cage as he gathered his thoughts and put them into a linear and cohesive diatribe that revealed the truth about everything that Samuel had been through that led him to this point in time.

When he did speak it sounded like a smug professor explaining to his students an idea that he understood but one that eluded his students.

"Athalia, have you told the young detective everything that you know about me? About where I come from? What I am?" he looked to Athalia for confirmation. She shuddered and nodded hoping to get his attention away from her as quickly as possible.

"Good. Well then Samuel. You should have paid very close attention to everything that Madam Athalia has told you. I am not a person, certainly not the person whose body I am so impeccably imitating right now. You see the real Captain Brigges was nothing more to me than a diversion at sea. The Captain on a ship that I was travelling on board. I tortured him in the same way that I have tortured you. And eventually he became a delectable meal. When I devoured him I absorbed everything that he knew. I have the ability to take on the forms that I have……let's say, had communion with. It is different to the simple satisfying of my hunger. When I ate the insides of those hapless women, my victims in Whitechapel, I was very choosy about what I ate. It was my way to nourish myself, nothing more. But when I completely devour a person, then that for me is the ultimate rapture. After the deed is done I am able to take on their form. At least that is how it started. I have grown and discovered all kinds of new abilities since I coupled with my first human."

Samuel could scarcely take in what was being said. He was supporting everything that Athalia had said about him. That he was in fact not a man but a monster that could pose as one. Samuel shook his head trying to make sense of it all. Brigges continued.

"And you should feel privileged Samuel, because I don't couple with just anyone, it is a small group, not defined by gender, age or race. I choose my lovers with care. They must be above all else be of use to me, they must amuse me, they must serve me by giving over themselves to me when I engulf them. Are you beginning to understand Samuel?"

Athalia was shaking her head violently.

"No; it's horrible, unspeakable!" she retorted. Her objection made Brigges laugh. Samuel for his part had a growing sense of horror welling up within him. This….*thing*, was basically telling him that he was going to be its next meal. He felt a tightness in his chest and it was becoming difficult to breathe properly. He was breaking out in a sweat even though it was cold. Brigges moved closer to the cage to inspect his prized possession. Samuel instinctively moved back from the bars to distance himself from the smiling mad-man.

"You're insane. You'd have to be to murder those women?" it was all that he could think of to say. Brigges moved back from the bars and began pacing once more.

"Still thinking of the victims of Jack the Ripper Samuel. Forget them, they would never be able to mean as much to me as you. And it has been great fun watching the police fall over themselves trying to apprehend me. Trying to even come up with a suspect. The most hilarious part of it all is that I have had a controlling interest in the investigation. And nobody has suspected a thing"

The sentence didn't make any sense to Samuel. But just as he was about to say something the most incredible thing happened. Brigges began to glow an unearthly glow that emanated from beneath his skin. As Athalia and Gates watched with horror his features and indeed his entire body seemed to soften and lose shape, his clothing too. Whilst they were still grappling with their comprehension of what was happening, he reformed into another person. It was the most amazing thing that Samuel had seen in his entire live. Standing before him was none other than Senior Detective Inspector Edmund Reid.

It took Samuel a few moments to collect his wits.

"No, it can't be?" he said incredulously.

"Oh poor Edmund Reid. I consumed him in July of this year. Not even his devoted and dithering old wife knows. She doesn't suspect a thing. Forever telling me about how happy she will be when I retire and no longer need to spend the exorbitant hours working that I do." Reid laughed. It was definitely Reid's laugh; it was simply uncanny.

"No that's not possible" Samuel said hoping that by saying it that it would become true. Reid was self-satisfied with his reply.

"Not only possible my dear Samuel; ingenious. Where else should I have been after beginning a series of callous murders than at the very head of the organisation that would be investigating them? I was so very pleased to see Scotland Yard send man after man to take over the investigation from me. It was very hard some days presenting the morning briefing and not laughing at the absurdity of the situation. The very man that they were all seeking was addressing them every morning. I was right in front of them all the time." Reid stopped his pacing to come back to the cage bars. Athalia and Gates recoiled.

"Thank you so much for alerting me to the letters that Madam Athalia had sent to the police. Without your information I may have never known that this old woman was a threat to my ingenious little plan"

Samuel and Athalia exchanged looks. The insidiousness of the turn of events gripped them both.

"I led him to you……I am so sorry….I don't know what to say" Samuel was close to tears. Athalia reached over and held his hand. She too had tears in her eyes. But something that Reid had said kept niggling at Samuel. He seized upon it.

"Threat?"

Samuel had voiced the key word in Reid's recent words.

"I beg your pardon?" said Reid in an overly-polite way.

“You said threat. Madam Athalia was a threat to you?”

“Indeed she was Samuel which is why I had to *kill* her” his smug explanation did nothing to actually explain what had happened. But Samuel had a feeling of hope now. The old psychic was perceived as a threat by this monster. That was a good thing. That meant that there was still a hope that Athalia’s premonition about him catching Jack the Ripper may still come to pass. He had to play for time to find out more about this monster. He was beginning to think clearly now. His detective training and instincts were working overtime.

“All very clever except for the obvious *Inspector Reid*” Samuel’s unexpected sarcastic response caught Reid by surprise.

“Oh?’ he said raising an eyebrow in distain at the tone of voice in which he was addressed.

“Well clearly Madam Athalia is not dead. Even a *master manipulator* such as yourself should be able to see the problem there. Athalia alive, therefore still a threat to your twisted little scheme; wouldn’t you say?” Again Samuel’s less than contrite toe annoyed Reid.

“That old bag had to be silenced so I kidnapped her.” With that he made a gurgling sound, his throat expanded like that of a bullfrog and he spat out a small black thing that landed on the floor. It was a disgusting display from Reid. Both Athalia and Gates regarded the small black round thing with multiple spikes coming from it with some revulsion.

“What is it?” asked Gates, almost afraid to hear the answer.

"This is how I convinced Athalia to accompany me here. One of these spikes touches your skin and you become very susceptible to suggestion; my suggestion". Reid pointed to the thing as he spoke. He turned back to address them both.

"Do you remember any of this Alice, anything at all?" Reid mockingly asked her. Athalia shook her head.

"Such a weak old mind, if you were younger, stronger, you may have had some hope of resisting my control. But alas. I broke into your room hit you with one of these and you were mine to control. You came willingly to my lair here. I had found a piece of human refuse on the streets, an old lady that I had similarly taken under my control. When I had her replace you in your bed I used a new little trick that I have learned. I refashioned her body into a likeness of yours".

The story just became more incredible with each new turn. Samuel and Alice looked at each other again in disbelief. Yet there was a knowing between them that this must be the truth. There was simply no reason for Reid to lie to them. After all they were his captives.

"That explains the body that was examined" said Gates. "You deliberately cut the poor old soul in a way that would seem like it was done by a Jack the Ripper impersonator" Samuel looked to Reid for confirmation that he was correct.

"And I assigned you to the case with the help of Police Commissioner Charles Warren. I told you that he had requested your help, but really it was me that had made your services available to him. It was such a neat and tidy little part of my overall plan"

“I have been a pawn in your sick game” Samuel declared. His admission pleased Reid.

“It was I that sent you out to search the streets for Jack the Ripper. It was I that almost allowed myself to be caught by you the first time. Do you see how ingenious I have been Samuel?’ Reid was wallowing in his own self-proclaimed brilliance.

“There is more if you want to hear it. I know that you do” Reid again began to glow and his form softened it reformed into another familiar person. Athalia and Gates were horrified at who the creature now looked exactly like.

“Burton!” Athalia cried out. She looked at the creature so adeptly imitating her long-time butler and companion. She closed her eyes tightly and began to cry.

“No, you didn’t!” she said sobbing loudly.

“I did, I absorbed the old man shortly before you interviewed him the second time Samuel” Burton said as he straightened up and put himself into a posture more befitting the butler that he looked like.

“It was I that directed you to Athalia’s Windsor house Samuel” Burton winked at them both.

Samuel had a familiar sinking feeling in his stomach again. A horrible thought occurred to him. One that he did not want to think. He turned to Alice and asked her.

“When was the last time that you were in residence at your Windsor property?” Samuel’s heart began to beat faster.

“I don’t really remember” said Alice feebly.

“Think please, it is very important. Was it in the last month?” he said urging her to give him what he needed.

“No, no, I haven’t been to my Windsor house for about three months” As Athalia said the words the realisation of what Burton was intimating fell upon Samuel. It felt like a crushing blow. He turned to look at Burton who during the exchange had once more altered his form. The house maid Hillary Harris was smiling malevolently back at him.

“No!” Samuel shouted in disbelief. Hillary burst into laughter at his distress. Gates clenched his fists and pounded the floor. This only made Hillary laugh all the more.

“It’s horrible what you are doing stop it, stop it!” screamed Alice at the imitation housekeeper.

“Oh it’s more horrible than you think Athalia, far more intricate than you know. Would you like to tell her Samuel or shall I?” she bent down and waited for his response.

Samuel was incapable of replying. He had begun to sob. He closed his eyes so tightly that it hurt. Athalia realised at that moment that something more horrible than the murder and replacement of her Windsor housekeeper must be affecting Samuel.

“Samuel what is it, what has happened?” she moved to comfort him as best as she could but he would not take solace.

“You are boring me Samuel. Don’t keep the old lady in suspense. Tell her about the premonitions that you read. The writings of the grand old psychic Madam Athalia, kept in her library at her Windsor house?” The assertion from Hillary made no sense at all to Athalia.

"What are you talking about vile creature. I have not written down any premonitions in my library at Windsor. Samuel please tell me what is going on?" Samuel felt everything slip away from him at that moment. He knew without doubt that he was facing death as surely as any of the other victims of Jack the Ripper. He had no hope left. He managed to stop crying for long enough to look into Athalia's eyes and tell her.

"I read what I thought were your premonitions of me, capturing Jack the Ripper in your library. Disjointed visions that seemed to point to a residence at Millers court in Whitechapel, on a particular night. But it was all a part of the plan to ensure that I was exactly where he, she, it wanted me to be." Samuel looked, sounded totally defeated.

"You followed everything that I had invented for you to decipher so ably Samuel. I cannot tell you how happy with your performance I was." She scorned him and it cut him as much as the sharpest knife. There was no premonition. It was a set-up from the beginning. He was completely taken in with everything that had been laid out for him to find and follow. He was directed as surely as a playwright manoeuvers actors on a stage. Samuel felt completely used. He felt violated and sick.

Athalia managed to gather enough strength to stand up and face the perfect approximation of Hillary Harris that the creature had become. Alice was angry and she bravely directed her vitriol at the monster.

"Don't you ever get tired of *pretending* to be someone else. You may look like Hillary but you could never be the caring and loving individual that she was. You may take a hundred faces of a hundred people but you could never be a human being because you lack even the most basic qualities that make us what we are. You could only ever be a pallid imitation of a *real* human being at best. Show us what you really look like to insidious thing! Or are you ashamed?"

The uncharacteristic brave and scathing attack from Athalia seemed to take Hillary aback somewhat. Hillary's eyes narrowed in anger. She did not like being spoken to in that tone of voice. More than that, she was particularly unhappy at being called a pallid imitation. Hillary's response was equal to Athalia's in bitterness.

"Do you think that I will inherit your psychic abilities when I absorb your body old lady? Hillary said with contempt. It made Athalia afraid again. Her momentary bravery waned. Hillary moved to the cage door and produce a key from somewhere. She slowly and deliberately unlocked the padlock and swung open the door.

Samuel jumped to his feet and stood with Athalia facing the beast.

Chapter 47: The Cage

Athalia and Gates had nowhere to run. They were already backed up against the bars. They held each other tightly. Hillary prolonged their torture by simply standing in the cage doorway. She very slowly took one step into the cage.

"Samuel" Athalia whispered to Gates. He could barely take his eyes from Hillary who had infuriatingly ceased her ingress to the cage.

"Samuel" Athalia's increased urgency somehow managed to break through to him and he looked at Alice. Something in her eyes made him take his notice away from Hillary.

"Let go of me. Let go of me" she said twice. It was then that he realised that he was still holding on to Athalia, but she had released her grip on him. He couldn't for the like of him figure out why. He looked back at Hillary who took another single step toward them clearly delighting in their terror at her approach.

"Please, Samuel, let me go, I am an old lady". Her insistence sparked his gentlemanly side and he managed to find the strength in the circumstances to do as he was told. But still he did not understand completely what was happening.

As he released his grip upon Alice she did the most noble thing that he had witnessed in his life. In a show of the ultimate self-sacrifice she shoved him as much as she could away from her and ran toward Hillary.

“Run Samuel!” she said as she hurled herself into the creature. He barely had time to take in what happened in those couple of seconds. Athalia collided with Hillary who almost immediately became gelatinous and absorbed the impact and began to form around the old woman. Athalia screamed in that instant. Samuel could scarcely believe what he was seeing but in that microsecond of realisation that Athalia had given her life so that he may have a chance of escape, he seized upon the opportunity.

Samuel ducked around the monster as it enveloped Athalia. He squeezed himself behind the mass of viscous gunge and escaped from the cage. He did not look back. If he had, he would have seen Athalia now completely encased in the gooey form.

***

Samuel didn’t recall selecting any particular door to exit all that he was thinking of was escape. He ran and ran. It was dark and he could barely see anything in front of him. A couple of times he thought that there was corridor in front of him when in fact it was a closed door or a wall and he painfully collided with it. It was pain that could wait for now though.

He moved as quickly as he could. He scrambled to find door handles in the darkness and looked back hoping to not see any glowing form chasing him. His thoughts were scattered, as if fragments of glass on a floor were each reflecting a different picture. Samuel pondered how Athalia had given up her life to give him the chance of escape. It was the most honourable thing that he had witnessed in his entire life. He worried that the creature was chasing him wanting him to be its next meal. There were thoughts of how to get out of the warehouse that seemed to go on and on. Samuel thought of how he had been completely fooled by the monster. It had posed as Edmund Reid, Butler Burton, House maid Hillary Harris all to lure him to find falsified writings that would lead him into this trap. He felt ashamed, betrayed by those people, the real ones, even though they would never have willingly participated in such a charade. He admonished himself for even thinking such dour thoughts of the poor victims of the creature.

Samuel realised that he could see a little better now. He looked up. There were windows above him at an impossible height. No chance of escape through them unless he could find a ladder. But there definitely was a small amount of light coming through. Perhaps it was from a street lamp outside. But it was enough for him to make out his surroundings.

He stopped moving. The loudness of his breathing as he tried to catch his breath bothered him. He wanted desperately to be completely silent. He did not want to give away his position to the monster. Samuel briefly wondered if it had superior night vision compared to him. If not, then the creature too would be at a disadvantage. If so, then he would be.

His surroundings were nondescript; a featureless corridor with filing cabinets here and there. Various doors leading to who-knows-where? He chose one and opened it as quietly as he could. Standing facing him was Madam Athalia.

"Samuel I was beginning to wonder if you'd ever find me in the maze of this warehouse?" the chilling facsimile of Alice Athalia smiled malevolently at him and then lunged toward him.

Samuel let out a cry and ran in the opposite direction. He could hear running footsteps behind him. He raced around a corner. A long stretch of the hall lay before him. He bolted down its length as quickly as he could. Reaching the end, he chanced a look behind him. Butler Burton was in pursuit of him now. The creature seemed to be delighting in taking on the various forms that it had used to set up this elaborate trap.

Samuel clutched at the door handle. His now sweaty palms slipping off the knob rather than turning it effectively. His heat skipped a beat as he madly grappled with the simple device and managed to open the door. He ran inside. It was where he had been before. The cage was there bathed in the light of the oil lamp that was still alight on the desk. Samuel looked at where he had last seen Athalia. There was nothing but a puddle of foaming mass now. He shuddered.

Choosing an exit he sprinted toward it. Just as he reached it he heard the doorway behind him open. Samuel looked around. Edmund Reid was now pursuing him.

"There's no escape Samuel. Give yourself over to me willingly. Why fight the inevitable" Reid hollered at Gates.

Samuel did not wait to hear the whole tirade. He moved as fast as his legs would carry him through the door slamming it shut behind him. Quickly he ran down another featureless hallway. Choosing a doorway at random he opened it quickly and smoothly and slipped inside closing it as quietly behind him as he could. He was in an office. There was thankfully another door for him to use as an escape route. But right now he wanted to hide and collect himself. He considered the desk, beneath it. But it was too exposed. There were no other cupboards or spaces in which he could secret himself. He listened at the doorway he had just closed, hoping to hear if the monster was nearing. There was nothing. No sound of pursuit at all.

Somehow this was more unnerving than having the monster directly behind him. Samuel checked for a way to lock the door. There was nothing. Not a chain, not a key in the door lock, nothing that would help secure it. He crept away from the doorway and over to the next. He wanted to get as many closed doorways between him and the thing chasing him as he could.

He carefully opened the next door and tried to peak through the crack to see what was waiting for him on the other side. He could scarcely believe what he saw. There was another cage similar to one that had held captive Athalia and himself. It was smaller though, in a smaller room, but similarly littered with wooden crates. In the cage was Florence Fairclough, in her sleeping attire. She looked frightened out of her mind.

For one instant he considered that it could be the monster again, but then thought that it simply couldn't possibly be, unless he had.....he did not want to even think about it.

Florence was staring wide-eyed at the opening door. She could be heard breathing quickly. He opened the door the entire way and stepped through.

“Samuel!” she screamed at him, unable to believe that her fiancé had just walked through the door.

“Dear God Samuel, help me please? Get me out of here!” she begged. Samuel could still scarcely believe his eyes. But the frantic pleas from Florence convinced him in that moment that she was the genuine article. He ran to her and clasped her hands as she held out her arms and desperately tried to hug him through the thick iron bars that imprisoned her.

“How did you get here?” he said as he tried to console her.

“I was taken from my bed by a madman! Samuel I have no idea how he got into the house or why I went with him. I was simply unable to resist; I cannot explain it. I lost consciousness in a handsome cab and woke up here only a few moments ago” She was almost blubbering out the explanation to him

“What are you doing here Samuel? Where are we? Who is that bearded man? What does he want?” Florence was again almost babbling with frantic questions about her bizarre situation.

“There will be time enough for explanations when I get you out of here Florence” he said as he looked around for anything that could help him free his betrothed from the cage in which she was imprisoned. He ran over to the desk that was nearby which resulted in Florence crying out that he had left her side.

“Samuel where are you going?’ she stammered in panic.

“I just have to find something to free you from the cage” he said back to her as he ripped open the draws to reveal nothing more than useless paperwork. He looked around frantically. Something made him look up. There was a pulley and rope system still attached to the cage that Florence was in. His eyes followed the mechanism up and down through other attachment points and pulleys to the rope and where it was tied-up at the side on the far wall.

"Just a minute Florence, I think that I can lift this cage off you with that rope and pulley. Fear not my love I shall have you freed in a few moments". He resolutely offered Florence the comfort of assurance that he had the situation well in hand. She responded with a great deal of relief in her voice.

"Oh thank you Samuel bless you, please hurry, I am terrified out of my mind".

Even as she was speaking Samuel raced over to the rope and began to unfurl it from the cleat that was fastened to the wall. He pulled the rope tightly and visually checked that it would do what he anticipated that it would. He was correct. It was designed to lift and lower the cage. Much like the larger one that Athalia and he had been imprisoned in, this smaller one did not have a base. Maybe they were slotted into place for transportation of whatever was in them. Whatever the reason Samuel didn't have time to think about it . He pulled with all of his might. The cage lifted a few inches, it was remarkably easy. The mechanical advantage was making the job easy. He pulled and pulled, it inched up further.

"That's it Samuel it's working!" cried out Florence in joy. Samuel needed no encouragement, he was working as fast as he could.

Soon the cage was off the ground enough for Florence to slip beneath it. Samuel was about to call out for her to do just that but she beat him to it. So desperate was she to be freed she scraped herself and her white nightgown on the grimy floor to free herself from captivity.

"That's it, good girl!" called out Samuel. He made sure that she was free before releasing the rope, the cage came down with a thump. It made Florence jump with fright. She ran to be with Samuel. They embraced tightly and desperately.

"Thank god you found me Samuel. I hate to think what my fate would have been otherwise. Who is this man? What does he want?" Florence was still in the dark about how and why she was here.

"It's a long story. I'll tell you as much as I know, while we try to find a way out of here" he said.

"That sound perfect Samuel. Which way?" she looked around her. The room had another door. Samuel chose it because he had not been through it before. It was no more scientific a decision than that, but he didn't want to alert Florence to the fact that he did not actually know the way out of this labyrinthine warehouse.

"Come alone this way" he led her toward the door. Now that he felt somehow more in control of the situation he allowed himself to be a little angry.

"The fiend! What did he hope to gain by brining you here?" he said aloud. They reached the door and Samuel bravely opened it. Just another featureless corridor lay beyond.

"This way" he said and pulled Florence along with him. They walked and talked.

"Whoever he was, he said that he had business with you. I remember that much. But not why I went with him Samuel. I cannot explain my actions. It was if he had some power over me".

“I am sure that he did Florence. He is not a normal man by any means. He has ways of making people do things against their will.” Samuel picked another door at random and opened it. Another corridor. He signed with exasperation.

“What do you mean not a normal man. Who is he?”

“Captain Benjamin Brigges, Edmund Reid, Hillary Harris; Burton Abberline and more recently Madam Athalia; whatever he calls himself, he is better known as Jack the Ripper” even as Samuel said the words he regretted it. Florence’s hold on his hand intensified. She stopped dead in her tracks. He turned to look at her. Her eyes were wide. She was shaking her head.

“No” she said weakly. “I was to be a victim…..”

Samuel cut her off, not wanting her to reflect on what may have been.

“We have to get out of here so that I can alert police that this is his den. Quickly Florence this way.” He hoped that the urgency would detract from her growing terror. She allowed herself to be pulled along by him. The news that he captor was none other than the Ripper himself had clearly affected her. She was silent. Hall after hall, room after room and then something that Samuel recognised.

“There!” he said and pointed with his free hand. It looked to be just another door to Florence. Sensing her non-understanding.

“It looks to be an external door not an internal one. See?” he explained. Indeed, it was

“Yes, yes I do see Samuel. Thank goodness”

Chapter 48: The End in Sight

Samuel and Florence surged forward as one anxious to get out of the warehouse.

"If we can just get outside I can alert the police" said Samuel as he fumbled with the door handle. It was locked. His heart sank in that moment and he almost swore. But he looked up and found that the locking mechanism was operated from the inside without a key. It was simple turn-knob. His heart felt like it started beating again and he breathed a huge sigh of relief.

"What is it? What's taking so long?" demanded Florence.

"Nothing, I have it" he assured her as he has flung the door open. It was very early morning outside. There was the first hint of light in the sky. Samuel breathed the air in as he hurried through the door dragging Florence with him. It felt that his ordeal was almost over. The relief was palpable. It flooded through him like a wave of ecstasy. He was still revelling in the moment when he felt Florence's hand tense. He turned around to see what was wrong. She was staring back at the doorway that they had just exited.

"I heard something" she said. She looked back at him, fear evident in her eyes. Samuel felt his body tense up again. The joy that he had felt only moments before deserted him. He looked around wildly for anything that he could use as a weapon.

The creature must have caught up with them. Frustratingly, there was nothing. They stood in an cobbled alleyway. A gas lantern the only other distinguishing feature. Samuel took only a second to make up his mind about what they were to do.

"Listen to me Florence. I will tackle the Ripper. You must run for help, scream at the top of your lungs until you get attention. With any luck there will be constables on foot patrol somewhere nearby. Bring them back here". His brief plan laid out he prepared to move toward the doorway pushing Florence away from him as he did so.

"I won't leave you Samuel"

"Please just go I don't want you in harm's way. Get help"

"I'm afraid"

"Go now!" he said forcefully. Florence still hesitated. Samuel crept forward expecting Brigges, or Burton or Reid to pounce from the shadowy doorway. He readied himself for the battle of his life.

Instead of a horrible creature, a small tabby cat emerged from the darkness. It seemed completely unfussed with the tension that had been building upon its approach. It looked up at Samuel and meowed before moving around him and trotting down the alleyway.

Samuel and Florence let out audible groans of exasperation and relief.

"Oh Samuel" said Florence as she held her arms out for him to embrace her once more. Samuel wanted nothing more than to hold Florence. He took the moment to enjoy their liberation and the reprieve from what he had anticipated would be the final fight of his life. Florence and Samuel embraced for a long time.

"Now let's get out of here" he said as he pulled back to once more look upon Florence's face. To his horror he was looking at Madam Athalia once more. Samuel screamed and stepped back instinctively, tripping and falling in heap on the ground as he did so. He had been fooled once more. It had been the creature playing its cruel game with him all along. In that gut-wrenching moment ,he realised that Florence must have been a victim of the monster too. He was crying and shaking his head. His entire world was crumbling beneath him. His stomach sank inside of him making him feel like he was about to vomit.

Samuel forced his tear-filled eyes to open. The monster had transformed itself into Edmund Reid once more. Samuel shook his head and managed to blubber

"No, no"

Reid took perverse pleasure in Gates' suffering.

"Yes Samuel, I have devoured your darling Florence. I *convinced* her to accompany me while her parent's slept soundly in the room next to hers. But not before having her write a note to them about how you and her were to elope in a secret place on the Continent before taking an extended honeymoon".

Reid laughed loudly. Samuel couldn't take in the meaning of what Reid was saying. All that he could think about was Florence being digested by that thing the way that it had eaten Alice Athalia.

Reid seemed to be taking pleasure in watching Samuel suffer. He bent down and stroked Samuel's head like a mother comforting her child.

"Dear Samuel. You have been more amusing than any of my other victims. I want you to know that. It is important for me that you understand that you mean more to me than all of those women that I tortured and killed. Do you understand?"

Samuel was past the point of comprehension. He was in a pit of emotional desolation so deep that he wanted nothing more than to die now rather than endure it for a second longer. He shook his head unable to understand anything that Reid was saying.

"There is something about feeding on a person that I have nurtured and formed the way that I have with you. It is somehow more satisfying to me than simply eating. It transcends the need for nourishment. You have given me a great deal of delight Samuel and I am very grateful to you. Thank you Samuel" Reid actually moved to embrace Samuel. Gates did not even have the strength to push him away.

Samuel could feel that the body of Reid was soft and pressing on him harder than he thought possible. He opened his eyes again to see that Reid was gelatinous now and enveloping him treacle over a scone.

Everything that was Samuel Gates was covered over, consumed and digested by the Siphonophore. Alone in an alleyway, nobody saw the creature feeding on the young man. The speed with which the monster absorbed him was incredible. Before long there was nothing left. Edmund Reid regained his form and straightened up.

Looking around him he decided to make the most of the day. After all it was his final day in the Whitechapel police department. Tonight, was his retirement party.

Chapter 49: Edmund Reid's Retirement Party

The retirement party was in full swing. People were laughing and dancing. There was a string quartet that was plying a waltz which had encouraged quite a number of people to dance. Missus Reid was busy telling a gaggle of women about their soon-to-be retirement in Derbyshire, far away from the madness that is central London.

The senior men of the CID all stood together and of course were talking about business. Frederick Abberline was the one of the group that put an end to the impolite conversation that was not centred on the man-of-honour Edmund Reid.

"Enough of talking shop everyone, we are being rude. We should be asking you more about what you intend to do with the freedom that you are achieving Edmund?" Frederick and his companions all focussed their attention upon Edmund awaiting his response.

"As little as possible I should think" he answered wryly. This provoked a chorus of laughter from the men.

"And so you should Edmund! Justly deserved it is too!" said Robert Anderson as he slapped Reid heartily on the back.

"Where is young Gates?" he said looking around him. The Junior Detective Inspector was conspicuous by his absence. Everyone else from the station had spent time congratulating Reid on his brilliant career and wishing him well for the future.

"I heard from his parents this morning actually" said Reid. The crowd listened intently.

"Apparently he and his faïence have run away to the continent to elope"

"Good heavens. Never thought he would have it in him. Always saw him as a very straight-laced chap." Henry Moore was surprised at the news.

"It does seem odd I must say, but a young man in love is apt to do impetuous things I suppose." counselled Walter Andrews.

"Do they know where?" inquired Donald Swanson.

"They suspect Switzerland, probably Andermatt, at least that is what his parents and those of Florence Fairclough thought from the note that she left behind". Reid explained the current thinking of both sets of parents.

"Andermatt you say? I've been there but didn't see a thing of it. Had a terrible case of food poisoning from the night we arrived to the day we left three days later. Couldn't tell you a thing about it." Robert Anderson quipped in a small anecdote. This produced a small wave of sympathy from the group.

"Terrible" said Donald

"Nasty thing; food poisoning" agreed Walter

"Switzerland, eh. I'm sure you didn't miss much" Henry was clearly not a fan of the awe-inspiring natural beauty of the country. It was Edmund Reid that rounded out the responses to Robert's tale of woe.

"I can honestly say that I have never eaten anything that has not agreed with me."

The End

The murder mystery trilogy:

1. Murder on the Mary Celeste

2. Jack the Ripper: The Murder of Madame Athalia

3. The Monster of Matlock

Connect with Aenghus Chisholme

Visit my website on www.aenghuschisholme.com

Other Books by Aenghus Chisholme

Merlin the Sorcerer AD491

King Arthur is facing a war with the murderous Saxon Lord Aelle over the artisan land of Anderidae. Unknown to him magical forces have conspired with Aelle to ensure Arthur's defeat.

Guinevere the Queen AD494

Queen Gwenhwyvar and Sorceress Morgan Le Fay pursue the stolen Excalibur to a magical labyrinth where it is guarded by powerful Minotaur.

Sir Gawain and the Green Knight AD499

An animated corpse has Sir Guaen in its sights. How can you kill something that is already dead?

Arthur the King AD517

Caught in an untenable situation King Arthur is manoeuvred into a battle he cannot possibly win.

The Best Things in Life Begin with the Letter B

Don't let consumerism make a meal out of you. Learn what is best about life whether worth millions or obtained absolutely free of charge.

www.ingramcontent.com/pod-product-compliance
Lightning Source LLC
LaVergne TN
LVHW091023080826
845145LV00002B/343

* 9 7 8 0 6 4 8 0 7 8 9 5 1 *